P9-DNY-660

"A tantalizingly beautiful epic."
—*Elle*

"Visceral and haunting."
—*The New York Times Book Review*

"[Filled] with suspense and surprises."
—*The Washington Post*

"Extraordinary."
—*Emily St. John Mandel*

"Powerful . . . Vibrant . . . Unique."
—*Los Angeles Times*

"Thrilling."
—*Time*

"Aching and poignant."
—*The Guardian*

"Enchanting."
—*Geraldine Brooks*

"Gripping."
—*The Economist*

"Fast, exciting."
—*The Wall Street Journal*

"Full of hope."
—*CNN.com*

national bestseller

Praise for *Migrations*

"Visceral and haunting . . . As well as a first-rate work of climate fiction, *Migrations* is also a clever reimagining of *Moby-Dick*. . . . This novel's prose soars with its transporting descriptions of the planet's landscapes and their dwindling inhabitants, and contains many wonderful meditations on our responsibilities to our earthly housemates. . . . *Migrations* is a nervy and well-crafted novel, one that lingers long after its voyage is over."

—*The New York Times Book Review*

"True and affecting, elegiac and imminent . . . The fractured timeline fills each chapter with suspense and surprises, parceled out so tantalizingly that it took disciplined willpower to keep from skipping down each page to see what happens. . . . There are many losses, but lives are also saved. Franny charts our course through a novel that is efficient and exciting, indicting but forgiving, and hard but ultimately hopeful." —*The Washington Post*

"Powerful . . . Vibrant . . . Unique . . . If worry is the staple emotion that most climate fiction evokes in its readers, *Migrations*—the novelistic equivalent of an energizing cold plunge—flutters off into more expansive territory. . . . McConaghy has a gift for sketching out enveloping, memorable characters using only the smallest of strokes. . . . *Migrations*, rather than struggle to convince readers of some plan of environmental action, instead puts humans in their place." —*Los Angeles Times*

"Thrilling . . . In piecing together who this mysterious protagonist really is, McConaghy creates a detailed portrait of a woman on the cusp of collapse, consumed with a world that is every bit as broken as she is. . . . In understanding how nature can heal us, McConaghy underlines why it urgently needs to be protected." —*Time*

"An aching and poignant book, and one that's pressing in its timeliness. It's often devastating in its depictions of grief, especially the wider, harder-to-grasp grief of living in a world that has changed catastrophically. . . . But it's also a book about love, about trying to understand and accept the creatureliness that exists within ourselves and what it means to be a human animal, that we might better accommodate our own wildness within the world."

—*The Guardian*

"A good nautical adventure . . . *Migrations* moves at a fast, exciting clip, motored as much by love for 'creatures that aren't human' as by outrage at their destruction."

—*The Wall Street Journal*

"[A] tantalizingly beautiful epic."

—*Elle*

"You can practically hear the glaciers cracking to pieces and the shrill yelps of the circling terns."

—*Vulture*

"Suspenseful, atmospheric . . . As much a mystery as an odyssey."

—*Vogue*

"Gripping . . . By merging cli-fi and nature writing, the novel powerfully demonstrates the spiritual and emotional costs of environmental destruction."

—*The Economist*

"At a time when it feels like we're at the end of the world, this novel about a different kind of end of the world serves as both catharsis and escape."

—*Harper's Bazaar*

"An ode to our disappearing natural world."

—*Newsweek*

"This page-turner is captivating, enlightening, and surprisingly full of hope."

—CNN.com

"Gorgeous . . . A personal reckoning that cuts right to the heart. This beautiful novel is an ode—if not an elegy—to an endangered planet and the people and places we love."

—*Literary Hub*

"*Migrations* is a gripping tale that ultimately celebrates the beauty and resilience of the creatures—human and animal—that endure."

—*Sierra* magazine

"An exceptional novel that is both elegy and page-turning thriller."

—*Maclean's* (Canada)

"Transfixing, gorgeously precise . . . [The] evocation of a world bereft of wildlife is piercing; Franny's otherworldliness is captivating, and her extreme misadventures and anguished secrets are gripping."

—*Booklist* (starred review)

"[*Migrations*] could be taking place in two years or twenty years, but it could just as well be happening today. . . . A consummate blend of issue and portrait, warning and affirmation, this heartbreaking, lushly written work is highly recommended." —*Library Journal* (starred review)

"At times devastating and, at others, surprisingly, undeniably hopeful . . . Brimming with stunning imagery and raw emotion, *Migrations* is the incredible story of personal redemption, self-forgiveness, and hope for the future in the face of a world on the brink of collapse." —*Shelf Awareness*

"*Migrations* is as beautiful and as wrenching as anything I've ever read. This is an extraordinary novel by a wildly talented writer."

—Emily St. John Mandel, author of *Station Eleven*

"This novel is enchanting, but not in some safe, fairy-tale sense. Charlotte McConaghy has harnessed the rough magic that sears our souls. I recommend *Migrations* with my whole heart."

—Geraldine Brooks, author of *March*

"*Migrations* is a wonder. I read it in a gasp. There is hope in these pages, a balm for these troubled times. Charlotte McConaghy's words cut through to the bone." —Lara Prescott, author of *The Secrets We Kept*

"An astounding meditation on love, trauma, and the cost of survival. Charlotte McConaghy weaves parallel stories of a woman and a world on the brink of devastation, but never without hope. Equal parts love letter and dirge, this is a true force of a book that I read holding my breath from its start to its symphonic finish."

—Julia Fine, author of *What Should Be Wild*

"*Migrations* is indeed about loss—but what makes it miraculous is that it is also about both the glimpses of hope and the shattering persistence of love, if we are only brave enough to acknowledge them. Written in prose as gorgeous as the crystalline beauty of the Arctic, *Migrations* is deeply moving, haunting, and, yes, important." —Caroline Leavitt, author of *Pictures of You* and *Cruel Beautiful World*

MIGRATIONS

Charlotte McConaghy

FLATIRON
BOOKS
NEW YORK

This is a work of fiction. All of the characters, organizations, and events portrayed in this novel are either products of the author's imagination or are used fictitiously.

MIGRATIONS. Copyright © 2020 by Charlotte McConaghy.
All rights reserved. Printed in the United States of America.
For information, address Flatiron Books, 120 Broadway,
New York, NY 10271.

www.flatironbooks.com

Designed by Michelle McMillian

The Library of Congress has cataloged the hardcover edition as follows:

Names: McConaghy, Charlotte, author.
Title: Migrations / Charlotte McConaghy.
Description: First edition. | New York: Flatiron Books, 2020.
Identifiers: LCCN 2020001233 | ISBN 9781250204028 (hardcover) |
    9781250774545 (international, sold outside the U.S., subject to rights availability) |
    ISBN 9781250204011 (ebook)
Subjects: GSAFD: Adventure fiction.
Classification: LCC PR9619.4.M3798 M54 2020 | DDC 823/.92—dc23
LC record available at https://lccn.loc.gov/2020001233

ISBN 978-1-250-20403-5 (trade paperback)

Our books may be purchased in bulk for promotional, educational, or business use. Please contact your local bookseller or the Macmillan Corporate and Premium Sales Department at 1-800-221-7945, extension 5442, or by email at MacmillanSpecialMarkets@macmillan.com.

First Flatiron Books Paperback Edition: 2021

10 9 8 7 6 5 4 3 2 1

For Morgan

Forget safety.
Live where you fear to live.

—RUMI

PART ONE

The animals are dying. Soon we will be alone here.

Once, my husband found a colony of storm petrels on the rocky coast of the untamed Atlantic. The night he took me there, I didn't know they were some of the last of their kind. I knew only that they were fierce in their night caves and bold as they dove through moonlit waters. We stayed a time with them, and for those few dark hours we were able to pretend we were the same, as wild and free.

Once, when the animals were going, really and truly and not just in warnings of dark futures but now, right now, in mass extinctions we could see and feel, I decided to follow a bird over an ocean. Maybe I was hoping it would lead me to where they'd all fled, all those of its kind, all the creatures we thought we'd killed. Maybe I thought I'd discover whatever cruel thing drove me to leave people and places and everything, always. Or maybe I was just hoping the bird's final migration would show me a place to belong.

Once, it was birds who gave birth to a fiercer me.

GREENLAND

NESTING SEASON

It's only luck that I'm watching when it happens. Her wing clips the hair-thin wire and the basket closes gently over her.

I sit up straighter.

She doesn't react at first. But she knows somehow that she is no longer free. The world around her has changed just a little, or a lot.

I approach slowly, reluctant to scare her. Wind screams, biting at my cheeks and nose. There are others of her kind all over the icy rocks and circling the air, but they're quick to avoid me. My boots crunch and I see a ruffle of her feathers, that hesitant first flap, the will-I-try-to-break-free moment. The nest she has built with her mate is rudimentary, a scattering of grass and twigs wedged into a crevice in the rocks. She doesn't need it anymore—her fledglings are already diving for their own food—but she returns to it like all mothers unable to let go. I stop breathing as my hand moves to lift the basket. She flaps only once, a sudden burst of defiance before my cold hand closes over her body and ceases her wings' movement.

I have to be quick now. But I've been practicing and so I am, my fingers swiftly looping the band over her leg, shifting it over the joint to the upper stretch beneath her feathers. She makes a sound I know too well, one I make in my dreams most nights.

"I'm sorry, we're nearly there, nearly there."

I start to tremble but keep going, it's too late now, you have touched her, branded her, pressed your human self upon her. What a hateful thing.

The plastic tightens firmly on her leg, keeping the tracker in place. It blinks once to tell me it's working. And just as I am about to let her go she turns very still so that I can feel her heartbeat pounding inside my palm.

It stops me, that *pat pat pat*. It's so fast and so fragile.

Her beak is red like she's dipped it in blood. It turns her strong in my mind. I place her back in the nest and edge away, taking the cage with me. I want her to explode free, I want there to be fury in her wings and there is, she is glorious as she surges. Feet red to match her beak. A velvet cap of black. Twin blades of a tail and those wings, the sharpness of their edges, the elegance.

I watch her circle the air, trying to understand this new piece of her. The tracker doesn't hinder her—it's as small as my little fingernail and very lightweight—but she doesn't like it. She swoops at me suddenly, giving a shrill cry. I grin, thrilled, and duck to protect my face but she doesn't swoop again. She returns to her nest and settles over it as though there is still an egg that she must protect. For her, the last five minutes never happened.

I've been out here on my own for six days. My tent was blown into the sea last night, as wind and rain lashed it from around my body. I've been pecked on the skull and hands more than a dozen times by birds who have been named the most protective in the sky. But I have three banded Arctic terns to show for my efforts. And veins filled with salt.

I pause on the crest of the hill to look once more, and the wind calms a moment. The ice spreads wide and dazzling, edged by a black-and-white ocean and a distant gray horizon. Great shards of cerulean ice float languidly by, even now within the heart of summer. And dozens of Arctic terns fill the white of sky and earth. The last of them, perhaps in the world. If I were capable of staying any place, it might be here. But the birds won't stay, and neither will I.

My rental car is blessedly warm with the heating on full blast. I hold my frozen hands over the vent and feel my skin prickle. A folder of papers sits on the passenger seat and I fumble through them, looking for the name. Ennis Malone. Captain of the *Saghani*.

I have tried seven captains of seven boats and I think maybe the persistently mad part of me wanted them to fail the second I saw the name of this last boat. The *Saghani*: an Inuit word for raven.

I scan the facts I've managed to learn. Malone was born in Alaska forty-nine years ago. He's married to Saoirse and they have two young children. His vessel is one of the last legally certified to fish for Atlantic herring, and he does so with a crew of seven. According to the marina schedule the *Saghani* should be docked in Tasiilaq for the next two nights.

I put Tasiilaq into my GPS and set off slowly on the cold road. The town will take all day to reach. I leave the Arctic Circle and head south, pondering my approach. Each of the captains I have asked has refused me. They don't abide untrained strangers on board. Nor do they like their routines disrupted, routes shifted—sailors are superstitious folk, I have learned. Creatures of pattern. Especially now, with their way of life under threat. Just as we have been steadily killing off the animals of land and sky, the fishermen have fished the sea almost to extinction.

The thought of being aboard one of these merciless vessels with people who lay waste to the ocean makes my skin crawl, but I'm out of options, and I'm running out of time.

A field of green stretches to my right, punctured with a thousand white smudges I think at first are stalks of cotton, but it's only the speed of the car blurring everything; in fact they are ivory wildflowers. To my left, a dark sea crashes. A world apart. I could forget the mission, try to swallow the compulsion. Find some rustic hut and hunker down. Garden and walk and watch the birds slowly vanish. The thought darts through my mind, inconstant. Sweetness would turn sour and even a sky as big as this one would soon feel a cage. I won't be staying; even if I were capable of it, Niall would never forgive me.

I book a cheap hotel room and dump my pack on the bed. The floor is covered with ugly yellow carpet but there's a view of the fjord lapping at the hill's foot. Across the stretch of water rear gray mountains, cut through with veins of snow. Less snow than there once was. A warmer world. While my laptop powers on, I wash my salty face and brush my furred teeth. The shower calls, but first I need to log my activity.

I write up the tagging of the three terns and then open the tracking software with a lungful of air I'm too nervous to let out. The sight of the blinking red lights melts me with relief. I've had no idea if this would work, but here they are, three little birds that will fly south for the winter and, if everything goes to plan, take me with them.

Once I'm showered, scrubbed, and warmly dressed, I shove a few papers in my backpack and head out, pausing briefly at the front desk to ask the young receptionist where the best pub is. She considers me, probably deciding which age bracket of entertainment she should recommend, and then tells me to try the bar on the harbor. "There is also *Klubben*, but I think it will be too . . . fast for you." She adds a giggle to this.

I smile, and feel ancient.

The walk through Tasiilaq is hilly and lovely. Colorful houses perch on the uneven terrain, red and blue and yellow, and such a contrast to the wintry world beyond. They're like cheerful toys dotting the hills; everything feels smaller under the gaze of those imperious mountains. A sky is a sky is a sky, and yet here, somehow, it's more. It's bigger. I sit and watch the icebergs floating through the fjord awhile, and I can't stop thinking about the tern and her heart beating inside my palm. I can still feel the thrumming *pat pat pat* and when I press my hand to my chest I imagine our pulses in time. What I *can't* feel is my nose, so I head to the bar. I'd be willing to bet everything I own (which at this point isn't much) on the fact that if there's a fishing boat docked in town, its sailors will spend every one of their waking moments on the lash.

The sun is still bright despite how late in the evening it is—it won't go down all the way this deep in the season. Along with a dozen snoozing dogs tied to pipes outside the bar, there is also an old man leaning against the wall. A local, given he isn't wearing a jacket over his T-shirt. It makes me cold just looking at him. As I approach I spot something on the ground and stoop to pick up a wallet.

"This yours?"

Some of the dogs wake and peer at me inscrutably. The man does the same, and I realize he's not as old as I thought, and also very drunk. "Uteq-qissinnaaviuk?"

"Uh . . . Sorry. I just . . ." I hold up the wallet again.

He sees it and breaks into a smile. The warmth is startling. "English, then?"

I nod.

He takes the wallet and slips it into his pocket. "Thanks, love." He is American, his voice a deep and distant rumble, a growing thing.

"Don't call me love," I say mildly as I steal a better look at him. Beneath his salt-and-pepper hair and thick black beard he is probably late forties, not the sixty he appeared at a glance. Creases line his pale eyes. He's tall, and stooped as though he's spent a lifetime trying not to be.

There is a largeness to him. A largeness of hands and feet, shoulders and chest and nose and gut.

He sways a little.

"Do you need help getting somewhere?"

It makes him smile again. He holds the door open for me and then closes it between us.

In the little entry room, I shrug off my coat, scarf, hat, and gloves, hanging them ready for when I leave. In these snow countries there's a ritual to the removal of warm gear. Inside the bustle of the bar there's a woman playing lounge music on the piano, and a fireplace crackling in a central pit. Men and women are scattered at tables and on sofas under the high ceiling and heavy wooden beams, and several lads are playing pool in the corner. It's more modern than most of the undeniably charming pubs I've been to since I arrived in Greenland. I order a glass of red and wander over to the high stools at the window. From here I can once more see the fjord, which makes it easier to be indoors. I'm not good at being indoors.

My eyes scan the patrons, looking for a group of men that could be the *Saghani*'s crew. I don't spot any who particularly stand out—the only group big enough has both men and women playing Trivial Pursuit and drinking stout.

I have barely taken a sip of my overpriced wine when I see him again, the man from outside. He's down on the water's edge now, wind whipping through his beard and against his bare arms. I watch him curiously until he walks straight into the fjord and disappears beneath the surface.

My wine nearly tips over as I slide off the stool. There's no sign of him returning to the surface. Not now, or now, or now. God—he's really not coming back up. My mouth opens to shout and then closes with a snap. Instead I'm running. Through the door to the deck, down the wooden steps so slippery with ice I nearly land on my butt, onto the cold muddy sludge of the bank. Somewhere near a dog is barking with high, panicked yelps.

How long does it take to freeze to death? Not long, in water like that. And he still hasn't resurfaced.

I plunge into the fjord and—

Oh.

Out flies my soul, sucked through my pores.

The cold is familiar and savage. For a moment it grips me and forces me into a cell, the painted stone cell I know like a lover, for I spent four years inside it, and because the cold sends me back I spend too many precious seconds wanting to be dead, just for it all to be over, right now, I can't wait any longer, there is no part of me that isn't finished—

Clarity returns with a punch to the lungs. Move, I order myself. I've always been good at cold—I used to swim in it twice a day, but it's been so long that I've forgotten, I've become soft to it. I kick my waterlogged layers toward the large body below. His eyes are closed and he's sitting on the bottom of the fjord, and he is unnervingly still.

My hands reach slowly to encircle his armpits. I press off the floor and drag him up to the surface with a mighty gasp. He is moving now, taking a great breath and wading free with me in his arms, like he is the one who has rescued me and not the other way around and how the hell did that happen?

"What are you *doing?*" he pants.

There are no words for a moment; I'm so cold it hurts. "You were drowning."

"I was just taking a dip to sober up!"

"What? No, you . . ." I drag myself farther up onto the bank. Reality sinks in slowly. My teeth are chattering so hard that when I start laughing I must seem like a lunatic. "I thought you needed help."

I can't quite recall the logic that brought me to this moment. How long did I wait before I ran? How long was he under?

"For the second time tonight," he says. Then, "Sorry. You should get yourself warm, love."

More people have emerged from the bar to see what the commotion is about. They are crowded on the balcony, looking puzzled. Oh, the humiliation. I laugh again, but it's more of a wheeze.

"You right, boss?" someone shouts in an Australian accent.

"Fine," the man says. "Misunderstanding."

He helps me to my feet. The cold is inside me and—shit, the pain. I have felt this cold before, but not for a long time. How is he standing it so well?

"Where are you staying?"

"You were under so long."

"Good lungs."

I stumble up the bank. "I'll get warm."

"Do you need—"

"No."

"Hey!"

I pause and glance over my shoulder.

His arms and lips are blue, but he doesn't seem bothered. Our eyes meet. "Thanks for the rescue."

I salute him. "Anytime."

Even with the shower on as hot as it will go, I'm still cold. My skin is red raw, scalded, but I can't feel it. It's the two toes on my right foot that I can feel tingling as though with the return of heat; strange because they were cut off some years ago. But then I often feel those phantom toes and right now I'm disturbed by something else, by how easily my mind went back to the cell. I'm frightened of how simple it was to dive into the water instead of shouting for help.

My drowning instinct.

When I'm wearing every item of clothing I own, I find my pen and paper, sit down at the crooked table, and write a clumsy letter to my husband.

Well, it's happened. I've embarrassed myself so thoroughly that there's no coming back from it. An entire village of people saw a strange foreign woman fling herself into an icy fjord to inexplicably harass a man who was minding his own business. At least it'll make a good story.

And don't even try to use this as another excuse to tell me to come home.

I tagged my third bird this morning and I've left the nesting grounds. Lost my tent, nearly lost my mind. But the trackers are working, and I've found a man with a vessel big enough to make the journey so I'm staying in Tasiilaq while I convince him to carry me. I'm not sure I'll get another chance and I don't know how to force the world into a shape I can manage.

Nobody ever seems to do what I want them to. This is a place that makes you very aware of your powerlessness. I never had any power over you, I sure as hell don't have any over the birds, and I have even less over my own feet.

I wish you were here. You can convince anyone of anything.

I pause and stare at the scribbled words. They feel silly, sitting there on the page like that. After twelve years I'm somehow worse at expressing how I feel, and it shouldn't be like this—not with the person I love best.

The water was so cold, Niall. I thought it would kill me. For a moment I wanted it to.

How did we get here?

I miss you. That's what I know best. Will write tomorrow.

F r

I put the letter in an envelope and address it, then place it with the others I haven't yet sent. The sensation is coming back into my limbs and there is an erratic pulse in my veins that I recognize as the marriage between excitement and desperation. I wish there were a word for this feeling. I know it so well, perhaps I ought to name it myself.

In any case the night is early and I've a job to do.

I'm not sure when I first started dreaming of the passage, or when it became as much a part of me as the instinct for breath. It's been a long time, or feels it. I haven't cultivated this myself; it swallowed me whole. At first an impossible, foolish fantasy: the notion of securing a place on a fishing vessel and having its captain carry me as far south as he is able; the idea of following the migration of a bird, the longest natural migration of any living creature. But a will is a powerful thing, and mine has been called terrible.

2

I was born Franny Stone. My Irish mother gave birth to me in a small Australian town where she'd been left, broke and alone. She nearly died in the birthing, too far from the nearest hospital. But live she did, a survivor to her core. I don't know how she found the money, but not long after we moved back to Galway, and there I spent the first decade of my life in a wooden house so close to the sea I was able to tune my swift child's pulse to the *shhh shhh* of the neap and spring tides. I thought we were called Stone because we lived in a town surrounded by low stone walls that snaked silver through the hilly yellow fields. The second I was able to walk I wandered along those curving walls and I ran my fingers over their rough edges and I knew they must lead to the place from where I truly came.

Because one thing was clear to me from the start: I didn't belong.

I wandered. Through cobbled streets or into paddocks, where long grass whispered *hish* as I passed between. Neighbors would find me exploring the flowers in their gardens, or out in the far hills climbing one of the trees so bent by the wind that its brittle fingers now reached sideways along the earth. They'd say, "Watch this one, Iris, she's got itchy feet and that's a tragedy." Mam hated me being critiqued like that, but she was honest about having been abandoned by my dad. She wore the wound of it like a badge of honor. It had happened all her life: people left her, and the only way to bear it was proudly. But she would say to me most mornings that if I ever left her that would be it, the final curse, and she would give up.

So I stayed and stayed, until one day I couldn't stay any longer. I was made of a different kind of thing.

We had no money, but we went often to the library. According to Mam, inside the pages of a novel lived the only beauty offered up by the world. Mam would set the table with plate, cup, and book. We'd read through meals, while she bathed me, while we lay shivering in our beds, listening to the scream of wind through the cracked windows. We'd read while we balanced on the low rock walls that Seamus Heaney made famous in his poetry. A way to leave without really leaving.

Then one day, just outside Galway where the changing light leaches the blue from the water and drapes it over the long grass, I met a boy and he told me a story. There was a lady, long ago, who spent her life coughing up feathers, and one day when she was gnarled and gray she stretched from a woman into a black bird. From then on dusk held her in its thrall, and night's great yawning mouth swallowed her whole.

He told me this and then the boy kissed me with vinegar lips from the chips he was eating, and I decided that this was my favorite story of all, and that I wanted to be a bird when I was gray.

After that, how could I not run away with him? I was ten years old; I packed a satchel filled only with books and I heaved it over my shoulder and set off, just briefly, just for a nose about, a wee adventure, nothing more. We rolled out with the storm that very same afternoon, and wound our way up the west coast of Ireland until his great sprawling family decided to turn their cars and caravans inland. I didn't want to leave the sea, so I snuck away without anyone noticing and spent two days on the stormy shore. This was where I belonged, where all the silver walls led. To salt and sea and wind pockets that could carry you away.

But in the night I slept, and I dreamed of feathers in my lungs, so many I choked on them. I woke coughing and frightened and knew I had made a mistake. How could I have left her?

The walk to a village was longer than any I'd tried, and the books grew so heavy. I started leaving them on the road, a trail of words in my wake. I hoped they would help someone else find their way. A kind fat lady in the bakery fed me soda bread, then paid for my bus ticket and waited with me until it arrived. She hummed instead of talking and the tune got stuck in my head so that even after I'd left her at the station I kept hearing her deep voice in my ears.

When I arrived home my mother was gone.

And that was that.

Perhaps the feathers had come for her, like they whispered they would in my dream. Perhaps my father had returned for her. Or the strength of her sadness had turned her invisible. Either way, my wandering feet had abandoned her, like she'd warned me they would.

I was taken from my mother's home and sent back to Australia to live with my paternal grandmother. I didn't see the point in staying in any one place after that. I only ever tried once more, many years later when I met a man called Niall Lynch and we loved each other with brands to our names and bodies and souls. I tried for Niall, like I did for my mother. I really did. But the rhythms of the sea's tides are the only things we humans have not yet destroyed.

TASIILAQ, GREENLAND
NESTING SEASON

Take two. There are no men outside the bar this time, only the dogs, who look at me sleepily and then lose interest when I stride past without offerings.

As I enter, an odd rustle moves through the patrons and then, almost in unison, they erupt into applause. I see him at one of the tables, smiling broadly and clapping along with everyone else. People thump me on the back as I head for the bar, and it makes me laugh.

Someone meets me there with a grin. He's maybe thirty, handsome, with long dark hair in a bun. His bottom teeth are noticeably crooked. "The lady's drinks are on us tonight," he tells the barman, and he's either a different Australian or the one who called out from the balcony earlier.

"No need—"

"You saved his life." He smiles again, and I don't know if he's taking the piss, or if he actually thinks that's what happened. I decide it doesn't matter—a free drink's a free drink. I order another glass of red and then shake his hand.

"I'm Basil Leese."

"Franny Lynch."

"I like the name Franny."

"I like the name Basil."

"You feeling all right now, Franny?"

I never like this question. Even if I were dying of plague I would dislike this question. "It's just cold water, right?"

"Yeah, but there's cold and there's cold."

Basil takes my drink and carries it back to his table without asking, so I follow. He's with the "drowning man"—who has also managed to change into dry clothes—and a few others. I'm introduced to Samuel, a portly man in his late sixties with a luscious head of red locks, then Anik, a slender Inuit man. Next Basil points out a younger trio playing pool. "Those two idiots are Daeshim and Malachai. Newest and dumbest members of the crew. And the chick is Léa."

There is a scruffy Korean guy, and a gangly black guy. The woman— Léa—is black, too, and taller than both the men. All three are in the middle of a heated argument about pool rules, so I turn to the drowning man last, expecting to be introduced, but Basil has already launched into a detailed complaint of the dinner he's been presented with.

"It's overcooked, heavy-handed on the oregano, and way too buttery. Not to mention the pitiful bloody garnish. And look—look at the piss-poor presentation!"

"You asked for bangers and mash," Anik reminds him, sounding bored.

Samuel hasn't taken his merry eyes off me. "Where are you from, Franny? I can't place your accent."

In Australia I sound Irish. In Ireland everyone thinks I'm Australian. Since the very beginning I've been flickering between, unable to hold fast to either.

I swallow my mouthful of wine and grimace at the sweetness of it. "If you want you can call me Irish Australian."

"Knew it," Basil says.

"What brings an Irishwoman to Greenland, Franny?" Samuel presses. "Are you a poet?"

"A poet?"

"Aren't all the Irish poets?"

I smile. "I suppose we like to think so. I'm studying the last of the Arctic terns. They nest along the coast but they'll fly south soon, all the way to the Antarctic."

"Then you *are* a poet," Samuel says.

"You're fishermen?" I ask.

"Herring."

"Then you must be used to disappointment."

"Well, now, I suppose that's true."

"Dying trade," I comment. They were warned, time and again. We all were. The fish will run out. The ocean is nearly empty. You have taken and taken and now there is nothing left.

"Not yet," the drowning man speaks for the first time. He's been listening quietly and now I turn to him.

"Very few fish left in the wild."

He inclines his head.

"So why do it?" I ask.

"S'the only thing we know. And life's no fun without a challenge."

I smile, but it feels wooden on my face. My insides are churning and I think of what this conversation would do to my husband, who has fought for conservation. His scorn, his disgust, would know no bounds.

"Skipper's got his heart set on finding the Golden Catch," Samuel tells me with a wink.

"What's that?"

"The white whale," Samuel says. "The Holy Grail, the Fountain of Youth." He makes such an expansive gesture that some of his beer slops onto his fingers. I think he's drunk.

Basil gives the older man an impatient glance and then explains, "It's a huge haul. Like they used to catch. Enough to fill the boat, and make us all rich."

I consider the drowning man. "Then it's money you're hunting."

"It's not money," he says, and I almost believe him.

As an afterthought, I ask, "What's your boat called?"

And he says, "The *Saghani*."

I can't help laughing.

"I'm Ennis Malone," he adds, offering me his hand. It's the largest hand I've ever shaken. Weather-bitten, like his cheeks and lips, and there is a lifetime's worth of dirt tattooed under the fingernails.

"She saves your life and you don't even tell her your name?" Basil says.

"I didn't save his life."

"You meant to," Ennis says. "Same thing."

"You shoulda left him in there to drown," Samuel says. "Serve him right."

"You could tie stones to his feet—that would drown him quicker," Anik offers, and I stare at him.

"Don't mind him," Samuel says. "Macabre sense of humor."

Anik's expression suggests there is no humor about him whatsoever. He excuses himself.

"He also doesn't like to be on land too long," Ennis explains as we watch the Inuit man's elegant passage through the pub.

Malachai, Daeshim, and Léa join us. The men look annoyed, sitting with identical frowns and folded arms. Léa is amused until she sees me, and then something wary chases its way through her brown eyes.

"What now?" Samuel asks the boys.

"Dae likes to pick and choose the rules he obeys," Malachai says with a broad London accent. "And when he's feeling really poorly he'll make up his own."

"Boring otherwise," Daeshim says in an American accent.

"Boredom's for people without imaginations," Malachai says.

"Nah, boredom's useful—it makes you innovative."

They look sideways at each other and I see them both fight not to smile. Their fingers entwine, argument concluded.

"Who's this then?" Léa asks. Her accent is French, I think.

"This is Franny Lynch," Basil says.

I shake their hands and the boys seem to brighten.

"The selkie, huh?" Léa asks. Her hand is strong and stained with grease.

I pause, surprised by the reference and all the echoes in a life.

"Seal people who take to the water, only they don't rescue folk like you did, they drown them."

"I know what they are," I murmur. "But I've never heard of a selkie drowning anyone."

Léa shrugs, letting my hand go and sitting back. "That's 'cause they're tricksy and subtle, no?"

She's wrong, but I smile a little, and my own wariness is kindled.

"Enough about that," Daeshim says. "A question for you, Franny. Do you obey rules?"

Expectant eyes rest on me.

The question seems sort of silly, and I could almost laugh. Instead I take a mouthful of wine and then say, "I've always tried to."

At one point Ennis goes to the bar for another round, Samuel disappears to the toilet for the fourteenth time ("When you get to my age, you won't find it so funny"), and Basil, Daeshim, and Léa go out onto the cold deck to have a cigarette, so I find myself cornered on the sofa next to Malachai, even though I'd prefer to be outside smoking. The bar has thinned out a bit—the piano player has knocked off for the evening.

"How long you been here?" Malachai asks me in his deep voice. He has a fidgety quality about him, like an excited puppy, and dark brown eyes, and fingers that tap along to music even when there's nothing playing.

"Only a week. You?"

"We berthed two days ago. Be leaving again in the morning."

"How long have you been with the *Saghani*?"

"Two years, Dae and me."

"Do you . . . like it?"

He flashes me the white of his teeth. "Ah, you know. It's hard and it hurts and some nights you just wanna cry 'cause you're so sore and there's no way off and it feels really small, fuckin' small. But you love it anyway. It's home.

We met on a trawler a few years back, Dae and me, but it didn't go down too good when we hooked up. This crew don't mind a bit, they're family." Malachai pauses and then his smile turns amused. "I'm telling you, it's an insane asylum."

"How's that?"

"Samuel didn't settle down 'til he'd had a child in every port from here to Maine, and he recites poetry because he wants people to know he can. Basil was on some cooking show in Australia but he got kicked out 'cause he couldn't make anything normal—just that weird micro stuff you get in fancy restaurants, you know?"

I grin. "Does he cook for you?"

"He's banned everyone else from the galley."

"At least you must eat well."

"We eat at midnight 'cause he spends hours stuffing around in there and then it's usually a plate of something that looks like sand covered in flower petals and there's only enough of it to leave a foul taste in your mouth. He can be a right prick, too. Then there's Anik, Christ, don't even get me started on him. He's our first mate—did you meet him? Yeah, well, he's like a reincarnation of a wolf. Except if you ask him on a different day he's an eagle, or a snake, depending on how shitty he's feeling. Took me ages to figure out he was making fun of me. He doesn't like anything or anyone. Like, for real. But that's what skiff men are like, you know? They're outsiders, every one of them."

I file skiff men away to ask about later. "And Dae?"

"God love him, he gets so seasick. I shouldn't laugh, it's not funny. But it's part of his daily routine now—wake up, have a puke, finish the day, have a puke, and go to sleep. Wake up and do it again."

I think Malachai might be making all of this up, but I'm certainly enjoying it. I can hear it in his voice, how much he loves them. "Léa?"

"She has a foul temper and she's the most superstitious of us all. You can hardly burp without her spouting some warning and last week we were two days late to depart 'cause she wouldn't set foot on the boat 'til the moon was right."

"What about Ennis?"

Malachai shrugs. "He's just Ennis."

"What's just Ennis?"

"Well, I dunno. He's our captain."

"But not part of the asylum?"

"Nah, not really." Malachai considers, looking awkward. "He's got his shit like everyone."

I can believe this, since I found the man sitting in a fjord. I wait for Malachai to go on. His fingers are drumming furiously.

"He's a wagering man, for one."

"Aren't all men?"

"Nah, not like this."

"Huh. Sports? Racing? Blackjack?"

"Anything. I've seen him lose himself completely. His reasoning—it just goes." Malachai stops speaking and I can tell he feels guilty for having said as much.

I ease off Ennis. "So why do you do it?" I ask instead.

"Do what?"

"Spend your life at sea."

He considers. "I guess it just feels like really living." He smiles shyly. "Plus what else am I gonna do?"

"The protesting doesn't bother you?" Lately I feel like all I see on the news is violent protest rallies at fishing ports around the world—*save the fish, save the oceans!*

Malachai looks away from me. "Sure it does."

Ennis returns with the drinks and hands me another glass of wine.

"Thanks."

"So what does your man think of you being out here?" Malachai asks, nodding to my wedding ring.

I scratch my arm absently. "He works in a similar field so he gets it."

"Science, right?"

I nod.

"What's the bird one called?"

"Ornithology. He's teaching at the moment, and I'm doing the fieldwork."

"I know which sounds more fun," Malachai says.

"Mal, you're the biggest pussy this side of the equator," Basil says, sitting down. "Bet you'd love to be holed up in some safe little classroom some- where. Although that'd require you to be able to read . . ."

Malachai gives him the finger, making Basil grin.

"What does he really think?" Ennis asks me.

"Who?"

"Your husband."

My mouth opens but nothing comes out. I sigh. "He hates it. I'm always leaving him behind."

Later Ennis and I sit at the window and watch the stretch of fjord that swal- lowed us. Behind us his crew members are getting steadily drunker and have taken over the set of Trivial Pursuit, which has incited numerous arguments. Léa doesn't participate in the ribbing, but smugly wins most of the rounds. Samuel is reading by the fire. Any other night I'd be playing with them, and I'd be pushing and prodding to see the make of them. But tonight, the task. I need to get myself onto their boat.

The midnight sun has turned the world indigo and something about the quality of the light reminds me of the land where I was raised, that special Galway blue. I've seen a fair helping of the world and what strikes me most is that there are no two qualities of light the same, no matter where you go. Australia is bright and hard. Galway has a *smudgeness* to it, a tender haze. Here the edges of everything are crisp and cold.

"What would you say if I told you I could find you fish?"

Ennis's eyebrows arch. He's quiet awhile, and then, "I'd reckon you're talking about your birds, and I'd say that's illegal."

"It only became illegal because of the trawling methods huge liners used to use, which would capture and kill all the surrounding marine life and birds. You don't use those anymore, not with a smaller vessel. The birds would be safe. Otherwise I wouldn't suggest it."

"You've done your homework."

I nod.

"So what are we really talking about, Franny Lynch?"

I retrieve the papers from my bag, then return to the stool beside Ennis. I place the papers between us and try to smooth out some of the wrinkles. "I'm studying the migratory patterns of the Arctic tern, looking specifically at what climate change has done to their flight habits. You know all about this, I'd say—it's what's killing the fish."

"And the rest," he says.

"And the rest."

He is peering at the papers but I don't blame him for not interpreting their meaning—they're dense journal articles with the university's stamp on them.

"Do you know of the Arctic tern, Ennis?"

"I've seen them up this way. Nesting season now, isn't it?"

"That's right. The Arctic tern has the longest migration of any animal. It flies from the Arctic all the way to the Antarctic, and then back again within a year. This is an extraordinarily long flight for a bird its size. And because the terns live to be thirty or so, the distance they will travel over the course of their lives is the equivalent of flying to the moon and back three times."

He looks up at me.

We share a silence filled with the beauty of delicate white wings that carry a creature so far. I think of the courage of this and I could cry with it, and maybe there's something in his eyes that suggests he understands a little of that.

"I want to follow them."

"To the moon?"

"To the Antarctic. Through the North Atlantic Sea, along the coast of America, north to south, and then down into the glacial waters of the Weddell Sea, where the birds will rest."

He studies my face. "And you need a vessel."

"I do."

"Why not a research vessel? Who's funding the study?"

"National University of Ireland, in Galway. But they've pulled my funding. I don't even have a team anymore."

"Why?"

I choose my words carefully. "The colony you've seen here, along the coast. It's reported to be the last in the world."

He breathes out heavily, and with no surprise. Nobody needs to be told of the extinction of the animals; for years now we've been watching news bulletins about habitat destruction and species after species being declared first endangered and then officially extinct. There are no more monkeys in the wild, no chimps or apes or gorillas, nor indeed *any* animal that once lived in rain forests. The big cats of the savannas haven't been seen in years, nor have any of the exotic creatures we once went on safari to glimpse. There are no bears in the once-frozen north, or reptiles in the too-hot south, and the last known wolf in the world died in captivity last winter. There is hardly anything wild left, and this is a fate we are, all of us, intimately aware of.

"Most of the funding bodies have given up on the birds," I say. "They're focusing their research elsewhere, in places they think they can actually make a difference. This is predicted to be the last migration the terns will attempt. It's expected they won't survive it."

"But you think they will," Ennis says.

I nod. "I've put trackers on three, but they'll only pinpoint where the birds fly. They aren't cameras, and won't allow us to see the birds' behavior. Someone needs to witness how they survive so we can learn from it and help them. I don't believe we have to lose these birds. I know we don't."

He doesn't say anything, eyeing the NUI stamp on the papers.

"If there are any fish left in this whole ocean, the birds will damn well find them. They seek out hot spots. Take me south and we can follow them."

"We don't go that far south. Greenland to Maine and back. That's it."

"But you could go farther, couldn't you? What about just to Brazil—"

"*Just* to Brazil? You know how far that is? I can't go wherever I please."

"Why?"

He looks at me patiently. "There are protocols to fishing. Territories and methods, tides I know, ports I have to deliver to, to get paid. Crew whose livelihoods depend on the catch and delivery. I've already had to shift my route to take into account all the closing ports. I change it any more and I might as well lose every buyer I have left."

"When was the last time you fulfilled your quota?"

He doesn't reply.

"I can help you find the fish, I swear it. You just have to be brave enough to go farther than you have before."

He stands up. There is something hard in his expression now. I have hit a nerve. "I can't afford to take on another mouth. I can't pay you, feed you, bed you."

"I'll work for free—"

"You don't know the first thing about working a seine. You're not trained. I'd be agreeing to pass you straight into the afterlife if I brought you aboard so green."

I shake my head, unsure how to convince him, flailing. "I'll sign a waiver so you aren't responsible for my safety."

"Can't be done, love. It's too much to ask for naught in return. I'm sorry—it's a romantic idea to follow birds, but life at sea is harder than that, and I got mouths to feed." Ennis touches my shoulder briefly, apologetically, and returns to his crew.

I sit by the window and finish my glass of wine. My chest is aching and aching and if I move I will shatter.

If you were here, Niall, what would you say, how would you do this?

Niall would say that I tried asking, so now I will have to find a way to take.

My eyes home in on Samuel. I go to the bar and order two glasses of whiskey and take one to his seat by the fire.

"You looked thirsty."

He smiles, chuffed. "It's been a long time since I've been bought a drink by a young woman."

I ask him about the book he's reading and listen to him tell me its story, and then I buy him another whiskey and we talk more about books, and poetry, and I buy him yet another whiskey, and I watch him get steadily drunker and listen to his tongue grow steadily looser. I can feel Ennis's eyes; now that he knows my intent I think he's suspicious of me. But I focus my attention on Samuel and when his cheeks are rosy and his eyes glassy, I steer the conversation to his captain.

"How long have you been working on the *Saghani*, Samuel?"

"Nearly a decade now, I'd say, or close enough to."

"Wow. Then you and Ennis must be close."

"He's my king and I his Lancelot."

I smile. "Is he as romantic as you are?"

Samuel chuckles. "My wife would say that's impossible. But there's a little romance in all us sailors."

"Is that why you do it?"

He nods slowly. "It's in our blood."

I shift in my seat, as intrigued by this as I am appalled. How can it be in their blood to kill unreservedly? How can they ignore what's happening to the world?

"What will you do when you can't fish anymore?"

"I'll be all right—I've got my girls waiting for me at home. And the others are all kids, they'll bounce back, find something else to love. But I don't know about Ennis."

"He doesn't have family?" I ask, even though I know otherwise.

Samuel sighs mournfully and takes a huge mouthful of his drink. "He does, he does. Very sad tale, though. He's lost his kids. Been trying to earn enough money to give up this life and get them back."

"What do you mean? He's lost custody of them?"

Samuel nods.

I sit back in my armchair and watch the flames crackle and spit.

I'm startled by the low rumble of a voice, and realize that Samuel has begun to sing a forlorn ballad about life at sea. Jesus, I've really tipped the poor guy over the edge. I try not to laugh as I realize half the pub is staring. With a signal to Ennis, I struggle to drag the big man to his feet.

"I think it's time for bed, Samuel. Can you stand?"

Samuel's voice grows louder, operatic in its intensity.

Ennis arrives to help me with the old man's considerable weight. I remember to grab my backpack, and then we support Samuel, still wailing, out of the bar.

Outside I can't help it. I start laughing.

A few moments later I hear Ennis's soft chuckle join mine.

"Where are you moored?" I ask.

"I can take him from here, love."

"Happy to help," I say, and he nods.

It's not yet dawn, but the light is disorienting. Gray and blue, with a pale sun hanging on the horizon.

We walk along the fjord to the village port. The sea opens up before us, dissolving into the distance. A gull squawks and caterwauls above; they're rare enough now that I watch it for long moments until it disappears from view.

"That's her," Ennis tells me, and I see it. A sleek fishing vessel, maybe thirty meters long, its hull painted black and scrawled with the word *Saghani*.

I knew it the second I read the name. That this was the boat meant for me. Raven.

We help Samuel stumble on board and guide him below deck. The corridors are narrow, and we have to duck to get through the doorways into Samuel's cabin. Small and sparse, with a bed on either side. He wavers and then crashes like a lopped tree onto his mattress. I wrestle with his shoes while Ennis goes to get him a glass of water. By the time it's next to his bed Samuel is already snoring.

Ennis and I glance at each other.

"I'll leave you to it," I say softly. He leads me back up onto the main deck. The smell of the ocean fills me as always and I stop, unable to walk away.

"You all right, love?" he asks.

I take a deep breath of salt and seaweed and I think of the distance between here and there, I think of their flight and mine, and I see in the captain something different, something I couldn't recognize in him before I knew about the children.

I reach into my pack for the map and go to sit by the railing. Ennis follows me and I spread the map between us.

With an invisible dawn approaching I quietly show him how the birds have always set out on separate paths, and where they come back together, each of them following a different route to the fish but always winding up in the same places, always knowing exactly where to meet.

"The spots are a little different each year," I say. "But I know what I'm doing. I have the tech. I can take you to them. I promise."

Ennis scrutinizes the map, and the lines carving their paths through the Atlantic.

Then I say, "I know how important this is to you. Your children are at stake. So we go for one last haul."

He looks up. I can't tell what color his eyes are in the light. He seems very tired.

"You're drowning, Ennis."

We sit for a while in silence, but for the gentle lapping of the waves against the hull. Somewhere distant the gull cries out.

"You're true to your word?" Ennis asks.

I nod once.

He stands and walks below deck, not bothering to pause as he says, "We depart in two hours."

I fold up the map with shaking fingers. A wave of such deep relief hits me that I could almost throw up. My footsteps sound softly on the wooden plank. When I reach land I turn to look back at the boat and its scrawled name.

Mam used to tell me to look for the clues.

"The clues to what?" I asked the first time.

"To life. They're hidden everywhere."

I've been looking for them ever since, and they have led me here, to the boat I will spend the rest of my life aboard. Because one way or another, when I reach Antarctica and my migration is finished, I have decided to die.

GARDA STATION, GALWAY

FOUR YEARS AGO

The floor is cheap linoleum, and very cold. I lost my shoes somewhere, before walking three miles through the snow carrying a bag of football uniforms. I can't remember how I lost them. I told the police, and they put me in this room to wait, and they have not returned to tell me.

But I know.

I pass the minutes and then hours by reciting passages of Tóibín in my head, remembering them as well as I can and trying to find comfort in his story of a woman who loved the sea, only it becomes too hard to try for prose, so I reach instead for poetry, for Mary Oliver and her wild geese and her animal bodies loving what they love, and even that is difficult. The effort of compartmentalizing is a steady scraping away at my mind. The long snaking curl of an orange being peeled in one skillful piece: that is my brain. What about Byron, *the heart will break*—no, maybe Shelley, *what are all these kissings worth*—no, Poe, then, *I lie down by the side of my darling, my darling*—

The door opens and saves me from myself. I am trembling all over and there is a puddle of vomit beside my chair that I don't remember supplying. The detective is a little older than I am, impeccably groomed, her blond hair tied into a neat twist, charcoal suit cut to fit all the right lines of her and shoes that make that *clop clop* sound that always reminds me of a horse. I notice these details with strange precision. She sees the mess and manages not to grimace as she sends for someone to deal with it, and then she sits opposite me.

"I'm Detective Lara Roberts. And you're Franny Stone."

I swallow. "Franny Lynch."

"Of course, sorry. Franny Lynch. I remember you from school. You were a couple of years below me. Always in and out, never staying put. Until you moved away for good. Back to Australia, wasn't it?"

I stare at her numbly.

A man arrives with a mop and bucket and we wait while he painstakingly cleans the vomit. He leaves with his tools and then returns a couple of minutes later with a cup of hot tea for me. I grip it with my frozen hands but don't drink—I think it might make me throw up again.

When Detective Roberts still won't speak, I clear my throat. "So?"

I see it then: the horror she has been working to hide from me. It slides over her eyes like a veil.

"They're dead, Franny."

But I already know that.

3

The *Saghani*, NORTH ATLANTIC SEA
MIGRATION SEASON

My hands have started bleeding to the touch. I spend six hours of each day tying ropes in knots. I am to do this until I can tie all ten of the most common sailing knots blindfolded or in my sleep. I have to know each one intimately, and I have to know which knot is used for which task. I was sure I knew all of this days ago, but Anik has made me continue tying anyway. The blisters formed first, and then they burst and the blood came free, and each night they begin to scab over, just a little, and each morning the scabs are worked off and they bleed again. I am leaving a smear of myself on everything I touch.

Knot tying, though painful, is relatively relaxing compared to my other tasks. I pressure hose the deck twice a day. I scrub it top to bottom, and tidy all the gear away, carrying heavy machinery and tanks of petrol. I clean all the windows, wiping away salt and grime from both sides of every glass surface. I clean inside, too, vacuuming cabin floors, mopping and scrubbing the kitchen, wiping down every surface and making sure there isn't a drop of sitting water anywhere, especially in the freezer area. Sitting water is a boat's nemesis. It causes rust. It makes things stop working.

The first few days after departing were spent unpacking and correctly storing supplies. There is food enough for an army aboard, as it needs to last us months. Yesterday I started learning about the nets. The *Saghani* is a purse seine, with nets 1.5 kilometers long, so the crew spends a great deal of time maintaining these nets, their weights, cables, and the enormous power block, which I think is a mechanized pulley system and rears into the sky like the claw of a crane. I have yet to see any of it in action, because we've been navigating our way through perilous waters in search of a school of herring that may not exist. The nets have "corks" along one edge, which are bright yellow floating devices, and these have to be coiled into a circular pattern so they don't tangle. This, too, cuts open the blisters on my fingers, but I coiled and coiled for eight hours, practicing so that when the nets are actually in use I'll be able to do this quickly and economically. After that I went back to cleaning what was already clean.

I think they're trying to break me.

The crew doesn't want me here. They were bewildered when they heard the new plan, the new path. They're frightened of sailing waters they don't know, that their skipper doesn't know. They resent me for it.

But what they don't suspect is that I love every second of the backbreaking, laborious eighteen-hour days. I have never been so exhausted in my life, and it's perfect. It means I sleep.

The *Saghani* powers slowly through thick ice off the coast of Greenland, splintering it into huge chunks that will be expelled from our path. The sound is like nothing I have ever heard. Great cracks rend the sky, huge whooshes, and always the persistent rumble of sea and engine combined.

I pull my windbreaker tighter about me; even with three thermals underneath I'm still cold, but it feels good. Freezing wind bites at my cheeks and lips, drying them, cracking them. I am being allowed a rare break from my duties to witness the passage. Up in the bridge stands Ennis, carefully navigating his vessel through the dangerous ice. I can see him through persistently salt-rimed glass and under an angry gray sky, just the thick dark beard. In fluorescent orange Samuel stands beside him, reading the gauges.

The others make a steady route from stern to bow, monitoring the ship's passage and watching for chunks big enough to cause damage to the hull. They shout in a language that seems foreign to me, as everything they say on board does. Things like *abeam* and *forepeak* and *belay*.

The terns haven't left Greenland yet. I've been watching the little red dots on my laptop obsessively, knowing it will be soon. Until they do we are staying in the *Saghani*'s normal waters, hoping for luck.

Ennis decides the route we take; he is the one who finds the fish, and so the livelihood of his crew depends entirely on his ability to scour this enormous ocean. I haven't spoken to him since I came aboard. I rarely see him, except at a distance behind the helm. He doesn't eat with us. Basil said this is normal—he's likely up there studying charts and weather reports and sonar tracking devices, the weight of his responsibility lying heavy upon him.

"He's in the heart of the hunt," Anik told me on my first day, as though I should have known this. "It makes him separate. Other."

"He's just making sure we don't all die, and thank the Lord for that," Samuel muttered, lighting two cigarettes at once and passing the second to Anik.

This is how I am learning about the captain of the *Saghani*—from afar, in the snippets his crew members offer up. He has skipper's quarters, whereas the rest of us share a cabin between two, the rooms all adjoining the small mess room and galley. I've been placed in Léa's cabin, and she's unused to having a roommate, to say the least. She doesn't speak to me, except to bark orders, and the cabin is barely big enough for both bunks. The only reason its tiny size has been endurable so far is because I've been too tired to lie awake in the heavy dark and imagine I am in a coffin.

"Franny, outta the way!" Dae shouts as he thunders past. I jump clear in time to hear him holler, "Berg at two degrees port!"

I peer over the railing to see what he's talking about. There's an iceberg jutting out of the layer of flat ice surrounding it, and we are angled directly for it. Presumably its shape means the bulk of it extends much deeper into the sea, whereas the rest of the ice sits mostly atop the water. The icebreakers can't cut through a berg. It doesn't look big enough to do proper damage but I suppose that's what everyone on board the *Titanic* thought. And given the noises being made by the crew, I'd say we're in trouble.

"Brace for impact!"

Basil wrenches me into his chest, pressing us roughly to the deck. The juddering impact sends us sprawling, and my shoulder connects heavily with the wall. I wince as the boat corrects itself once more. If Basil hadn't grabbed me I might have been flung overboard. He's already bolting off down the ship. I struggle to my feet and keep a firm hold of the railing. We're past the iceberg and angled away—we must have clipped the edge of it. I can see ice-free ocean up ahead and my hammering heart doesn't know whether to speed up or slow down.

It's not that I want us to sink or anything, but that was exciting.

"Clear!" Ennis booms from his balcony once we're out of the ice.

"Aye, Skip!" Léa calls.

"Nicely done!" Mal shouts.

Ennis heads down the stairs and I watch him stride to the point of impact, throwing a heavy rope ladder over the side. I lean over to watch him climb down and check the damage to the hull, completely at ease on that rope. Water sprays his body, but he only climbs lower, reaching to touch the long scrape and judge its depth. When he's satisfied he swings up and over, landing with a heavy squelch of boots. "Cosmetic," he tells the waiting crew, who let out a stream of relieved curses.

"You all right, love?" he asks me, the first words he's spoken to me since the night we met.

"Look at her face," Mal says, and as they all clock my expression, whatever it is, they crack up laughing. Even Léa is chuckling, though Anik only rolls his eyes.

Ennis smiles as he passes me, clapping me on the shoulder. "It's got ahold of you now."

"Hey, Franny, wake up."

No.

"Come on."

Someone is dragging me from my bed. It can't be dawn already. I blink blearily and see Dae.

"What are you doing? Let me sleep."

"Dinner's on."

"I'm too tired."

"You'll never survive if you don't eat."

I can see he's not going to be deterred so I haul myself to my feet and stumble into the mess. Malachai makes room for me to slide in next to him at the corner table. The booth seats are a sticky, peeling brown leather and when all seven of us are wedged in it's a tight fit. A small brick of a television is mounted on the wall above us and we all crane our necks to watch one of the four DVDs they have on board—tonight's screening is *Die Hard*, which they can all, without exaggeration, recite word for word. I rest my head on the back of the seat and let myself nod off.

"What the hell are you doing in there?" Dae shouts at one point, wrenching me from my doze.

"What time is it?" I ask groggily.

"One a.m.!" Dae shouts, not for my benefit.

"Patience!" Basil's voice comes from the adjoining galley.

"Can't I please just go to bed?" I ask.

Mal and Dae find my sleep-addled state highly amusing.

"Not coping too well, princess?" Léa asks me coldly.

I sink lower in my seat and ignore them all.

Samuel sits heavily, placing a shot glass in front of me. "This'll help, lass."

I don't have it in me to argue, so I do the shot. It burns so outrageously that I spit half of it over the table and cough until my eyes water. Which makes them all laugh even more. I eye Samuel suspiciously. "Was that revenge?"

He grins. "I am a peaceful man. *An eye for an eye will only make the whole world blind.*"

Samuel pours shots for the others.

"I hate the stuff, too," Malachai sympathizes as he lifts his to his lips.

"Good luck," I mutter.

Someone gasps. "*Putain de crétin!*" Léa snarls.

"What?"

"Don't say good luck, moron!"

"Why not?"

"It's bad luck."

They're all staring at me. I spread my hands. "Well, how was I meant to know?"

"You don't know shit," Léa spits.

"So tell me."

"First lesson," Samuel announces.

"Don't ever step onto the boat with your left foot first," Léa says with a horrified shudder.

"Don't leave port on a Friday," says Dae.

"Don't open a tin upside down," says Samuel.

"No bananas," Léa says. "Or whistling."

"No women on board," says Basil as he emerges from the galley with a plate in each hand. He winks at Léa as he says it. "Don't worry, we live dangerously on the *Saghani*."

Samuel and Dae stare at the plates they've been delivered. And rightly so. There is a small, slender S-shaped curl of spaghetti, artfully painted with delicate swirls of red and yellow sauces and finished off with shards of what looks like parmesan, wedged perfectly between the pasta so they stand aloft. To be honest I'm surprised there's much fresh food at all, but we've only just begun the journey—according to Dae the menu will go steadily downhill over time.

"What . . ." Mal can't even finish. He appears to be swallowing the urge to scream, or possibly having a stroke.

"What's this meant to be then?" Samuel demands.

"Spag Bol," Basil says as he returns with more plates. "You said you wanted something normal so here you bloody go."

"But . . . *how?*"

"It's deconstructed."

"Well . . . can it please be reconstructed?"

I can't help it. I cover my mouth and laugh.

Dae manages to grab all the leftover bits and pieces and heap our plates with a normal-sized serving, while Basil grumbles about overeating in the American populace. I'm handed a bowl with plain spaghetti because they know by now that I'm vegetarian. "Not even fish?" Basil demanded when he found out.

"Not even fish." This piece of information was met with a great deal of suspicion.

After dinner I do the washing up and wipe down the kitchen, and then, because the food has woken me up a bit, I pour myself a few fingers of whiskey to quiet the noise in my head, and go up onto the main deck to smoke.

We've left the midnight sun behind. Night has found us.

I wander to the bow so I can watch the endless stretch of black sea. It's calm now, mostly, and quiet but for the engine's rumble and the ocean's *shhhhh*. We glide along at a cracking pace, headed south. I light a cigarette, knowing that when I start I can't stop, and that I'll likely stand here and smoke an entire packet, one after the other in an effort to survive the night. The poison of the smoke feels good in my lungs; it feels damaging.

"Ennis says this is the only true wild left."

Samuel appears beside me.

I gaze at the dark expanse of it and know what he means. I'm glad now that Dae woke me—I haven't had a moment to think since I boarded a week ago.

"Do you think your wife will forgive you for being away longer?" I ask.

"Sure. Not so likely to forgive you, though."

I'm unsure what to say. I could apologize, but I'm not sorry.

"So she doesn't like you leaving?"

"No."

"Then why do you do it?"

"*There is pleasure in the pathless woods. There is rapture on the lonely shore. There is society where none intrudes, by the deep sea, and music in its roar.*"

I smile. "Byron."

"Bless you, dear, I do love the Irish." He pauses and grins. "And by God I love to fish."

But why? I want to ask. *Why?*

I can understand wanting to be at sea. Of course I can. I have loved the sea all my life. But fishing? Maybe it's not exactly the fishing these people love, but the freedom, the adventure, the danger. The respect I have for them wants to believe that.

"I could do without the coming and going, though, and the months away. You know what I'd really like?" Samuel asks.

"What would you like?"

"I'd like to take my reel down to the beach on my little stretch of land and spend all my hours with a line in, drinking wine and reading poetry."

"Any in particular?"

"*Do you not see how necessary a world of pains and troubles is to school an intelligence and make it a soul?*"

I search my memory, and take a stab. "Is that Keats?"

"You get bonus points for that one."

"It sounds perfect. Why don't you?"

"I have a lot of children to feed."

I consider this. It's not the pathless woods or the lonely shore that guides him from his home, then, but necessity.

"Does he find much anymore?" I ask.

Samuel shrugs, uncomfortable. "He used to. Everyone wanted to work for Ennis Malone. Herring aplenty. Now it's no easy task. The turning o' the world, right there. Things grow dire." He looks at me. "Don't have time to be chasing birds all over the world."

I don't repeat myself: I've already told them the birds will lead them to fish. They don't believe me. They believe in superstition, and in routine. They believe in knowing the oceans you sail.

"Today with that berg—that was nothing," Samuel says. "It'll get much worse as we reach the Gulf Stream."

"Why's that?"

"It connects with the Labrador Current, which'll give us a lift south. They're two of the great currents of the world, moving in opposite directions." He takes a drag of his cigarette, the butt glowing red in the dark. "When you reach that spot, where they brush against each other . . ." Samuel shakes his head. "You can't count on much. It's a beast of an ocean, the Atlantic. Ennis told me once that he's sailed it for most of his life and he still knows next to nothing about it."

"Ennis seems to say a lot of things to everyone except me."

Samuel looks sideways at me, then reaches to pat my shoulder kindly. "You're brand-new, kid. And he's focused."

"He's pissed."

"If he regrets his decision he won't take it out on you. He's not that petty. Look, what I mean to be asking is if you're really sure about all this, lass. Quick way to the grave, hopping aboard a deep-sea vessel without the skills to survive it. Even if you do have the skills, come to think of it."

"You've survived." I suspect he's hiding nimble feet under that rotund figure.

"And I expect Lady Luck to change her mind about that most every day."

I shrug. "Well, Samuel, what can I say. If I die on this boat, then I guess it's just my fate, isn't it."

"Huh."

"Huh what?"

There's something gentle in his eyes as he looks at me. "What makes a young thing like you so tired of life?"

When I don't answer he hugs me. I am so surprised that I don't remember to return the embrace. There are very few people, in my understanding of the world, who offer tenderness so freely.

I don't follow the old sailor back inside. Instead I think about what he has perceived in me and know it isn't true. It's not life I'm tired of, with its astonishing ocean currents and layers of ice and all the delicate feathers that make up a wing. It's myself.

There are two worlds. One is made of water and earth, of rock and minerals. It has a core, a mantle and a crust, and oxygen for breathing.

The other is made of fear.

I have inhabited each and know one to feel deceptively like the other. Until it is too late, and you are watching the eyes of the other inmates to see if there is death in them, watching every face you pass, listening to the angry hum for a hint you are its next target, clawing at the walls of your cell to get free, to get out, for air and sky and please, not this shrinking tomb.

The fear world is worse than death. It is worse than anything.

And it has found me once more, way out in the Atlantic, inside this rocking cabin.

Tonight is the first night I haven't been able to sleep.

"Primary coverts," I whisper through chattering teeth, "greater coverts, median coverts, scapular, mantle, nape, crown—*shit*." I lurch upright because even the mantra isn't helping me tonight, it's not calming or centering me, there's no distraction from the queasy terror of this skyless room.

I click on my travel torch and wedge it on top of my pack so its beam lights my notebook.

Niall, I scribble. I have to forestall a full-blown panic attack. *Where are your lungs when I need them? Where is your sense, your perpetual calm?*

It's been over a week and we've escaped the ice. We're headed for the Labrador Current, which Samuel says is dangerous. He says this whole ocean is dangerous. I'm not sure you'd like it. I think you enjoy having your feet on solid ground too much, but the sea is like the sky and I can't get enough of either. When I die don't bury me in the ground. Scatter me to the wind.

I stop because tears have blurred my eyes. This won't be one of the letters I send. It would frighten him to hear me speak of dying.

"Turn that fucking light off," Léa snaps at me from her bed.

I riffle through my pack until I find the sleeping pills. I'm not meant to take them with alcohol but at this point I don't give a shit. I swallow one and then squeeze my eyes shut. *Primary coverts, greater coverts, median coverts, scapular, mantle, nape, crown—*

I wake hanging two inches above the sea. It roars black and bottomless, its spray icy against my face. For a moment it must be the most perfect dream and then the moment passes and I realize I'm awake and my body lurches with such shock that I nearly fall.

I'm clinging to the rope ladder I saw Ennis use. Swaying precariously against the ship's hull. My knuckles are white and frozen in their grip, and I am not wearing enough layers, not even close.

I have sleepwalked here.

I am about to haul myself the hell up when instead I stop. I've found myself in strange places before, but never this extreme, this perilous. I feel abruptly alive, for the first time in years. For the first time, if I'm being honest, since the night my husband left me.

To be fair, I left him first, more times than I can count.

"Yours is a terrible will," he told me once. And that is true, but I have been a casualty of it far longer than he has.

The rope's ascent drags me from the sea. Someone has turned on the crank and now I rise without having decided to do so. For a second I hate whoever is pulling me up. Then thoughts blur as the cold finds its mark. Hands haul me over into a bundle of limbs. The flash of moonlit skin tells me this is Léa, her long frame strong enough to support my useless body. My legs can barely hold me upright, so she does that for me.

"What the *fuck*."

"I'm okay."

"You're goddamn freezing." She starts pulling me over the deck, catching me when I stumble. "What the fuck are you doing, Franny," she says, but not really like a question. "What is wrong with you."

We manage to get down the ladder and below deck. My teeth are tiny jackhammers. Into the little bathroom with its shower so narrow I have to step out to wash my hair. She wrenches off my sweater and shoves me under a stream of hot water. It burns so badly I bite my tongue and taste copper. Knees give out, and she catches me in time to sink with me to the floor, both of us soaked and scalded now, a tangled mess of extremities freezing and burning and everything in between.

"What is wrong with you?" she asks again, but really asking now.

I give a breath of laughter. "How much time do you have?"

Her arms tighten about me, shifting to an embrace.

I don't have the energy for more, so I say only, "I'm sorry," and I mean it.

4

NATIONAL UNIVERSITY OF IRELAND, GALWAY, IRELAND
TWELVE YEARS AGO

"*We ate the birds*," he says. "*We ate them. We wanted their songs to flow up through our throats and burst out of our mouths, and so we ate them. We wanted their feathers to bud from our flesh. We wanted their wings, we wanted to fly as they did, soar freely among the treetops and the clouds, and so we ate them. We speared them, we clubbed them, we tangled their feet in glue, we netted them, we spitted them, we threw them onto hot coals, and all for love, because we loved them. We wanted to be one with them.*"

There is silence in the enormous hall. He is small, down there behind his lectern. And big enough to fill the space. Loud enough, powerful enough. We are hanging on his every word, even if the words don't belong to him, even if he is only saying to us what Margaret Atwood said first.

"They have been here for two hundred million years," he says, "and until recently there were ten thousand species. They evolved to go in search of food, traveling farther than any other animal to survive, and thus they colonized the earth. From the oilbird, which lived in pitch-black caves, to the bar-headed goose, which bred only on the desolate Tibetan plateau. From the rufous hummingbird, which survived in the freezing altitude of fourteen thousand feet to the Rüppell's griffon vulture, which could fly as high as a commercial airplane. These extraordinary creatures were undoubtedly the most successful on earth, because they courageously learned to exist anywhere."

My heart is beating too fast and I will myself to be calm, to breathe more slowly, to really take this in. To savor it and remember every detail because too soon I will be gone from the circle of his perfect words.

The professor moves out from behind his lectern and spreads his hands beseechingly. "The only true threat to birds that has ever existed is us.

"In the 1600s the Bermuda petrel, of the Procellariidae family, the national bird of Bermuda, was hunted for meat so catastrophically that they were thought to be extinct. Until, in 1951, by sheer accident they were found again, only eighteen pairs of them. They were hiding, nesting in the cliffs of small islands. I imagine that day a great deal." He pauses as though to imagine it now, and I marvel at the command he has over the hall. I am with him on those cliffs, discovering those lonely little birds, the only survivors of their kind. He goes on, and his voice is hard now, demanding. "They did not survive our second attack. This one was crueler, far more pervasive. With the burning of fossil fuels we changed the world, we've killed it. As the climate grew hotter and the sea levels rose, the Bermuda petrels were washed from their burrows and drowned. That is one species of a very great many. And it's not only birds that suffer—as I've said, birds tend to be the most resilient. Polar bears are gone, thanks to that rise in temperature. Sea turtles have gone, the beaches where they once lay their eggs eroded by those same rising seas. The ringtail possum, which could not survive temperatures above thirty degrees Celsius, was decimated by a single heat wave. Lions perished in never-ending droughts, rhinos were lost to poaching. And on it goes. Those are simply a few you know of, the stars of the animal kingdom, but if I started listing the creatures destroyed by habitat destruction we would be here all day. Thousands of species are dying right now, and being ignored. We are wiping them out. Creatures that have learned to survive anything, *everything*, except us."

He walks back to his lectern and turns on his projector. He is tall and lean, maybe even thin, with short, dark hair and an impeccably tailored navy suit. A lime-green bow tie makes him seem a man of another time, as do glasses that can really only be called spectacles. Despite his strange appearance he is the darling of the university staff. Adored by his students. Almost young enough to be one of them. There is a table with a covering over it, its image projected large onto the wall. He slides the calico off with a magician-esque flourish to reveal a bird.

It takes me a moment to realize that it is real, dead and stuffed and pinned to some sort of apparatus so that it appears in flight. A gull, white and gray and too much. Like that, I am no longer with him; I have fallen behind. I stand and move awkwardly past the other students in my row, causing a mild rustle of annoyance but not caring, needing out.

His voice follows me. "This semester we will be looking not only at the anatomy of birds, but their breeding, feeding, and migration patterns, and how these have been affected over time—both negatively and positively—by human interference—" The door falls shut with a slight bang that they will have heard inside. I run, sandals slapping the lino. Out into the sunshine, down the steps to where I've locked my bike. I work the code with unsteady fingers and then I ride as fast as I can, my hair streaming behind me, through cobblestone streets and all the way to the sea.

The bike crashes to the ground and I hop to get my shoes off, flinging them to the grass and sprinting until I hit the water and dive beneath the surface.

Here is the sky. The salty weightless sky. Here I can fly.

I genuinely consider not going back. I'm growing restless—I don't like being so close to the house my mother and I once shared. I'm tired of Galway. But being in the university is serving a purpose: it allows me access to their genealogy software, and that is how I'm going to do it, that is how I will find my mother.

"You're late."

"My gift to you, Mark, since you take such pleasure in pointing it out." I dump my bag in the locker and pull on my janitor's jumpsuit. Mark does not look impressed, so I grab the mop and bucket and get moving.

"You're on the film buildings."

"Can't I do the labs?"

"Franny—"

"I'll do overtime," I promise as I wheel my bucket out. "Thanks!"

Someone has made a revolting mess in the male bathroom in the biology building. I pull my T-shirt up over my nose and try not to gag as I clean it. Three young men are waiting to use the bathroom as I emerge, expressions full of distaste and maybe a little disdain, as though I am responsible for the mess. They don't look me in the eye as I pass, they don't even glance my way—hardly anyone in this school does. Being a cleaner is like having the power of invisibility. So I make a game of it. I smile at people. Mostly they seem to think I must be a wee bit touched, and hurry on by. But sometimes, occasionally, they return the smile, and those smiles are sweet enough to collect.

I use my key card to enter the lab itself. I can't see anyone, which would make sense as it's after hours, except the lab usually contains the huddled forms of the obsessive, those uninterested in the outside world and unwilling to leave here no matter the time of day. I don't turn the lights on, but move into the quiet, cool space wreathed only in the red glow from the security monitors. Specimens are kept in even lower temperatures, in metal refrigerated drawers that hiss as they are opened and closed. I run my fingers over the edges of them, imagining all the little treasures inside and wanting so much to peek. I can't risk it—I'd hate to damage something—so I wander on, my cleaning gear forgotten at the door. Mostly the lab is filled with desks covered in different types of testing machinery, but there are also shelves holding hundreds of glass jars and bottles and tubes, and these glitter a little in the dim winking light. I move past the empty glass to the insects and reptiles held in ethanol, as fascinated by them as I am repulsed. They don't look real, floating motionless in there. Or maybe they look too real.

These are easier to consider than the bird in the lecture hall this morning. I should know better: thoughts conjure their like. As I turn my head a fraction I see it. There, in the corner of my eye.

I have always been frightened of dead things, birds more so than anything else. There is nothing so disturbing as a creature born to flight being bound to dull lifelessness.

I turn from the white shape of it and come face-to-face with a person. A yelp escapes my mouth. "Jesus." I lift a hand to my pounding heart.

It's the professor, watching me in the dark.

"The girl who fled my class," he says. His gaze goes to the cleaning trolley near the door, then back to me. "Come here."

I am momentarily stunned as he takes my elbow and steers me toward the dead gull. The presumption of his touch makes my mouth dry, but since I will always be a person who craves boldness, I am also thrilled by it. Then I am looking at the creature and I have no thoughts for touch, I am empty of any thoughts except the one telling me to get away from here. I go for the door but he—astonishingly—grabs my arms and holds me in front of him, holds me firm, traps me before this macabre thing.

"Don't be frightened. There's nothing here but flesh and feathers."

Doesn't he know? That's the problem.

"Open your eyes."

I open them and look. The bird is frozen and staring. Its feathers are clean and smooth. Eyes lifeless. It's such a sad, still thing that my chest aches. Delicate and sweet and all the worse for it.

The professor lifts my hand and guides it to the carcass. I want nothing less than to touch it but I've entered a dreamscape and no longer have control of my limbs. The pad of my index finger is pressed ever so lightly to the edge of a wing feather.

"Primary coverts," he says softly.

He traces my finger for me, up the length of the feather to different feathers of the wing, "greater coverts, median coverts, scapular," then up over the body, the shoulder area, the neck, "mantle," he murmurs, "nape," and up to the soft shape of the bird's skull, "crown."

He lets me go and my hand drops away. And yet, in the quiet weightlessness of the moment, I feel it itching to go back, to touch the creature again. To join my skin with its feathers, breathe air back into its lungs.

"The vessel is as graceful as the life was," the professor says.

I wake from the dream. "Is this how you seduce your students? With scientific terms in a dark lab?"

He blinks, surprised. "It's not."

"I didn't say you could touch me."

He steps back immediately. "Forgive me."

My pulse is thrumming and on fire and I want to punish him for making me feel out of control, except that I also love being out of control and the whole thing is so confusing that it becomes repulsive and I turn for the door without looking at him.

"Don't be late to class," he calls as I grab my trolley and shove it into the corridor. But I don't have any intention of ever nearing Professor Niall Lynch again.

The car that picks me up is a rusting old Ford, driven by two young women. I have rules about hitching: no vans, no trucks, no cars driven by single men. I learned this rule after stupidly climbing into a panel van when I was fourteen and being ordered to give the middle-aged driver a blow job.

There are two surfboards tied to the roof and sand all over my seat: the girls are surfers. They take me south along the coast and stop at a hostel, where we drink ourselves numb and talk about our fears. Their names are Chloe and Megan and they follow the swells. Outside a murmuration of starlings throbs its glorious way through the white sky.

I go in search of the water. It doesn't take me long to catch the scent, to feel the tug. There's a compass in my heart that leads me not to true north but to true sea. No matter which direction I turn, I will find myself being persistently corrected. The low roar reaches me first, as always, and the smell.

The girls follow me and I lead them down to it. We drink red wine that stains our mouths black and I gather sea spaghetti for later, when it can be cooked in a billy pot and eaten sloppily with fingers straight from the fire. There are empty shards of shells shining silver in the moonlight, and they grow into a shimmering trail I must follow, leaving behind the warmth of voices and laughter. The trail leads me into the water, so I take off my clothes and dive in, the cold a knife to my lungs and laughter flying from me in birdlike screeches.

This is the stretch of coast—the Burren, it's called—where my mother's family is from. They have dwelled here where the hills are silver with slate for hundreds of years. When I was sixteen I came back here, but found no one. I tried again at nineteen. And once more now, at twenty-two. This time I am determined to stay as long as it takes; I have rented a room in a shared house and found myself a job, and each minute I'm not working I spend in the library trying to sketch out a family tree. It's been difficult because so many people share the same names and I have no idea which lines I belong to or even which Iris Stone is actually my mother. It's my deepest hope that if I find even just one member of her family, they will lead me to her.

At sunrise I watch Chloe and Megan pull on their wet suits and run into the surf to press their powerful bodies into the teeth of it. I could watch the paddle and rise and twist of them all day long. They know the ocean well, but they fight it, somehow. They pound and bash against it as swimmers don't, cleaving their waxed weapons through its walls. It's violent.

I join them without a wet suit or a board, just my own thin skin. The ocean washes away anything bitter left upon me, remaking me fresh. I am smiling so widely as I emerge that it must almost split my face. The three of us collapse onto the warm sand; they unzip each other and wriggle free.

"Nine degrees in there," Chloe says with a laugh. She shakes her matted locks and a kilo of sand pours free. "How do you do it without a suit?"

I shrug, grin. "Seal blood."

"Oh, aye, you've the dark look of them, too."

I've been told this before. It's the black hair and the black eyes and the pale, pale skin. It's how the black Irish used to look, back in the days when folktales were true and people might really have come from the sea. It's how my mother looks.

"Where are we headed today?"

"I'll walk from here," I say. "Thanks for the ride."

"How will you get back?" Megan asks.

"Back to where?"

"Galway. Your life. Isn't that where it is?"

I don't know the answer to that. I had thought my life was just here, with me.

. . .

The Bowens live in a pink cottage outside Kilfenora. They own the town pub, Linnanes, and they are all in the Kilfenora Céilí Band, which has traveled the world. I've watched videos of them online, and I found two of their CDs in an underground music shop in Galway, much to my delight. These I have been listening to on repeat for a month. Now that I'm here I can hardly speak for nerves. It takes all my courage to knock on the front door, but it isn't answered and when I peek around the side I'm fairly sure no one's home.

So I hop the fence, a woman possessed. I want to understand where my mam comes from. I want to know if she ever lived here, or even just visited. These would be her cousins, I think, maybe second or third cousins. A great-aunt, maybe? Or perhaps I have it wrong and they are even further relations than that, perhaps the branches skewed apart generations ago, but I know that in some small way they are family, and that is enough for me.

There is washing on the line and the back door is open a crack. Something barks seconds before it crashes into me and I find myself accosted by a black-and-white sheepdog, all tongue and eyes and paws of excitement. I wrestle the dog off me with a grunt and a laugh and that's when—

"Who's that?"

I look up to see an old woman in the back doorway. She has a violet woolen pullover on, and short white hair and glasses and slippers.

"I . . . Hi, I'm really sorry, I . . ."

"What's that?"

I go closer, which is tricky with the dog leaning against my legs as though she's missed me all her life. "I'm looking for Margaret Bowen."

"That'll be me."

"My name's Franny Stone," I say. "Sorry to just come in."

"Stone? You'll be a relation, then?" And just like that she smiles and then laughs with delight and ushers me in. And she keeps laughing all the while she makes me a cup of tea, and while I tell her how I got here, by hitching and walking, and she laughs all the more when she starts calling round to her family and telling them they have to come over tonight. And I know that she's not laughing at me, she's laughing for happiness, for life, and I know just as well that she laughs like this all the time, every day, every minute. She is an absolute joy of a human being and I almost start crying right here in her kitchen as she jokes about needing a hot toddy instead of a boring old cuppa tea.

"Who is it then, love, which bit of the family do you come from?"

I panic, suddenly, and say, "I'm from the Australian branch."

"Australia?" This seems to confuse her. "Goodness, you've come a long way then. What is it brought you here then?"

I don't tell her that I'm Irish, too. It feels fraudulent. As though she is the real Irish and I am only a pretender. I say instead that our family left Ireland five generations ago and settled in Australia, which they did on my father's side, I'm told. I say that I've always wanted to come back here and find the other side of the family, those descended from the ones who stayed, instead of the ones who left. This is truer to my nature, surely, and maybe this is why it feels right to share. That I am of the leavers, the searchers, the wanderers. The ilk of those taken by the tides, instead of the steadfast, the true. But that a part of me has always wanted to belong here.

She tells me of the other relations who've made the journey over from Australia, more cousins, seemingly an endless string of them, all fascinated by what they see as their heritage, and she says, with a laugh, that she's never rightly understood the fascination, why they come here in droves to see this small windy stretch of land, where life is as plain as it comes. I don't know how to answer her, except to agree that it is somewhat inexplicable, but has, I think, to do with music and stories and poetry and roots and family and belonging and curiosity. She takes this for truth and then goes right ahead and makes me a hot toddy regardless of the time. Her husband, Michael, is sitting in an armchair nearby and when Margaret introduces us I see that he can't speak, nor can he move well, but he smiles as widely as she does, with the brightest eyes I have ever seen, and she tends to him with the tenderness of a lifetime's worth of love.

The family arrives soon. Her three sons and four daughters, and several of their partners and children, too. It's clear none of them have any idea who I am, but they all shake my hand or kiss my cheek, and they chat and laugh happily, all of us pressed in around the small kitchen table, everyone making room for Michael to be wheeled into pride of place, and we eat chocolate biscuits and drink from enormous bottles of Coca-Cola and then without preamble they draw free their instruments and begin to play.

I sit in stunned silence as the music unfolds around me. Three fiddles, furiously sawed or plucked, a set of pipes, hand drums, a flute, two guitars, and several of them singing. It swells to fill the kitchen, every inch of it and more, it is a bursting of life, of soulfulness, of fun. I'm watching half the bloody world-famous Kilfenora Céilí Band performing in a kitchen. Margaret bops up and down in her seat, her eyes shining with enjoyment. Without warning she takes my hand. I whisper, "Does this happen every night?"

And she says, "No, dear, this is for you." And I do start crying then.

Later they take a break and demand that I sing, and it's with no small measure of shame that I admit I don't know the words to any songs.

"None?" Margaret's son John asks. "Come on, you know something, all right. Shout out a name. Or just start away and we'll follow you."

"I'm . . . It's not like this in Australia. We don't really learn songs, not any worth singing. I'm so embarrassed."

There's a surprised silence.

"Well, then you've a homework task to complete. Next time you come to visit us here we expect you to have learned a song to share with us."

I can't nod vigorously enough. "I promise."

It ends too soon. They all have to get home, and Margaret needs to get Michael to bed. I don't know what to do or where to go. I keep lying and telling them I already have somewhere to stay, and I have no idea why I do this. I think the idea of imposing any further is mortifying.

It's with a swelling of desperation that I pause at the front door, even though poor Margaret is so tired. "Do you know Iris Stone?" I ask finally.

She frowns and thinks, and shakes her head. "I don't believe I do. Is she one of yours?"

I swallow. "My mother."

"Ah, lovely. If she's ever this way, love, you tell her to visit us."

"I will."

"No, 'tis a shame I don't know more of you. The only Stone I know, come to think of it, was a Maire Stone, married to old John Torpey, my dear husband's cousin. They were living up north a ways, last I heard."

I'm not sure who these people are but I'm certainly going to find out.

"You get home safe tonight, dear," Margaret tells me. "You're sure I can't make you up a bed?"

"I'm sure. Thank you, Margaret. Tonight meant a lot to me."

I walk out into the dark night. I'm a long way from town, but I don't mind. The night is mild with summer and the moon wide, and I like to walk. And perhaps this walk wasn't one my mother ever made, but I feel a step closer to finding the ones she did.

It's time to return to Galway, to where I'll find Maire Stone and her husband, John Torpey.

And to where there's a man, with his coverts and scapulars, with mantles and napes and crowns and birds dead or alive. Without my permission, something in me seems to have turned itself toward him.

5

The *Saghani*, NORTH ATLANTIC OCEAN
MIGRATION SEASON

There are bodies gathered around mine, pressing against me, elbowing for space. Everyone wants to see: on the laptop screen are three little red dots.

And they're moving south.

"So these are what we're gonna follow?" Mal asks.

I nod.

Samuel sees my expression and laughs, patting me on the back. "Well done, lass."

"How reliable are the trackers?" Léa asks skeptically.

"They're geolocators," I say. "They measure light levels, which the software uses to measure latitude and longitude and get the location."

"That doesn't sound reliable at all."

Given that's the extent of my knowledge of the trackers, I can't help but agree with her.

"Get your head out of the way," Basil says, shoving Dae to the side so he can see better.

Together we watch the dots. After resenting the hell out of me, the sight of movement on the screen has the crew wriggling with eagerness. The birds are still farther north than we are, having only just left Greenland, but they'll catch up to us soon, cleverly using the winds to hurry themselves along. After a while the three dots diverge a little, converge again, and then seem to be setting off in different directions.

"That'd be right. What do we do now?" Mal asks.

I take the laptop up to the bridge. I haven't been in here before, have only spied from a distance and wondered at the decisions made within. Ennis sits alone at the helm, gazing out to where sea meets sky. This room is higher than anywhere else on the boat, save for the crow's nest, and I'm struck for a moment by the sight of the world spread before us. Sunrise has cast both sea and sky a startling red.

"I've never seen a sunrise that color," I murmur.

"Bodes a storm," Ennis says. Then without looking at me, "How can I help you, Franny Lynch?" There is a crispness to his tone, his posture. Something in him mistrusts me, resents me, even dislikes me a little. I don't exactly know why, but I can feel it.

"The terns have left Greenland."

I place the computer on the big round desk at the center of the bridge. Ennis joins me and we peer at the dots. "See how they're diverging?" Two of the trackers have headed east, while the solitary tracker has veered west.

"Is that unusual?" he asks.

"No. It happens. They usually take one of two paths. They'll either travel alone or in small groups, and some will go east, down the coast of Africa. Some west along America. But never straight. They curve in big S shapes."

"Why travel farther than they have to?"

"They follow wind and food, as you follow the currents."

"The hot spots you mentioned."

"Aye."

"Can you predict where they'll go this time?"

"I've got old maps of where they once flew, but the data's outdated. There were fish then. It'll be different now, with an ocean nearly empty."

"What are you telling me to do, Franny?"

"I think we should follow the two birds along Africa. Better odds."

He thinks for a long time, watching the screen.

My heart beats a little too quickly when I follow his gaze and see where that path might take the birds first. To Ireland, or just past it.

Ennis shakes his head. "We'll follow the one traveling west. I know the waters better."

"It's a bigger risk," I warn. "Half the likelihood it'll find fish."

"I'm not following red dots on a wild-goose chase to the other side of the Atlantic."

Rather than reminding him that this is the whole point of what we're doing, I bite my tongue. "You're the boss."

"Leave that with me, will you."

I open my mouth to argue, to tell him the software won't be leaving my side, then realize how foolish this is. He can't follow the bird without seeing it. With a last look at the dots, I relinquish the laptop and head for the door.

"Tell me," he says, staying me. "I have the trackers, so why do I need you?"

I turn around and meet his eyes. It's the first time he's looked at me since we left Greenland. There's a challenge in him, bristling to his surface. He wants to take me back to shore, I can see it, and it stirs my ferocity. I want to snarl at him, *dare* him to try to leave me behind, tell him the truth that I'd burn this fucking boat to ash before I let it follow the birds without me. I've come too far, survived too damn much.

But I've a calmer heart, too, living alongside the savage one. Its voice often sounds a lot like my husband's, and it counsels caution, it warns me that there is a very long way yet to travel and that cunning will serve me better than fury.

I clear my throat and say, "You don't. But I need you. And I guess you gotta work out what your conscience will allow."

Ennis's gaze drops away, grip returning to the helm. "How are your hands?"

I don't bother replying. He knows how my hands are. And I won't play at beholden any more than I have to.

The skipper dismisses me.

. . .

"Why's he so pissed at me?" I ask around the mess table tonight.

The crew look up at me from their hand of poker. Léa rolls her eyes, returns her attention to her cards.

"He's not pissed—" Samuel starts.

"Is anyone going to tell me the truth? What exactly have I done?"

"It's not what you've done," Mal says uncomfortably.

"It's what you are," Anik says bluntly.

I look at him, at the blank expression I'm never able to read. "And what am I?"

"Untrained," he says. "Dangerous. Too wild for a boat."

Words dissolve on my tongue.

There's an airless silence.

"It's not your fault," Dae says gently.

But it is, of course it is.

I'm not meant to, but I return to the bridge twice a day to check on the terns. Their red lights blink steadily, busily tracking their journeys. The bird we're following is guiding us south and west toward the coast of Canada. Ennis is charting a course he thinks will intercept the tern, as long as it holds fast to its trajectory. He doesn't speak to me of anything else, and he doesn't much look at me, but it doesn't matter; with each visit to the bridge I grow fonder of the little red dot, more concerned for it, more in love.

This afternoon is calm, the sky cloudless. We're moving slowly through flat glassy water.

I'm tying knots. Surprise, surprise.

"Show me a rolling hitch," Anik says.

I loop the smaller rope around the thicker one, make another coil, a half hitch, and then finish the rolling hitch by pulling it tight.

Anik looks unimpressed. "What's it for?"

"When you need to pull something lengthwise. Or slacken a tensioned sail line if the winch gets jammed."

He watches my face. "Do you have any idea what that means?"

"No."

I think he *almost* smiles. Then the bastard tells me to do fifty more before I switch back to sheet bends.

When Anik's out of sight I lower the ropes, tilt my face back, and enjoy the sun. The deck beneath me is warm and the air is still cold but for the first time I'm not wearing fifty layers. Thoughts drift to Niall, always. I wonder how he would take to this life, to the physicality of it. His mind, always working so swiftly, seeking answers to unanswerable questions, would probably be numb with boredom, but I think it might be good for him to have a break from so much thinking. It would be good for him to live more in his body than in his head. His hands, though. They are smooth and slender and unblemished. They are upon me now as vividly as anything I've felt, tracing my sun-warmed skin, my dry lips, tired eyelids, massaging my aching scalp in just the way they do. I'd hate to see them suffer the punishment mine have

A voice floats down from the sky.

I squint up at Dae in the crow's nest. He's laughing and pointing.

The ropes fall from my hands, forgotten. My feet hurry to the railing, heart swelling. And I see them, white shapes in the distance, flying ever closer.

6

When I was six years old my mother used to sit with me in our back garden to watch the crows perch in the huge willow tree. In winter months the long hanging leaves would turn white like the snow on the ground, or like the wispy whiskers of an ancient man, and the crows hiding among them were stark spots of coal. To me they were the presence of something profound, though at six I didn't know what. Something like loneliness, or its opposite. They were time, and the world; they were the distances they could fly and the places to which I could never follow.

Mam told me never to feed them or they'd grow dangerous, but when she went inside I did it anyway. Crusts from my toast or pieces of Mr. Hazel's orange cake, carefully concealed in pockets and then scattered covertly over the frost. The crows began to expect the offerings and came more often; soon it was every day. They would perch in the willow and watch for my crumbs. There were twelve of them. Sometimes fewer but never more. I would wait until Mam was occupied and then slip outside to them, to where they waited.

The crows began to follow me. If we walked to the shops they would fly alongside and perch on the roofs of houses. When I trailed the stone walls into the hills they circled above. They followed me to school and waited in the trees for me to finish my day. They were my constant companions, and my mother, maybe intuiting that I needed them to be a secret, pretended all along that she didn't notice my devoted dark cloud.

One day the crows began to bring me gifts in return.

Little stones or shiny sweet wrappers were left in the garden or dropped near my feet. Paper clips and bobby pins, pieces of jewelry or rubbish, sometimes shells or rocks or bits of plastic. I kept each in a box that year by year had to grow bigger. Even when I forgot to feed the birds they brought me gifts. They were mine, and I theirs, and we loved each other.

So it went for four years, every day without fail. Until I left not only my mother but my twelve kindred spirits, too. Sometimes I dream of them waiting in that tree for a girl who would never come, bringing gift after precious gift to lie unloved in the grass.

The *Saghani*, NORTH ATLANTIC OCEAN
MIGRATION SEASON

The birds are tired already, even so early in the journey, so it's lucky that we've come to find them. They make a beeline for us and as though the sky has shattered into falling flapping pieces they land on the boat, all over it, at least twenty of them. They fold their wings and gaze calmly at the passing world, happy to catch a ride. My muscles lock me in place, I'm terrified of startling them, but the longer I stand here, holding my breath, the clearer it becomes that they won't be startled by anything—they're utterly unbothered by my presence. Dae comes down from the crow's nest, and the others stop what they're doing to join us on the deck and watch the birds, to be near them.

"You forget, until you see one . . . ," Basil says, and we know what he means. Easy to forget how many there once were, how common they seemed. Easy to forget how lovely they are.

Anik loses interest first and tries to order me back to chores, but when I give him the finger he leaves me to it.

I only go inside when it reaches the coldest part of deep night, but for the rest of their visit I sit with the birds, as close as I can get, and write letters to Niall. It's my method of logging everything: describing the terns to him in great detail. How they use their beaks to scratch beneath their feathers, and how they call to each other across the boat using a language I would give anything to speak. How, when they feel a draft, they spread their wings and let it lift them off their perches, and they just hover there, airborne, as though for no reason at all but the fun of it. I write it all down for him, so that when he reads the words he will be filled with the courage of the birds just as the wind fills their feathers.

The terns have been with us for twenty-four hours when Ennis emerges to sit beside me on the deck. He alone hasn't come to spend time among them. The gray at his temples glistens in the afternoon light.

"Guess you were wrong about the storm," I say.

"Where's yours?" Ennis asks.

I point her out, sitting on the roof of the bridge, the piece of plastic on her leg poking free of her plumage. Her eyes are closed; I think she's sleeping. Her mate is probably one of the other birds on the boat—they're unlikely to attempt the long journey separately.

"Why aren't they moving?" Ennis asks.

"There's hardly any wind. They're using the boat to rest."

"Can we shoo them along?"

I shoot him a look. "No, Ennis, we can't shoo them along. They'll go when they want to, and we can follow." If I had the power, I'd carry the birds all the way. Protect them from the journey's difficulty. Then again, it's a fool who tries to protect a creature from its own instincts.

Ennis leaves without another word, returning to the bridge. I watch him briefly through the salty glass, and then I go back to watching sweeter things.

By dusk the wind has picked up. I haven't moved from my spot, unable to waste a single precious moment. The crew has been taking it in turns to bring me food, sparing a little time to sit with me and ask questions about the birds. How do they know where to go? Why do they fly so far? Why are they the last, why *these* ones, what makes them luckier than the others? I don't know the answers, not really, but I do my best and, anyway, it's not really answers they want, it's simply remembering what it feels like to love creatures that aren't human. A nameless sadness, the fading away of the birds. The fading away of the animals. How lonely it will be here, when it's just us.

I'm not the only one who's spent as much time as possible on deck. Last night Malachai became convinced he needed to wrap the terns in blankets and take them into his cabin to keep them safe and warm. I had to assure him captivity was no way for the birds to spend their last migration and that it's early yet, they're still strong, still happy to be in flight. I caught Léa singing to one, and, despite orders, Basil has been sneaking them bread crumbs they have no interest in, even though feeding the birds is moronic since we're meant to be following them on their hunt for food.

The crew appears now. I warned them that when the weather changed the birds would leave, so they've come to say goodbye.

The first to rise is mine. I have taken to thinking of her as mine because she has burrowed inside and made a home in my rib cage. With the sun setting golden, she lifts and spreads her wings, hovering. Testing the air, her hunger, perhaps, her desire. It's right, whatever she feels, because she flaps once and it's as if she floats up into the sky, effortlessly higher and higher and unbound.

As the others of her kind follow her, the crew members wave, call their farewells, wish the birds a bon voyage.

Samuel uses meaty fingers to dash away his tears. When he sees me looking, he spreads his hands and says helplessly, "If they're the last . . ."

He doesn't need to finish.

"Don't go too far," I hear Anik tell one of the terns softly as it takes flight.

I find mine in the sky again, leading the way. She is smaller and smaller, halved and halved again.

Don't, I whisper, inside. *Don't leave.*

But I know she must. It's in her nature.

7

NUI, GALWAY, IRELAND

TWELVE YEARS AGO

"You skipped my class," a voice says as I'm scrubbing the bowl of a toilet.

I glance over my shoulder, then get back to work.

"What's the point of cleaning this shithole if you're not even attending your lectures?"

"It's called a job. There are worse places to clean."

"Why clean at all?"

I flush the toilet and straighten, annoyed at his privilege. He's blocking the stall door, taller here before me than he was behind his lectern. "Excuse me."

Professor Lynch tilts his head to better study me. His eyes probe the way they must probe a specimen he can't figure out. He's wearing a lilac bow tie with his suit today. It looks stupid, but I think that might be the point. "If you skip again I'll have to mark you absent and your credit goes way down."

I smile. "Good luck with that. Now move or I'll smear my shitty gloves all over you."

He rears back. "What's your name?"

My gloves come off with a snap and I throw them in the rubbish, before removing the whole bag and carrying it in the direction of the bins.

"What are you doing here?" he calls.

It's a damn good question.

The next time I see him I'm sweeping the courtyard outside the university café. He's with several of his colleagues, drinking Americanos in a rare moment of sunshine between the clouds. His eyes fix on me across the courtyard; I don't know how I know because I'm very careful not to look at him. I just feel it. I start sweeping closer because it's my job, I have to, and so I reach the table next to his, where a mound of hot chips has been spilled. I stoop to sweep them up, laughing as a seagull lands and tries to pinch them from me.

"All right, then, you win, greedy guts." I leave the chips for the bird, realizing as I do that it's been quite a while since I've seen one in this courtyard, when once you could barely eat a meal out here without getting invaded by a flock of them. It's much quieter now, without their raucous battling for scraps.

"Excuse me," a woman's voice says and I look up to find a plate being shoved in my face. It's one of the women from Professor Lynch's table, and her plate is covered in half-eaten food. I've seen her around—she's another professor in the science department, thirties, charming, apparently racked with impatience.

"I'm not a waitress," I say. Plus everyone knows they have to take their own tableware inside.

"What are you?"

"A cleaner."

"So . . . *here*." She thrusts the plate even more forcefully so I have no choice but to take it.

"I'll take it inside for you, shall I?"

Her eyes swivel back to me, surprised. They narrow, as if she's only just noticing me for the first time and not liking what she sees. "That'd be great."

"Want me to accompany you to the toilet, too? I'm great at wiping arses."

Her mouth drops open.

I carry her plate inside, and I don't know what possesses me but I wink at Niall Lynch as I pass him. His expression, for the briefest moment, is utterly mystified and makes the whole thing worthwhile.

My front tire is punctured, which is why I'm walking my bike along the headland tonight when I see him for the third time in one day. Seated on the bench I love, he holds a pair of binoculars with which to watch the seabirds caterwaul and fish for their dinner. The diving cormorants, forcing their way bravely through the dark water.

I stop beside him. The sun is beginning to set, but this time of year it's a little too far north to see where it hides behind the headland, and a veil of clouds besides. The light of the world is ashen, the sea at this hour rough and impassioned and searching.

After a little while I say, "Hey."

Professor Lynch jumps half out of his skin. "Jesus. Fuck. You scared me."

"Payback."

My eyes graze his binoculars and without a word he passes them over. And like that the birds are no longer smudges, but elegantly detailed and purposeful and *real*. They steal my breath as they always do, these creatures who think nothing of having wings.

"I'm Niall."

I don't take my eyes from the birds. "I know."

He stands with the kind of jerking speed that tells me immediately something is wrong. I lower the binoculars, follow his pointed finger to the shape, lift them once more and see. It's a rowboat. I recognize the little vessel as the one that lives down on the shore, years beyond its capabilities in the water, its work now purely to advertise Nan's Florist. There is all the strange paraphernalia about its hull, the plastic flowers and streamers and the like, and there, yes, the golden scrawl about its nose that reads *Nan's*. Usually there's an anchor keeping it on the rocks, but perhaps it's been lost or removed because that boat is no longer safely beached but drifting swiftly out into the water, tugged along by the red-and-yellow beach umbrella that has been opened to catch the wind's teeth. In the rowboat's belly sit two boys.

"Wind's got them," Niall says.

"That rip will be next." I can see it out there, waiting patiently and mercilessly for its prey. The dark line where waves meet.

Niall starts removing his shoes.

"Are you a strong swimmer?" I ask him. Inside I'm already moving. My body knows.

"Not really, but—"

"Get help. Find a boat and call for an ambulance."

"Hey!"

My useless bike hits the ground. I leave my shoes on to run. Entering the water here would be foolish—along the headland a delicate finger of land reaches into the sea; from its end the swim to the boat will be easier, less directly against the current. The earth is uneven and thoughts flicker through my mind: how glad I am to have worn sneakers this morning, how I must try not to waste all my breath on the run when I will need it more for the swim How cold the water will be. How far the boys have already been lured and how very fickle that boat looks.

Several minutes pass before I reach the white-tipped tongue. My discarded jacket tumbles behind me, caught on an eddy. My shoes scatter and my first few running steps into the sea are a familiar shot of adrenaline to the heart. I've swum this ocean all year round, at any time of day in any weather. I swim it morning and night as often as I can. Which has taught me not how to best it nor even, truly, how to survive it, but simply to be aware of its capriciousness even after so many years. It could take me tonight just as it could have done when I was a child or may do when I'm gray. *Only a great fool*, my mother once told me, *does not fear the sea*.

When I'm far enough out I take a deep breath and dive under. It's cold but I've felt worse. Problem is how quickly my own temperature will drop. Nothing for it now, no use worrying about that. Focus instead on the lift and reach of arms, on the smooth arc of shoulders, the swift kick of socked feet and always, always the air feeding my lungs. The breaths must be perfect, the tick of a metronome, as steady and sure.

I stop often to find the boat ahead and adjust my trajectory. It seems farther from me each time. The current is dreadful. I have dread of my own, begging me to turn back. I don't want to die. There are far too many adventures yet to be had. Over and over I think, *Now, now's the point of no return, now you will probably drown out here with the children,* and what would that be for? But I keep swimming until the boat is near enough for them to hear me over the wind.

"Shut the umbrella!"

The boys struggle to do my bidding but the wind shrieks and they're no match for it.

My fingertips at last find the tin of the hull, then the edge of the boat. My arms shake with the effort of pulling myself into the dinghy. It feels too much, and I imagine the relief of sinking back into the water's embrace, until—small hands clutch at my wrists, trying to help me. They bolster me for the fight, and then I am hauling myself up and over with a low animal groan.

I grab for the umbrella and wrestle it closed. Our passage slows considerably. There are oars, thank god. I strike out for land but quickly realize I'll never get us there.

"There's an inlet south," one of the boys says.

I look at them for the first time. Eight or nine, maybe. One with ginger freckles, the other a dark fringe obscuring darker eyes. Both astonishingly calm.

The ginger boy points south and I realize he is right, the inlet isn't far now, and will be easier to reach on the waves. I angle the boat south, leaving one oar submerged to give us a wide arc around the headland.

"The boat's not gonna last," I say. "Can you swim?"

"A little."

We come around and I start rowing properly, hard and fast toward the closest line of land. But the boat takes on water, as it was always going to. Our ankles swim, then our knees.

"Right, jump in, stay close to me."

We roll into the sea and strike out, and oh, these boys and their courage, and oh, their uselessness in the water, their tiny flailing limbs and "a little" turning out to be not really, not in any way that will help us. So in my left hand I take the backs of their jackets, the scruffs of their necks, and with my right arm I paddle, and with my feet I kick like a mad creature, like a hell-beast, dragging them along with me at this snail's pace.

Land finds us in twenty minutes, an hour, two—who knows—and though I would never admit it aloud, I'm not sure I could have kept swimming. Not with the extra load hitched to my muscles, muscles I had thought were strong but now seem feeble. There's no easy end to this, because there's no gentle sand waiting to catch us as there is on the beaches in Australia; there are only hard-edged rocks and sullen waves to deliver us. I do my best to land first, pulling the boys atop me and saving their bodies from the impact, but fire erupts in my side as I'm dragged along the sharp teeth.

There's no time to dwell because the next wave that comes will slam me harder and I have to get us out of its reach. I hurl the boys up toward the shallow end and tell them to crawl and quickly, and they do—they slip and slide and make their way onto the dry rocks, and I scramble clear, too, just as the next wave dumps, and the three of us sink onto our bums and could just as easily dissolve into the earth, I think.

We sit quietly, not speaking. Over the roar of the sea I can hear the distant ambulance siren.

It's fucking cold.

Professor Niall Lynch arrives with my bike. "You guys all right?"

The three of us nod.

"Your parents are coming," he says, and I realize belatedly that he's managed to ride my bike to reach us, despite its flat tire. There's a flock of figures approaching along the hill. Niall puts his jacket around the two shivering boys, but it doesn't really fit and starts sliding off.

I stand. My body hurts, but only as a vague afterthought. I suspect the pain will find me later, and strip me bare, but for now I am dazed and too aware of my teeth.

"You're bleeding," Niall Lynch says.

"Nah," I say, even though I am.

I bend for my bike; he reaches for it a second later and we lift it together. He hands me my shoes and jacket, which I didn't realize he'd collected. "Thanks," I say, and then he's watching me too closely, so I look back to the boys.

They meet my eyes. Smile. And it's enough, it's more than enough. I don't want the parents and the ambulance and the hospital and the questions. The smiles are plenty. I flash them a grin of my own, a quick wave, and then I start pushing my bike back up toward the grassy hill.

I glance back once. Niall is staring at me in a way that seems to imply I should have said something, so I say the only thing I can think of, which is "Seeya," and head for home.

Blood sluices down the drain. My toes are pruned, mind blank. I'm curled on the floor of the shower and the hot water is starting to fail; in moments it will be gone and I'll be frozen again, but still I can't move.

I forgot to ask the boys' names. I suppose it doesn't matter, only now I wish I knew. I wish I were back in the sea.

Two shards of rock are embedded in my hip; my ribs and thigh have a layer of skin scraped free. Bruises are forming. The ache of the swim is bone-deep.

When I can put it off no longer I get awkwardly to my feet and turn off the taps. Even the act of drying myself takes effort. I perch on the toilet lid and use a pair of tweezers on the gravel in my flesh. I don't have any disinfectant so I pull on undies and singlet and search the kitchen for tequila. A splash for my hip, a shot to swallow.

My housemates find me sitting on the kitchen bench, halfway through the bottle. It doesn't surprise them. They reach for glasses and join me, but soon trickle away until I'm left, alone again, only now my tequila bottle is empty and the pain has melted into the background and there is a pounding beat of adrenaline in my pulse. I'd like to be outside but I'm glued to the spot, swaying just a little, too astonished by life and the world to move.

I think of my mother: she was always aware of life's marvels and its perils, and of how closely entwined the two are. I ponder what led her across the ocean and into the bed of a monster. I wonder if she knew what he was all along, and I think that she might have. I think she might have thrilled at what he was, even though it would see her abandoned once again. I wonder if anything was able to press through the wall of anger that led my father to tighten his hands around another man's neck. Was there a flicker of regret, even as he did it? A momentary revelation of the horror of the thing he was making of himself? I wonder what he thinks of, in prison, and if his anger feels like a worn old friend or a passionate lover even now. Perhaps he hates it, perhaps he left it buried in the throat of the man he killed.

Fuck. I'm drunk. These are the things that creep in uninvited.

I slide off the bench and drift to the bedroom I share with Sinead and Lin. They're asleep, Sinead's soft snoring evidence. I think of the sea to fall asleep, but tonight her rhythms are uneasy and offer no calm. I am altogether too alive for calm.

At 3:00 a.m. someone knocks on our front door. I know because I'm awake and staring at Lin's alarm clock when the sound reverberates through every paper-thin wall of the house. Whoever's responsible for that will be in trouble. All seven other occupants of Wall Manor, as we have named it, let free a stream of filth the likes of which would make a sailor blush.

Henry, who is closest to the front door, gets up to answer it and we all listen to his feet pounding along the floorboards.

"What? You know what time it is, man?"

"I believe it's 0302," a voice replies, and I know that voice. "Sorry to disturb."

I sit blearily upright.

"Does Franny Stone live here?" the voice says, and a chorus of groans travels through the Manor.

Sinead and Lin throw their pillows at my head while I stumble to the door.

Niall Lynch is on our front step, bathed in silver Galway moonlight. He's in the same clothes he was wearing earlier tonight, and he's smoking a cigarette. He looks lean and pale. What is it about him that so enamors everyone? I can't see it. Not when he isn't talking about birds.

"What are you doing here?"

"I'm not coming in."

I blink. "Correct."

"Want one?" He holds up his self-rolled ciggie.

"Yuck. No."

"Here, then." This time it's a calico bag of things. I look through it curiously and make out a few items: bandages, disinfectant, painkillers, and a bottle of gin.

"Thanks. I mean I have stuff . . ."

"I assumed." He spreads his hands helplessly. "You did that and then you just walked off and you looked like shit and no one even said thank you."

I process this. "So you're saying thank you?"

He shrugs. "Aye. I guess."

"Okay."

He finishes his cigarette, stamps it beneath his shoe, and reaches for his tobacco pack.

"Are you gonna leave that there?"

His gaze follows mine to the butt. He smiles a little. "Why, you want it?"

"Just pick it up, will you? It's disgusting."

He laughs as he bends down. "Jesus, I was going to. Forgive me for being a wee bit slow at this hour." He's not laughing as he straightens. "I thought you were going to die tonight. And those boys."

Silence. I shrug, no idea what he wants me to say.

"Do you have a death wish or something?"

I frown because the question pisses me off. Wasn't he also preparing to go into the water? Wouldn't anyone? "What are you doing here, Professor?"

Niall Lynch hands me a folder. In the dark it takes me a moment to make out the words on the front page. *NUI Enrollment.*

My cheeks start to burn unpleasantly. "What is this?" Then, "How do you even know where I live?"

"I asked your boss. He told me you're not a student."

"So?"

"So I'm going to generously invite you to continue to attend my class until you've properly applied and enrolled, because I'm that kind."

"No, thank you."

"Why not?"

"None of your business. And while we're at it, this"—a hand gesture to encompass his presence—"isn't cool. I never even told you my name."

I try to hand the papers back but he won't take them. He doesn't need to know I never finished year ten. There'll be no university for me.

There's a second, pre-rolled cigarette in his pouch, and I watch him light a match and hold the flame to its end, and I watch the little round glow of the burn, and I watch him inhale deeply, his eyes drifting closed as though the act is a religious one. I imagine the foul taste of his mouth and tongue.

"Chuck them out or burn them, or whatever," he says. "But have a read first. And keep coming to my class." He smiles a little. A smile too dangerous to keep. "I won't tell."

As he walks away I think, *Don't ask don't ask don't ask*, and then I ask. "Why'd you do this?"

Niall pauses and looks over his shoulder. His hair and eyes are very black, his skin silver. He says, "Because you and I are going to spend the rest of our lives together." Then he adds, "Seeya."

Inside the Manor I can hardly breathe. I lie on my single mattress on the floor and ignore the giggles of my roommates, who have heard every word.

I am in the sea's grip once more: within the pages of the enrollment forms he has hidden a single black feather.

I wait for the house to fall back to sleep and then I touch the feather's burning tip to my lips, and I touch myself to the thought of Niall Lynch.

8

The *Saghani*, NORTH ATLANTIC OCEAN
MIGRATION SEASON

A horn sounds throughout the boat and all I can think is *Thank god*. Even if it means we're sinking, even if there's another iceberg or a perfect storm, I don't care—anything to get me out of this box. I scramble to my feet and wrench my windbreaker on over my thermals. I hop to get my boots on, always off balance on my maimed right foot, and then follow Léa at a run. The other crew members are already bolting past, headed for the stairs to the deck.

Basil grins at me. "He's bloody found something."

I return the smile, thinking it's not Ennis who's found something, but the birds. I follow the others up into the glaring beams of the spotlights. Two illuminate the boat, which has stopped moving, while one beam swings smoothly out over the water. We all dash to the railing to see what he's found. The black ocean glimmers faintly silver; what look to be hundreds of fish swim just beneath the surface, and there above them are the terns, diving in and out of the water to eat their fill.

The men's voices roar their excitement. This is a rare thing indeed.

"Let's move!" Ennis booms from his balcony, and I twist my head to see the flash of his smile.

Mal and Dae hurry to crank two levers and I realize there is a smaller skiff being lowered into the sea. Anik swings over the railing and lands gracefully in the boat, his motions those of a dancer. He descends onto the sea and disconnects the cables. I watch him maneuver the boat out into the water, and I see that there is a thick ream of net being pulled along behind him. Léa stands at the crank, making sure the net unrolls without snagging or tangling, while Anik drags it far out into the darkness, its top edge buoyed up by yellow corks I know so well, the bottom edge weighed down by the lead line. Anik pulls the net in an enormous circle around the school of fish.

"What happens now?" I ask.

Mal, who's beside me, points to the net. "When Nik's done and Skipper gives the go-ahead, we'll sync those weights together—like pursing 'em—to stop the fish swimming out the bottom. Then the block'll lift the net up onto the deck. Get ready, Franny-girl. You thought it was tough before? This is when the work really starts. We're gonna have fish to pack."

Anik makes the circle and joins the ends. I'm amazed at how swiftly he's done it, maneuvering that tiny skiff through the water like he was born to it. A kilometer and a half of netting. Malachai said all skiff men are outlaws; they have to be to set out on their own like they do. I can see what he means now, watching the solitary passage of that small boat.

The cables pull taut.

"Pursing," Ennis calls.

We all watch as the cables begin to pull the weights. I can't see what's happening underwater, but the corks jerk and twist as though the net below is moving. Silver scales grow frantic, cresting the surface and churning in panic. There is something monstrous about it, as though a mighty sea beast has been caught and dragged out of the depths.

The birds rear up and away, their feast interrupted.

I'm filled with sudden anxiety.

The crank stops. "Ready to lift!" Léa calls.

Mal and Dae haul Anik and his skiff back up onto the deck, then all three hurry to pull on plastic overalls and big rubber gloves. They signal their readiness and wait on deck for the net.

Ennis is controlling the power block, and yells down for everyone to stand by before the crane gives a jerk, slowly lifting the heavy net from the ocean. Water gushes out with a roar and I see the fish take shape—hundreds, maybe thousands—those on top flapping helplessly as they're lifted out. I wasn't expecting the volume, even after having seen the size of the net.

I don't want to watch this. I can't look away. I have to stop it somehow. Of course I can't stop it.

Basil gives a whoop of victory and I could throw up. Am I really going to stand here and watch as these creatures are slaughtered? How are they different from the birds, whose lives I might very well give my own to protect?

My eyes alight on something inside the net, a different texture from the rest. I frown and lean closer. It's hard to see through the darkness, but it's not a fish, I'm sure of it.

"What's that?"

Mal and Dae follow my pointed finger and frown.

"Light!" Dae yells.

Samuel, who is up with Ennis, swings the spotlight around to where Dae's pointing, and we all see it, clear as day. A huge sea turtle, caught in the net.

"Stop!" Dae and Mal both yell at once. "Skip!"

Ennis hears them and stops the crane. The net swings above the ocean, its magnificent weight swaying the boat. Ennis thunders down from the balcony and runs to the railing. "Loosen the purse!" he orders Basil.

"What? Boss, that's a big catch!"

"Loosen it."

Shock makes me grip the railing so hard one of my hands cramps. I work it quickly with the other while watching the poor creature, its flippers moving only very slightly beneath the suffocating weight of fish. Half of it protrudes out of the net and I'm frightened it will be too entangled to get free again.

The purse line begins to loosen, opening the gap at the bottom to let the fish flood out. They slap back into the water, thousands of them at once, creating a swell that rocks the boat. Many get caught in the net, wriggling uselessly. And along with them is the turtle, unable to work its way free.

"Bring it in, Sam!" Ennis calls. *"Gently!"*

The giant claw is swung slowly around and then lowered onto the deck. The net pools around the turtle and everyone rushes to help until Ennis roars at us to stop.

He picks his way to where the turtle is buried in reams of netting, and he lifts the spools away until the creature is revealed. My heart is in my mouth as I watch Ennis sink to its side and ever so carefully untangle the turtle's limbs and head. She snaps at him, but he is so gentle, so wary of damaging her. I see his hand rest once on her enormous shell, stroking tenderly.

"What are you doing so far north, my girl?" he asks softly.

Her hooked mouth opens and closes, her head lifting as much as she can. Once Ennis has her untangled we drag the netting away, clearing a path to the railing. She's a big thing, and it takes Ennis, Basil, Mal, and Dae to lift her.

I laugh in relief as she goes overboard, diving into the water with a huge splash. With the back of my hand I dash the tears from my cheeks and watch her disappear into the depths. I imagine going with her, down into the dark.

The men are freeing the stray fish from the net and throwing them back, too.

Ennis watches the ocean quietly. Anik rests a hand on his shoulder. It's the first kindness I've seen him offer.

"Just the way it goes," Ennis says with a shrug, and Anik nods. "Let's get the net done," he tells the rest, who move tirelessly back to the task of untangling and recoiling the huge net.

Ennis glances at me. "Why so surprised?"

I open my mouth but no words come. Because you're a fisherman, I want to say. I didn't know there were limits to your hunger.

"Get some rest," Ennis responds to my silence.

"I can help. I've been training."

"You're in the way, love. Get some rest." He barely spares me a glance as he dismisses me.

I stand on the deck, embarrassed. I am also relieved, though, I'm so relieved for the fish, which have swum away beyond our reach, and for the birds who have already moved off to hunt the next school. And for the turtle. I think about her as I ignore the captain and join the rest of the crew. It's her eyes I think of as I coil the corks, round and round. The look in her eyes as she hung there, trapped in the net and assuming her end had come for her.

There is grease caught under the flaps of my blisters, and nothing to be done about it, for today the engine needs my hands. Léa's doing something with the bilge pump, whatever that is. "Pumps any excess water out of the boat," she grunts, bent over something greasy as she always seems to be.

"And what are you doing to it?" I ask, lifting my voice over the low roar of the engine.

"Unclogging it. All kinds of rubbish gets stuck in the impeller. Pass me the wrench."

I do so, and watch her open up the pump and shove her hand deep into it. She pulls out a mess of greasy debris that smells like crap and lumps it straight onto my lap.

"Oh. Cool."

"Put it in the bucket and throw it overboard."

The bucket's right next to her; she could have dumped it straight there instead of onto me, but hey, sure. I catch her smirking as I head off to do as I'm told. I have to carry several more buckets of ripe fishy-smelling muck up to the main deck before we're finished and with each intake of breath my stomach churns. As Léa cleans the mechanisms of the pump I watch her muscular arms work and feel envious of her strength.

"Have you always been a sailor?" I ask her.

She shrugs. "Been fixing boats for a decade. Been a mechanic longer."

"What drew you to it?"

Another shrug.

"Where in France are you from?"

"Les Ulis, in Paris. My family moved there for my brother's football career," she adds.

"He's a footballer? That's cool."

She shakes her head, but doesn't elaborate.

"Where were you before there?"

"Guadeloupe."

"What was that like?"

Léa shrugs again.

"How chatty you are." I sigh, but actually it's kind of nice. I've had Malachai in my ear for the last few days, and he could talk the hind legs off a donkey.

He grew up in Brixton with three sisters after his single mother moved them from Jamaica to London. He was obsessed with girls, and got into fishing boats in order to chase after one in particular, who was ten years older than he was and totally un-gettable, but he boasts he's never turned down a challenge. This was obviously long before he fell for Dae and they were kicked off their last boat for wanting to be together. Daeshim's parents left a small village in South Korea for the most bustling, liberal place they could think of: San Francisco. Dae says they had no idea what they were getting themselves into, but went with the flow and were soon encouraging him to become an experimental performance artist or a feminist philosopher if he wanted to be. He did not. In his rebellion he became a marine engineer and hopped his way onto the first shrimp trawler he could find, despite suffering horrendous seasickness, and, much to his dismay, his parents were ecstatic. Malachai's not the only one who likes to talk—if Samuel gets even a whiff of drink you can't shut him up, and he weeps *all the time*. He's from Newfoundland and no, he doesn't have children in every port but he does have an unreasonable number in one house. As he puts it, he has a lot of love to go around. Basil's story is less amorous: he spent his childhood on boats and was determined not to wind up a sailor like his dad. I suspect that Dad was a hard man. Basil really was on a cooking show in Sydney but after he lost his temper he got fired and pretty much fled the country to avoid the scandal, returning to the inevitable course his life was always set on. Seafolk are always drawn back to the sea, whether they want to be or not. As for Anik, the others have filled me in on a couple of snippets here and there—he's been on the *Saghani* with Ennis longer than anyone, and there's definitely something mysterious about how they came to be working together, only no one will tell me what it is. They will say that Anik's mother used to lecture in physics in Anchorage, while his elderly father, fabulously, still takes people on sled dog tours, and loves huskies more than he loves any humans.

Even though they are as varied as a group of people can be, I can tell they are the same, all of these sailors. Something was missing in their lives on land, and they went seeking the answer. Whatever it was, I don't doubt for a second that they each found it. They are migrants of land, and they love it out here on an ocean that offered them a different way of life, they love this boat, and, as much as they may bicker and fight, they love each other.

In their own private ways they are all grieving the end of this life, knowing it must come to an end, not knowing how they'll survive that.

I can no longer ignore my seasickness. The smells and sounds of the engine room have done me over. Léa snorts as I head to the toilet to heave my guts up. The growing swell knocks me sideways into the wall of the cubicle and I have to grab onto the toilet bowl. Throughout the night the waves grow crueler and I find myself fighting Dae for the toilet, much to the crew's hilarity. Everything inside me is painfully expelled over and over again; vomiting is a singular hell. I guess Ennis was right about the approaching storm after all.

Samuel takes pity on me with a motion sickness tablet that knocks me out for a few hours, and when I wake it's still night but the sea is calmer. I find my way up onto the deck. Anik is standing in the prow but I don't think he'd welcome my presence.

"He doesn't like coming south," Basil says, and I notice him sitting in the dark, rolling a joint. "He never does."

I'm not in the mood for Basil, but I never am, and maybe irritation will do to keep me company. I sit beside him and we listen to the ocean. "Why?"

"The north's his home."

Basil offers me the spliff and I take a drag. The warmth touches me quickly, blurring me.

"So why does he leave, then?" I ask.

"Dunno, really, except it's something with him and Ennis. They have some deal or pact that goes way back, and it's why Anik sails with the skipper no matter what."

Curious.

"Did I sleep through the storm?" I ask, smelling the air for rain, but it still just smells of salt and grease.

"Hasn't even started yet," Basil says.

I gaze up into the clear sky. Stars abound.

"It's getting ready," Basil adds, recognizing my skepticism.

"Should I be worried?"

"Have another toke instead." After a while, he says, "My family's Irish. Way back."

"Convicts?"

He grins. "Couple of generations after that. They were just people looking for a better life."

"Than what?"

"Than poverty. Isn't that the way of all migrations? Poverty or war. Which half of you is Australian?" he asks.

"My dad's side."

"How'd your parents meet?"

"No idea."

"You never asked?"

I shake my head.

"But your mum, she's Irish, right?" Basil presses.

"Aye."

I watch him exhale a heavy plume of smoke. He sounds very stoned. "I knew a woman who lived and died by the slate-gray stones of County Clare. You could have carted her body across the ocean but you'd never be able to take her soul from that stretch of coast." Basil looks at his hands, tracing the lifelines as though searching for something. "I've never felt that. I love Australia and it's my home, but I've never felt like I could die for the place, you know?"

"That's because it's not yours."

He frowns, affronted by that.

"It's not mine, either," I add. "We don't belong there—we came from someplace else and we put our ugly flag in the ground and we slaughtered and stole and called it ours."

"Christ, we got another bleeding heart right here, folks," he says with a sigh. "So then how come I didn't feel at home in Ireland, either?" he asks me as though it's my fault. "I went there when I was eighteen thinking I'd find that homeplace." He shrugs, takes another drag. "Can't find it anywhere."

I can no longer hold in the question. "How long are you gonna keep doing this, Basil?"

He looks at me and smoke billows from his mouth into my face. "I dunno," he admits. "Samuel's so sure of it all. He says God will provide for us, the fish'll come back. That man's been fishing as long as we've been breathing. I used to listen to him. But there's too much talk now about sanctions."

"Do you think that's likely?"

"Who knows."

"Don't you . . . Why don't any of you seem to care about what you're doing?"

"'Course we care. It used to be such a good way to make money." He folds his arms, lets that sink in, and then he tops it off by saying, "And it's not us, you know. Global warming's killing the fish."

I stare at him. "Aside from also fishing to excess and contaminating the waters with toxins, who do you think caused global warming?"

"Come on, Franny, this is boring. Let's not talk politics."

I can't believe him, I really can't, and then it's like standing at the bottom of a mountain I have no way to scale, and I'm exhausted, I'm exhausted by Basil and his small selfish world, and I'm exhausted by my own hypocrisy because I'm just as human and just as responsible as he is, and so in the end I slump back in my seat and close my mouth.

You decided this. You decided the destination was worth spending the trip on a fishing vessel. So suck it up.

"How 'bout you, then?" he asks.

"How 'bout me what?"

"Where's your place?"

If I have a place, I think, *it was left behind long ago.*

Basil hands me the spliff and our fingers touch. Oh, I remember you. Skin. A pained thing inside me rears up. The rushing sound of the ocean rises.

"Where's your place, Franny?" Basil asks me again, and I think, Why would I ever tell you, and then I kiss him. Because I don't like him even a little and it feels destructive. He tastes of tobacco and marijuana and smoke, but I must taste of the same, and maybe worse after all my vomiting. His free hand grabs at my arm, a fumbling surprised motion that seems to reflect a great need inside him, one maybe he didn't know he harbored.

I end the kiss and sit back. "Sorry."

He swallows, running the hand over his long hair. "No worries."

"Night."

"Night, Franny."

My sleep is interrupted again, first by nightmares of my mother and second by the warm liquid sliding down my wrist. I sit up blearily, disoriented. I'm moving and there's pain, and the wetness is familiar, its rusty smell like a memory in the night.

I take a breath and let my head calm. You're not in prison. You're on the boat.

The swaying has grown much worse. Back and forth the boat rolls, in great woozy lunges, pulling my wrist so hard against its rope binding that blood has trickled wetly down my arm.

With one hand I untie the slipped constrictor knot. I'm quite proud of this knot because it wasn't easy to learn. I've decided to start binding myself to the bed at night, because there's obviously a version of me that wants to escape this cabin and find the ocean, and the least I can do is make it hard for her.

Untied, I tumble off the bed like a rag doll.

"You okay?" Léa asks. Then, "Are you awake?"

"I hope so." I untangle myself from the sheet and hurry through the locked cabin door, pinging off the walls like a pinball, careening into the stairs and gashing both my shins on the bottom rung. "Franny? What are you doing? Don't!" Up I go onto the deck, into the violent lash of rain and the howl of wind and the black sky despite the morning hour, and I can barely remain upright, almost plucked and carried off with the storm, almost stripped of my very skin by the sudden savagery of the world. For a moment I stop, stunned. Then my feet slip and I am nearly overboard, nearly gone, it's only my fingers grasping the railing that hold me to the world. I find my footing and lunge for the second stairwell. I have to get to Ennis, to the chart and the tracking dots, to my birds. The climb is perilous; my fingernails break where they scratch at the rungs and shoulders bruise against metal and my feet keep slipping, again and again, scraping my already tender shins but soon I arrive at the bridge, I am flinging open the door and being wrestled into the dark and the quiet. The door slams behind me and for a moment I am shell-shocked, the scream from outside echoing in my ears.

"The fuck are you doing?" he asks me.

I look away from Ennis's thunderous expression. "Is this . . . This is bad, isn't it?"

Sway, goes the boat, and we both careen into the wall. I can see it now, what's happening. The storm is pushing us up and down over the swell of the mighty waves. Up the wall of one and then—*whoomph*—down the other side of it.

"Got both anchors down, engine full throttle, still being forced backward. Be lucky if it's only miles we lose."

"And if it gets worse?"

"We'll take on too much water." He squints at me. "You deserve to be thrown overboard, wandering about like that."

"I wasn't wandering, I was coming here, to you."

Something I can't recognize fills his blue eyes. "Why?"

My stomach bottoms out as we go over a massive wave and I have to catch hold of the back of his chair.

"The birds," I say.

Ennis retrieves a life vest and places it over my head, and there's pity in the motion.

"Ennis, where are the birds?"

He nods to my feet. "Take off your boots, love."

"Why?"

"In case we have to swim."

And here it is, even now, even after everything. The return of that mad thrill, the one I have been seeking all my life. It's not right to be excited by danger, but I am. I am, even still. The only difference is that once I was proud of this and now it shames me.

9

GALWAY, IRELAND
TWELVE YEARS AGO

I've spent the afternoon on the computer in the university library, trying to find Maire Stone and John Torpey. Maire is almost nonexistent online—or at least the right Maire Stone is—but I've come up with a number of John Torpeys in the correct area and age bracket. I'm writing down the addresses when Niall Lynch walks past the row of computers with a pile of books in his arms. He doesn't look at me but my eyes are pulled to him as if by gravity, or perhaps something less scientific, something for which I don't yet have a name. We haven't spoken since the night he came to my house almost a month ago and said that absurd thing. I've been to his lectures but he hasn't looked at me once and maybe this is all part of his design because he has turned me effortlessly into a creature made of obsession.

I jerk upright, computer search forgotten. The bit of paper is crumpled into my jeans pocket, an afterthought now, and without conscious decision I am following the professor from the library. His winding path takes him through various buildings and I feel myself stepping his steps, making his choices, donning his life for these precious few minutes. Who is he? Where did he come from? What is he thinking of in this very moment? *Why* did he say that thing, that wrecking ball of a thing, and did he mean it? Did he know, somehow, that I've been waiting for someone to smash me to bits, to do the wrecking so I mustn't always do it myself? I draw his skin upon me and nestle down into his self. I wonder if he has ever wanted free of it, like I do mine, and if he has ever imagined leaving his life for another. Who would miss him? Who are the people that love him?

He doesn't spot me in the hallways or rounding corners, or lurking behind a tree in the evening sunlight. He unlocks his bike, spares a moment to chat with a student, then mounts and pedals away.

I unlock my bike and follow.

The professor rides at a good pace, but I have no trouble keeping up. On the contrary—several times I'm forced to slow so I won't draw too near. He leads me through the city, pausing at traffic lights and then dismounting to walk his bike through the cobblestoned outdoor mall, catching the vibrant snippets of musicians taking advantage of the sun. Then he rides out beyond the city's edge to where the grass is long and the sky is wide. Farther from the sea, but there's beauty out here nonetheless, in the gold-drenched green of the fields. He slows around a winding hill and each time I lose sight of him I come to my senses and decide to turn back and then each time I see him again I just keep following. Who else can I honestly say has had this effect on me? Who else, ever? It's the fantasy he's created, no more. I know this, and still I follow. Huge trees appear to line the narrow road, blocking the paddocks on either side. They turn the world darker. A tunnel with no end in sight.

Niall reaches an arched gate, unlocked, and rides through onto a driveway. I stop and lower a foot to take it in. Before us is some sort of brick manor, a castle, almost, with several stories and enormous grounds and a Lexus parked out front.

He could turn around now and see me plain as day, framed by the curled iron and ivy. I wonder how I could explain it, if I could bear to try. But he doesn't turn, and curiosity gets the better of me. I ride through the gate, embracing my insanity and ensuring humiliation. Up the winding driveway and around the stone fountain, all the way to the side path down which I saw Niall disappear. I leave my bike hidden behind a large, perfectly manicured hedge and creep along the perimeter of the house.

The back of the property is unlike the front. Out here it's overrun, uncontained. There are tall trees and unruly plants and too-long grass. A lake spreads silver, at its edge a gently rocking dinghy. Niall disappears into a small building in the distance, hidden by draping vines. Up close I see that its roof is made of cobwebbed glass, and the windows on all sides are almost too dusty to see through. If I squint I can make him out, moving through plants and workbenches. There he is now, between hanging succulents, now gone, and now there again, appearing and vanishing. He draws me to the back of the greenhouse; I am so magnetized to his passage that I step into a ditch and twist my ankle. Biting my lip to keep from swearing, I clutch the windowsill and find him again, and I forget about the pain because at the back of the greenhouse is a tremendous cage, and it is filled with birds.

All the blood rushes to my cheeks and I step away from the window, trying to catch my breath, only I can't, so I walk back to the entrance of the greenhouse, and then inside, through the vibrant colors as though in a dream, and the sound of the birds, what must be dozens of them, is echoing inside me and I can feel the flap of their feathers against my ribs. Niall doesn't hear me over the racket of chirps and squawks. There are finches and robins and blackbirds and wrens and those are just the ones I can identify at a glance. He's inside the cage feeding them grain, and the flutter of their colored wings is a whirlwind around him, and then suddenly, as though I haven't decided it myself, I too am inside the cage, and he's looking at me, surprised and also not surprised, and then I am kissing him amid the feathers.

We cling to each other, feverish. Perhaps it's the recognition of a second will, one to rival my own, but in his certainty I find mine awakening, I find true adventure, at long last, one that might just be enough to keep me.

He pulls away to say, "Let's get married," and I burst into laughter and he does, too, but we are kissing again and again and I am thinking that we have lost our minds and that this is ludicrous, foolish, absurd, but I am also thinking that this must finally be it: the end of loneliness.

The *Saghani*, NORTH ATLANTIC OCEAN
MIGRATION SEASON

"Be easy," Ennis says a while later when the storm has lulled us both into an uneasy stupor. "It won't come to that."

"To swimming?"

He nods. "We'll be all right."

He's sitting in his captain's chair because it's bolted to the floor. Every few seconds he braces himself against the lurch and sway. I kept being toppled off my seat so now I'm lying on the floor in order to avoid injuring myself. My feet break my forward impact, and Ennis has put a life vest behind my head for when I slide backward. He doesn't want me here, but he wouldn't risk me trying to get belowdecks.

The cabin feels small with the dark rain lashing at its windows and the two of us trapped here until the storm passes. There is a sky beast outside, intent on our destruction. Or maybe it doesn't notice us at all, small as we are.

My eyes are fixed on the laptop screen, on the red dot in the storm's path. How the terns will survive this is beyond me, but I know they will. I can feel it. I've never been more certain of anything.

Ennis reaches for the computer, moving it so he too can watch the dot.

"How'd you lose your kids?" I ask.

He doesn't reply.

"What happened between you and their mother?"

Ennis gives no sign that he's heard me, until—a slight shrug. Progress.

"Who ended it?"

He glances at me like he wants me to shut up. "She did."

"Because you went to sea?"

"No."

"Anik said you don't like me because I don't have the training to be here. He said it's dangerous."

Ennis grunts.

"Is that all it is?"

Silence.

I lick my dry, cracked lips. "Okay. We can do this, you and me, we can do this whole thing with you hating me for some reason and that's all right, I can deal with that. Or we can just talk and maybe make things easier for us both."

Long moments pass and I guess that means he's chosen the first option. Truth is I'm not sure why it bothers me. Of all the things that matter, Ennis's regard is not one. Not in the scheme of things. And yet with each passing day his dislike digs deeper under my skin. Maybe it's because I've been working my ass off on his boat, and I'd kind of hoped he might respect that.

"It's not just that," Ennis finally admits.

I wait.

He doesn't look at me as he says, "I know your kind."

"My *kind*?"

"Greenies."

"Oh, Jesus, now you sound like fucking Basil."

"I don't care what you believe in. That's your business. But why come on my boat with those eyes and look at us like that?"

"Like what?"

"Like we're scum. Like I'm scum."

I pause, astonished. "I don't think you're scum."

He doesn't reply.

"Ennis, I don't."

Again, nothing, and it's clear he doesn't believe me. My mind whirls, trying to figure out if he's right. I haven't said a word to any of them about what I think, except to Basil last night. But I guess I haven't needed to. I don't think they're scum—against all my better judgment I'm actually starting to *like* these people—but there'll always be a part of me that's disgusted by what they do. Maybe once upon a time the world could tolerate the way we hunted, the way we devoured, but not anymore.

I swallow, sitting up and holding the leg of the desk. "I didn't mean to," I say. "I'm sorry. I just don't understand."

"You got the luxury of not understanding."

My grip slips and I forget to protect my head in the backslide, clunking heavily. Pain pricks my eyes and blurs him. "I thought you were a hard old sailor who didn't get bruised by anything," I admit. "I thought you couldn't care less what I thought. I mean I'm no one, Ennis. I'm no one."

He looks at me once and a flash of lightning streaks his eyes, but he doesn't say anything, because that's mostly what he does, the not saying anything.

Exhaustion sets into my bones. I could sleep dreamlessly now, I'm sure of it, swayed into a lull broken only by the walls. If I were a deep-sea creature the storm would be nothing to me but a vista above, a painted roof to the world.

"Is it often like this?" I ask tiredly.

"It's just a bad day," he says, misunderstanding. "There'll be worse, and plenty of good."

I nod and it comes in a wave, as it does, the rupturing force of missing my husband. He too loves storms.

"I've been reading," I say. "Can I tell you what I've learned of the ocean?"

Ennis is silent again, and I think this means no, so I close my eyes and imagine the words.

But he says, "Go on, then," and a tense part of me uncoils within.

"It never stops moving around the world. It edges its way slowly down from the polar region, and some of it forms into ice. Some of it gets saltier and colder and starts to sink. The water that sinks into the deep cold makes its way south along the ocean floor, through the black twelve thousand feet down. It reaches the Southern Ocean and grazes the icy water from the Antarctic, and then it gets flung across into the Pacific and the Indian. Slowly it thaws, warmer and warmer and rising to the surface. And then at last it turns for home. North again, all the way to the mighty Atlantic. Do you know how long it takes the sea to make that journey around the world?"

"How long?" He is humoring me, but gently, so I smile.

"A thousand years."

Ennis shares my expression. How could he not? Who was it that discovered this extraordinariness? Someone like my husband, who has dedicated his life to the questions by which others are dwarfed.

"This ocean that's tossing us about?" I say. "She wasn't here sixty million years ago, but the earth moved enough to make her and now she's more boisterous than most. More stubborn. That last bit wasn't from a book. Samuel told me." I let my eyes drift shut as I speak. "We don't know her at all, really, or what she holds in her depths. We're the only planet that has oceans. In all the known universe, we're the only one sitting in the perfect spot for them, not too hot and not too cold, and it's the only reason we're alive, because it's the ocean that creates the oxygen we need to breathe. It's a miracle we're here at all, when you think about it like that."

"Your parents teach you how to tell stories?" Ennis asks, startling me.

"I . . . Yes. My mam."

"What's she think of you being out here?"

"She doesn't know."

"'Bout your dad?"

"No. But he doesn't know much. I'd be surprised if he knew my name."

Silence. Wind howls.

"Do you have children?" Ennis asks me.

I shake my head.

"You're young. Plenty of time for that yet."

"I never wanted them. We fought about it for years."

"And now?"

I think for a long while. The truth is a wound I can't speak. "Do you know the ocean, Ennis?" I ask instead.

He grunts noncommittally, his eyes falling closed.

"I know her a little," I say. "I've loved her all my life. I could never get close enough, or deep enough. I was born in the wrong body."

Something of him shifts, I know it. I can feel it upon the prickle of the air. A defrosting.

We sway back and forth, and I'm not anxious about the birds anymore, and maybe that's because the storm is easing or maybe it's because I'm talking. Niall has always wanted me to study the things I love, to learn them in a way he understands, like this—in facts. But I've always been content to know them in other ways, to know the touch and the feel of them.

"There's a spot," Ennis says, slow like he says all his words, "way out at sea. In the Pacific. It's called Point Nemo."

"Because of *Twenty Thousand Leagues Under the Sea*?"

He shrugs. "It's the remotest place in the world, farther from land than anywhere else." His voice is a deep rumble. I think, abstractly, that this must be what it feels like to have a father, if only he could thaw all the way. That this is what children are meant to have in a storm.

"This place is thousands of miles from safety," he says. "There's nowhere crueler or lonelier."

I shiver. "Have you been there?"

Ennis nods.

"What's it like?"

"It's quiet."

I roll over and curl into a ball. "I'd like to go there."

Perhaps I imagine it, but I think I hear him say, "I'll take you one day."

"Okay."

But there won't be any more journeys after this one, no more oceans explored. And maybe that's why I am filled with calm. My life has been a migration without a destination, and that in itself is senseless. I leave for no reason, just to be moving, and it breaks my heart a thousand times, a million. It's a relief to at last have a purpose. I wonder what it will feel like to stop. I wonder where we go, afterward, and if we are followed. I suspect we go nowhere, and become nothing, and the only thing that saddens me about this is the idea of never seeing Niall again. We are, all of us, given such a brief moment of time together, it hardly seems fair. But it's precious, and maybe it's enough, and maybe it's right that our bodies dissolve into the earth, giving our energy back to it, feeding the little creatures in the ground and giving nutrients to the soil, and maybe it's right that our consciousness rests. The thought is peaceful.

When I go there will be nothing of me left behind. No children to carry on my genes. No art to commemorate my name, nothing written down, no great acts. I think of the impact of a life like that. It sounds quiet, and so small as to be invisible. It sounds like the unexplored, unseen Point Nemo.

But I know better than that. A life's impact can be measured by what it gives and what it leaves behind, but it can also be measured by what it steals from the world.

10

We married the very same evening of our kiss in the aviary. Tripping onto our bikes and riding all the way back into town, stopping by the thrift shop to buy him an old-fashioned brown suit. For me a long silk dress of palest, softest peach, the feel of which will never leave me. Niall paused by someone's front garden to pick white flowers for my hair and his lapel, and he knew all their names, but chose only an array of sweet peas. Our next stop was at Joyce's supermarket to get a loaf of bread and a bottle of champagne. He made murmured phone calls all the while, using his money and connections to get us a fast-tracked marriage license and a celebrant who could be available on the spot. Not for Niall Lynch a merely ceremonial wedding, no, certainly not.

I kicked off my shoes at the harbor and we walked barefoot to its very edge, out to meet the sea. He'd asked me where I would like to get married and I'd said here, in this spot, exactly where I was once told about a woman who became a bird. Something of me had been left here that day. I didn't know if I would find it now, or leave another piece. Blue draped over us, saturating the world and our skin with it. The celebrant came and married us legally and we even spoke vows we conjured on the spot, vows we later found mortifying and laughingly rewrote, and from the corner of my eye I could see the elegant curve of white swan necks gliding through, waiting for the bread we'd brought to feed them, and I could see a mole beside his ear, and a dimple on the right side of his smile, and flecks of yellow in his dark hazel eyes, flecks I hadn't seen before. We thanked the celebrant and sent her away so we could sit with our feet dangling over the edge and drink champagne and feed the swans. The birds honked softly. We spoke of nothing in particular. We laughed at ourselves and swigged from the bottle. We had moments of incomprehensible silence. He held my hand. The sun went down, the swans swam away. Tears found my cheeks and his lips in the dark.

It was utterly mad. And still. I had not one doubt, not one question, nothing but a sense of inevitability. This had been designed and I would ruin it one day but for now it was mine, and his, and ours. Niall didn't see it that way, but instead as a choice I'd made. He said Franny Stone makes choices and the universe bends. She makes her own designs and always has; she is a force of nature and he the quiet thing that looks on and loves her for it, even then, still now. Funny, that. For to me it always felt as though I were the one following him.

Niall told me on our wedding night, as we gazed into the wild Atlantic, that for him it was because he'd dreamed of me before we met.

"Not you, exactly. Of course. But something that felt as you did that night in my lab, when we touched the gull. And then again when I watched you save the boys from drowning. It was so familiar. I recognized you."

"What did it feel like?"

He thought for a while and then said, "Something scientific."

This, I accepted—a tad disappointed—was his cynicism. But I was wrong. It remains to this day the most romantic thing he has ever said to me, only I didn't know that until much later.

UNIVERSITY HOSPITAL GALWAY, IRELAND
FOUR YEARS AGO

They think me asleep but in the dark I hear their soft voices.

"We don't know what really happened."

"She confessed. She said she was trying to do it."

"She was in shock. It might not count."

"It better fuckin' count."

"Do you understand how far she walked?"

"Don't be going soft 'cause you went to school with the bitch. She's bound for bars and you getting torn up about it won't help."

"I'm not torn up. I just don't understand it."

"Aye and that's a good thing, Lara—you're no killer."

I roll over, longing for sleep, but my wrist is shackled to the bed and the pillow is lumpy and my feet, oh god, my feet burn and burn and burn and they said I might lose some of the toes and still it's as nothing to the screaming, ravening burn of my mind.

The *Saghani,* NORTH ATLANTIC OCEAN
MIGRATION SEASON

Something shrieks.

I jerk upright, woken by the high-pitched grind of metal against metal. Ennis is talking quickly into an intercom, more urgently than I've heard him.

I climb to my feet in the small captain's office to find that the storm hasn't yet passed. It rages on, as violent as it's been all day. It takes me a moment to register what I've heard Ennis say.

"—nets are going in, prepare stations. Repeat—we have fish, nets are going in."

"*Now?*"

Ennis glances at me and nods grimly. The *Saghani* is barely holding anchor in the gale-force winds and I can see ten-foot waves crashing onto the deck. It will be slippery as hell down there, the simplest thing in the world to be washed overboard. On Ennis's monitors I see sonar circles that measure the depth of the ocean and any change of volume. There's a red spike to which he points that I assume indicates a large body of marine life two hundred meters under the surface, although I could be wrong because he doesn't explain.

Through the wall of rain I can barely see the crew members venturing onto the deck, just their bright orange overalls and parkas. They are wearing white helmets today, and they move quickly into action, hauling the cables into place and connecting them to the nets. It is Anik who seems to be in the most danger as he is lowered down onto the rocking sea in his skiff.

"He'll be killed," I say.

Through his radio Ennis is in constant communication with Daeshim on the deck, who relays everything that's going on and takes orders from his captain.

"He's down!" Dae reports. "I'm checking the winch cables now. Ropes are going out. Everyone stand clear! Bas—"

The radio goes off. I saw it: Basil slipped. I lose sight of him for a moment and then spot him again, clinging to a piece of rigging.

"Report, Dae," Ennis says calmly.

"He's all right, Skip. He's up."

Ennis studies a different monitor closely.

"What's that one?" I ask.

"Sensors on the net so I can see where they are." He goes for the radio again, but this time it's connected to an earpiece in Anik's ear. "You good to give me a wider loop, Anik?"

"Roger that, Skip. It's . . . rough down here . . . my best."

"Fuck," I breathe, closing my eyes. I can't see Anik's skiff through the storm. He's down there somewhere, tossed about and trying to maneuver the enormous one-ton net on his own.

"He's fine," Ennis says. "He's got it. We're in place. Dae, get him back in."

The men work quickly to haul Anik back onto the boat and then they rush to deal with the catch, pelted by rain and wind and waves. It's a kind of nightmare and it feels surreal to be up here out of harm's way, watching. I feel *wrong*.

"Pursing," Ennis warns, and starts to work his controls. "Nets up." He goes slowly and I feel the boat tilt alarmingly. "Fuck," he says, so softly I almost don't hear it. "Big catch."

"Skip, I got a lotta strain on the block," Dae reports. "The cables are stretched to their limit."

"Hold steady."

"How much weight's in that thing?" Dae asks incredulously.

"'Bout a hundred tons."

There's shouting on the deck and I press my nose to the glass to try to see what's going on down there. The net is almost out of the water when one of the cables snaps.

"Cover!" I hear someone shout and every crew member hits the deck. Too late for one of them: the cable whips out and cracks into a body, flinging it against the bulwark. A doll, a toy, something weightless and lifeless and fragile. I gasp in horror and listen to the shouts of panic from below. Whoever it is doesn't move.

The net, meanwhile, holds, but only just. More strain works at the power block and all the pulleys, and I feel the boat tilt farther. Someone is climbing the A-line to reach the top of the power block, and I recognize Malachai's tall athletic frame as it nears the top, swaying precariously with the waves. He could go over at any moment, and water this cold can kill.

"What's he doing?" I demand.

"Attaching the backup cable."

"Can't you just put the fish back and end this?"

"Too good a haul."

"Are you fucking kidding?"

Ennis ignores me so I bolt out into the gale.

"Franny!" I hear him roar but I'm ducking and hammering down the metal steps, holding on for life. I am drenched to the bone, my parka seems no help against that, and the cold is shocking. It is worse than when I dove into the fjord to save Ennis. It is worse than the winter mornings in our freezing little wooden house on the beach, with wind howling through the slats in the wall and you thought you would die of it, you honestly thought you would—oh, it is worse than that by far. Water streams inside my parka, down my spine and into my gloves, turning my fingertips to ice. My ears, I think, have dropped off. I have the lucidity to think of these poor people who work in this madness, who must function at their best in it. On deck the shriek of the storm is deafening. I press myself to where Anik is huddled over the crumpled body of Samuel. Léa, Basil, and Dae are still struggling heroically with the winch, holding it in place with nothing but sheer muscle, a constant stream of curse words spewing from their mouths all the while, as Mal tries to reconnect the cables.

I focus on Samuel, who is unconscious. "Help me get him inside!" Anik yells and so we take an armpit each and drag the big man over the lurching deck. My feet slip out from under me and I hit the deck hard. Air goes from me. I remember this. It's drowning. I gasp, panicked, trying to find a breath but there are none. The sky spins and falls onto my face. Anik's hand rests between my ribs and he says, "Slow, slow, easy," until I can breathe again and I'm not drowning and then we are moving, dragging, slipping, and finally inside the top of the ladder.

"How do we get him down?" I pant.

Anik is shimmying down the ladder and disappearing, and he seems to take a disastrously long time to emerge with a first-aid stretcher. Together we roll Samuel onto it and strap him in and I'm worried about his spine but there's nothing for it. Anik goes a few steps down and catches Samuel's feet, and then we slide the stretcher down the stairs to the bottom. The next task is to lift it, and it seems to weigh a thousand tons, a million, it's far too heavy for me, I can't—

"Franny," Anik says calmly. "No one is coming to help—they're too busy. You must lift him."

I nod, and bend my knees. I'm stronger than I've been before, stronger than even the days when I was a swimmer—prison will do that, it will carve you tough. We haul him up and stagger down the corridor. As the boat heaves the wall slams into us and there goes the air from my lungs again. "Keep going," Anik pants, and we do, crashing into the kitchen and dropping him on the bench.

"He's not breathing," I pant. "I don't think he has a pulse."

"I'm getting the paddles."

But he's taking too long, searching through a cupboard, so I duck to blow air into Samuel's mouth and then because he's too high and too large I climb up onto the kitchen bench and I straddle his large girth, and I start pumping his chest as hard as I'm able. I don't feel as though I'm making any difference. He is too firmly built, the bones and muscles too protective of his heart for me to get to it. I give him another breath of air, a long one, feeling him inflate beneath me in a way that unnerves me deeply.

"Off, quick."

I scramble down and Anik unzips Samuel's parka and cuts his shirt open. Then he places the small patches over where the heart should be. They connect with wires to a small black box with a monitor.

"Do you know what you're doing?" I ask.

"No."

"I think you have to put one to the side and one to the bottom."

"How do you know that?"

I shrug helplessly.

He hesitates, unsure, then does as I've said. The pack is energizing itself, and we watch the charge climb higher and higher until the light goes green.

Anik's eyes are frantic. He reaches for the button but he doesn't need to press it—the device automatically shocks if it can't detect a heartbeat. Electricity jolts through Samuel's large body. He is immediately a thing of meat and blood. But Samuel isn't dead—this isn't that, it isn't—he gasps and returns to consciousness, more quickly than I would have imagined possible. He groans and vomits all over himself, and we have to roll him onto his side so he doesn't choke.

"The fuck happened?" he asks.

"No clue," I say. "You got hit and your whole body shut down. Your *heart* stopped, Sam."

He rolls onto his back once more and stares at the ceiling. We watch him, frightened. I don't know what kind of injury could cause your whole body to shut down like that, and I imagine jumping back onto his chest and pumping it once more, blowing my breath between his cold lips once more. If he goes again I will have to.

But instead Samuel says, "*Like a shipwreck we die going into ourselves . . .*"

And I laugh, startled—because even now—and I say, "*As though we were drowning inside our hearts.*"

Samuel says, faintly, "You Irish." And then he closes his eyes and continues to breathe.

The catch is lost to the storm and the broken cable. Samuel has a laceration from the cable that cuts clean across his back. The crew is exhausted and heartsick over the lost catch, worried for Samuel. Ennis is so furious with himself that he's stopped speaking altogether.

And me?

I'm no longer the thing with feathers.

Because the tracking light for my tern has blinked out, snuffed away by the storm, dragged into the deep below where no sun can find it. Just as she must have been.

11

WOMEN'S PRISON, IRELAND

FOUR YEARS AGO

I flinch at every sound. My nerves are shot. The numbness has worn off and now there are sharp edges everywhere.

Because I'm on remand my lawyer can visit me any day of the week. I am led by a guard into the open meeting room and shown to a table. The glass windows are set high into the walls, right up near the ceiling, and they're open only a crack. It's better than my cell, though.

I wait what feels an age for Mara Gupta. She is a tenacious fiftysomething barrister, and she's brought her handsome and extremely clever young assistant, Donal Lincoln, who I'm fairly certain must be at least thirty years her junior. From previous meetings with them I've got the impression they might be sleeping together. A distant part of me loves them for it, loves *Mara* for it. But the part of me that loves anything is right now being resoundingly silenced. My heart has gone cold.

Because.

The world of fear. My new home. Fear that I won't survive this, fear that I will.

"How are you?" Mara asks me.

I shrug. There aren't words for what I am.

"Do you have enough money?"

I nod blankly.

"Franny, we need to talk about new evidence that's come in from forensics."

I wait, noticing her delicate gold watch. I wonder what it's worth. Having spent a painful eight years getting to know Niall's parents, I can say with certainty that it's probably a lot. The thought occurs to me to fire her again. I have done so twice already. She has been rehired. The Lynch family gets what they want, and they want me out of here.

I used to want enormous, unrealistic things, too. Now I only want my husband.

"Franny?"

I realize I've missed what Mara said. "Beg your pardon?"

"Focus on what I'm telling you because this is serious."

Serious. Ha. "Can you get me time outside? They won't let me outside."

"We're working on that but as I've said, you need to speak clearly with a psychologist about your claustrophobia."

"I did."

"Franny, she said you sat in silence for thirty minutes and she couldn't diagnose you."

I don't remember that.

"I'll arrange another session and this time try to speak, okay? We're going to talk about the evidence now." Mara's eyes are enormous. Someone coughs and I jump, shattered, exhausted, so fucking terrified I can barely function. Mara takes my hand and centers me, forces me to concentrate on her next words.

"There's new forensic evidence and the prosecution are claiming it means this wasn't an accident. You and I both know it was, but it now *looks* premeditated, and I'm going to need your testimony to help me argue against it. So I need you to tell me again what really happened—"

"Premeditated."

"You wanted to do it," Donal supplies. "You made plans and carried them out."

"I know what premeditated means," I say, and watch him blush. "What's the evidence?"

"We'll get to that, Franny, just listen for a second. This changes things," Mara says. "They don't want you for manslaughter. They want you for two counts of murder."

I stare at her and stare at her. Neither of the lawyers says anything, perhaps letting me process this. But I have processed it a thousand times over. I've been waiting for it. I squeeze Mara's hand and say, "You shouldn't have taken this job. I tried to tell you. I'm sorry."

The *Saghani*, NORTH ATLANTIC OCEAN
MIGRATION SEASON

"I'm sorry," Léa says when I tell her of the drowned terns. If mine couldn't survive the storm then it's unlikely any of the others in her group did. "I'm so sorry," she repeats, and I can see that she too is stricken by what's happened.

I nod, but can't think what to say. I've only told her so that she'll inform the crew for me. There's a yawning mouth in my chest. When I close my eyes I see the birds, one after the other, sinking into a watery grave.

Dinner is quiet tonight. Poor Samuel can't get up from his bed so we're without his comforting presence. Basil's large knee is digging into my leg and I hate it, I hate his touch, but there's no room for me to move.

The course has been decided. We're for St. John's, Newfoundland, and Labrador. It's where Samuel's family waits for him, where we can get him medical attention and repair the cable that snapped. From there I don't know. Ennis said he didn't want to cross the Atlantic—it's a long way, and an unknown sea—but they're the only birds we have left to follow.

Maybe he's tired of following birds.

I don't know if I can convince him again, but I let my feet carry me up to the bridge anyway.

It's the first time Ennis hasn't been at the helm. Anik stands in his place, eyes on the horizon. "Where is he?"

"On break. He hasn't slept in days. Leave him be, Franny."

I slump into a chair, and I don't open the laptop screen to check on the dots. Anik's gaze pins me a little. There's something heavy about it.

"Are you gonna tell me to get back to work?" I ask.

"Would you listen?"

"Probably not."

Anik's wide mouth curls into a smile, the first real smile I've seen him offer. He says something in another language. I wait for him to explain, but he turns back to the helm.

"What language was that?" I ask.

"Inupiat."

"Is that Inuit?"

He nods. "Northern Alaska."

"Is that where you met Ennis?"

Another nod.

"How did you meet?"

"On a boat. How else?"

"What's it like up there?"

"So many questions."

"I have millions."

His perpetual scowl is back in place. But he surprises me by saying, "It's death, up there. And life. The truest of each."

I watch the stretch of ocean before us, expecting at any moment to see land on the horizon. "How long will it take to get there?" I ask.

"Two days, maybe. What will you do, now that the birds . . ."

"They're not all dead," I say. And yet . . . "I don't know." I can't stop picking at my scabs and making my hands bleed. "If Ennis doesn't want to keep going . . ."

"You'll find another way," Anik says simply.

But he doesn't understand. I tried for months before I found a captain to agree.

"They're not all dead," Anik echoes.

I take a breath. He's right, but I can't stop seeing the bodies sinking down into the blur, and I can't stop remembering the hollowness of Samuel's chest as I blew air into it. It sends a shudder through me. "That moment before he woke up. Before we shocked him . . ."

Anik looks sideways at me.

"It was frightening."

"Yes."

"He was gone for a second. He didn't seem in his body anymore. I breathed into his mouth and it filled him up like a balloon. He was just this . . . just an empty thing."

Anik nods. "My grandmother would say that for a moment he visited the spirit world. We called him back and perhaps he'll thank us for that and perhaps he won't. Some think it unkind to be forced from such a place."

"Have you spoken to people who've returned from there?"

"They say they have."

"Do you believe them?"

I want him to say yes, I want it so badly, but he only shrugs.

"How do they describe it?"

Anik thinks for a time and I realize I have leaned so far forward I'm in danger of slipping off the seat.

"They say it is free of rules or punishments," he says. "They call it weightless, and very beautiful."

And suddenly I am crying. "Everyone goes there?"

"That's what they say."

"Even us? Even me?"

"Yes."

"And the ones we love?"

"Of course."

I close my eyes and tears spill down my cheeks, and the spirit he speaks of, my spirit, I can feel it trying to get free, trying to find its way there, only my body won't let it, not yet. "She's waiting for me, then."

"Who is?"

I open my eyes and meet his brown stare.

"My daughter."

His shoulders drop as he breathes out. His eyes are full now, too.

"Franny," Anik says, reaching to place a hand on my hair. We watch the sea, waiting for land and wishing we never had to reach it.

12

The *Saghani*, LABRADOR CURRENT OUTSIDE NEWFOUNDLAND
MIGRATION SEASON

The mood is bleak this morning as we near the coast of Newfoundland. We have abandoned any search for fish, and I didn't expect the profundity of their loss. It's easier to see how much the sea drives this crew, how much they belong to the hunt, when they are no longer in it.

Samuel warned me about the Labrador Current and what it would be like to reach where it meets the Gulf Stream. Still I couldn't have imagined it. We have been flung at such speeds that I fail to believe anything could stop us. Furthermore, the two currents running alongside each other, one freezing cold and the other warm, have created a shroud of heavy fog as we approach land. I stand at the bow, unable to see my hand before my face let alone the rocks we careen toward.

The bell sounds overhead. I imagine the shrill cry of a gull, and the sound of its wings swooping through the fog. There should be hundreds of gulls on a shore like this.

We are slowing. The crew members on deck shout to each other now, and the sweep of the lighthouse beam makes a path through the fog. The bell tolls in a steady rhythm to which I can match my breathing. Ennis guides us into the harbor of St. John's with what seems little effort. But I know the stress such a berthing has caused the crew. They've been tense all morning, unable to control the weather or the skill of their skipper.

I am nervous for a different reason: my passport is fake.

Well, that's not exactly true. It's not fake, it's just not mine.

The sound of it reaches me before anything else. I start to notice more voices adding their shouts to the wind. Shapes form through the fog. Bodies with signs held aloft. *Stop the massacres! Oceans belong to fish, not people! End the killing!*

I take a breath, a gasp; a fist connects with my chest. The shouting is almost violent, it is filled with a fury I know well: it is my husband's rage they embody as they chant and cry, as they try to do what little they can to stop the maddening inevitable doom we have built.

Léa moves to my side. Her eyes are cold, jaw hard. "Don't look at them," she says, flat.

I see one sign, larger than the rest—*What more must we destroy?*—and a bottomless shame opens within me. I'm on the wrong side of that sign.

It's strange being on land again, even after only a few weeks at sea. Already it feels unnatural. The earth is too hard under my feet, as though it will compound me a little with each step. I move down the gangway to the customs terminal, making sure to tuck myself between the crew members of the *Saghani*. I am handed a customs form to fill out and I do so using Riley Loach of Dublin's information. An overzealous customs officer watches me with hawk eyes the whole time. But the man behind the counter only gives me a cursory glance—I make sure to smile widely at him, obscuring my facial features a little—and then he stamps the passport and lets me through.

There is a corral separating us from the protesters but I can hear them so clearly, can make out their individual faces, each one watching us in disgust, bearing the same disbelief I've struggled with. A man near the end of the group wears a striped beanie and brandishes a sign that reads *Justice for fish, death to fishermen*. It sends a chill through me, and that's when our eyes meet, just for a moment, and it's as though this man can see straight inside me and has judged me monstrous.

"Come on," Basil says, pulling me by the elbow. "Don't give them the satisfaction."

We walk until the street is clear and then we wait for an ambulance to transport Samuel to the hospital.

"You okay?" Léa asks me softly, the two of us standing a little apart from the others.

I cast her a sideways glance. "Why wouldn't I be?"

"Just seem jumpy."

She has begun to watch me, this French mechanic. I feel her dark eyes on me often, and sometimes when I catch her gaze she turns quickly away. I have not been sure until this moment if what lives in her interest is concern for my sanity, or something more intimate, more painful.

Ennis travels in the ambulance with Samuel while the rest of us divide into cabs. I spend the drive staring through the window at the winding city, brightly colored houses built into craggy hills. Everything is still blanketed in heavy fog, giving the day a sense of unreality.

We find Ennis sprawled tiredly in the waiting room and sink into chairs around him. "He's being looked at. I've called Gammy, she's on her way."

Forty minutes pass before Samuel's wife, Gammy, arrives. She strides through the doors in thick leather boots, riding leggings, and a shaggy woolen sweater to cover her robust form. Her hair is as red as Samuel's, plastered with sweat to her forehead and flushed cheeks. Blue eyes dart worriedly as she takes Ennis in a bear hug and thumps him on the back. "Where is he?"

Ennis shows her the way and then we are quiet once more, waiting. I am not good at waiting.

"How long have they been married?" I ask Dae.

"'Bout thirty years. Think they're up to about a dozen kids now."

"No way."

"Yeah. Samuel's got a lotta love to go round. Just ask him."

"I have and he's told me the same thing multiple times already."

We while the day away, keeping ourselves occupied with a pack of cards Dae thought to bring. Léa and I go on a food run and return with egg rolls and coffees. Gammy finally reappears midafternoon, looking wan.

"They're keeping the idiot overnight. He's on some hefty antibiotics for the infection, and they want to monitor his heart. Think there might be a problem with it."

"From the defibrillator?" I ask.

Gammy's eyes find me and soften. "No, darl. The heart condition was from before he got injured. You saved his life." Gammy glances at Ennis. "Goddamn cable that hit him probably saved him as well. Otherwise we wouldn't have known about the bad ticker until it was too late. Never thought I'd thank you for anything, Ennis Malone."

I expect it to be a joke but no one smiles. Ennis inclines his head a little in acknowledgment. Gammy watches him for a good long moment, her expression unreadable. Then she spreads her hands. "Right. Let's get off, then. I've got ravenous beasts at home who need feeding and I'm sure you lot could do with a proper wash and feed."

I wind up in Gammy's car with Ennis and Léa, while the others all head off to find a rental car. Gammy and Samuel's place is out of town somewhere.

"I hope this'll be enough for you now, Ennis Malone," Gammy says. Maybe she's one of those people who find authority in using full names. Her accent is the same as Samuel's, the distinct "Newfie" mix of Irish and Canadian. "Although losing your men to the waves has never stopped you before," she adds coldly. "Anyone'd think you'd started tossing them overboard yourself."

This is an immensely cruel thing to say, and I wonder at the poor people she's talking about; I wonder at Ennis's involvement in their deaths and his regret. It shouldn't surprise me. He sent Anik into a storm, didn't he? Wasn't it his determination to catch fish that nearly got Samuel killed? And the rest of us, besides?

I find myself coming to an uneasy understanding of the captain's will. Twice before I've recognized something similar—in myself and then in my husband—and I know it to be destructive. How far will Ennis go to get what he wants, this mythical Golden Catch? What will he sacrifice?

"He's home now, Gam," Ennis says quietly from the back seat. I steal a look at him in the side mirror. His head rests on the window and he watches the ocean to our left. The burden of his desire weighs heavily upon him.

"Too late, Ennis Malone. Too fucking late. And if you've brought any trouble with you I'll be giving you a hiding."

"We'll stay in town if it makes you more comfortable."

"Don't be ridiculous."

"It wasn't Skipper's fault," Léa speaks up, obstinate. "We all know the risks. It's a fool who steps onto a vessel and assumes he'll leave it breathing. You know it, Samuel knows it."

Gammy looks in her mirror at the much younger woman. "And do you think it's fair, to use people's devotion against them? To pull at their hearts until they do as you say, and take bullets for you as well?"

Nobody speaks.

Gammy looks at me and I brace myself for her next blow. "Who's this one, then? How'd he rope you into his mess, darl?"

"I roped myself in."

"Good luck to you, then. Lord knows you'll need it. Now if you keep an eye on the hills ahead, you'll see our place coming up a little ways."

As we round a curve in the road a lighthouse appears on the headland, rearing into the sky.

"No," I say. "Do you really—?"

Gammy laughs at the look on my face.

The lighthouse is remote enough that it's not automatic, but still manned, and as Gammy tells me the story of her family and how they've always kept it, passed from generation to generation, I feel her deep sense of home. I can feel it in the earth, too, when I get out of the car and walk upon the rocks. It's in the sky and the roaring ocean and the keening of the wind, it's in the way she strides over her land and into her lighthouse; she owns this place and it owns her, tangible and unarguable. What must it be like to be bound so deeply and willingly to a place?

"You right, love?" Ennis asks me, handing me my backpack from the trunk.

I nod and follow him inside. The house adjoining the lighthouse is normal, really, not a relic of the past but an ordinary house, low-ceilinged, fire-placed, messy enough that it must harbor children.

And what children they are.

For an instant I try not to stare, and then I give up and do so with delight as they emerge from their shared rooms or come in from the hills outside. There are, not a dozen, but six identical daughters, the littlest six, the oldest sixteen, each with the same unruly red hair and pale freckled skin. None of them wear shoes. They look strong, a little dirty, very free. And they gaze at me with the same expressions of interest, with intelligence and mischief. I love them even before I've learned their names. Maybe it's their Irishness, their familiarity. Maybe it's the fabulousness of their sameness, or the strangeness of it.

They each hug Ennis excitedly, then Léa, and then the rest as they pile out of the rental car. Me they are watchful of.

"Hally," the oldest introduces herself as she shakes my hand. She has the most disheveled hair of all and eyes a deeper blue than the sea on a clear day.

"And this is Blue, Sam, Coll, Brin, and Ferd."

I say hello to each, trying to commit their odd names to memory.

"Don't worry, nobody ever remembers us all," says the one I think is called Brin.

"I'll try my best."

"Sometimes I make them wear name tags," Gammy admits.

"You're Irish?" Hally asks me.

I nod.

"We're Irish!" says Ferd.

"A long way back," Blue adds. Then, "Which part are you from?"

"Galway."

"The republic," Hally says. "So did you support the end of the War of Independence and the British colonization of Northern Ireland?"

I blink. "Uh . . . How old do I look, exactly?"

Hally makes an impatient sound and decides I'm not worth questioning further on the matter.

The rest of the adults are all gathered around the big kitchen table, while I've been surrounded by children in the living room. The fire is raging, even now with the sun high—the wind out here cuts through the house, turning the air frigid.

"You should visit Ireland one day," I tell the girls, sinking into one of the deep leather armchairs. "You'd suit it."

"Can we stay with you?" Hally asks me.

Surprised, I say, "Of course."

The littlest one, Ferd, climbs onto my lap and makes herself comfortable. "Hello."

"Hi," she says, curling my hair around her tiny fingers and humming contentedly.

"You like history, huh?" I ask Hally.

She nods.

"Mom wants her to study it in college," Blue says.

"Leave Franny alone, hounds," Gammy calls from the kitchen. She's taken off her huge woolen sweater and I can see that her arms and shoulders are thick with muscle.

The girls are reluctantly drifting away when I say quickly, "No, don't go."

From then on I have six shadows. Hally pummels me with questions. Ferd seems to want to always be cuddling. Coll doesn't speak a word but she watches my face like it holds the secrets of the universe. Blue and Brin seem more interested in mucking around with each other, but stay close, and Sam laughs kindly at anything anyone says.

"Would you like to see our garden?" Ferd asks.

In the kitchen I can see Basil and Gammy arguing about the food they're cooking for dinner. It seems Basil is rude enough to order people around in their own homes, and Gammy is the first one with enough moxie to stand up to him. Dae and Mal are playing cards again and baiting each other into fights. Léa is with the cars—I can hear her tinkering with Gammy's engine. Anik has disappeared outside somewhere and I don't know where Ennis has gone.

I smile because there's nothing I'd like more than to see the garden. Ferd decides she will be piggybacked, so I hoist her up and march outside. Her little hands gently circle my throat.

"We've been harvesting for months," Sam explains as we head up onto a hill covered in a marvelous, sprawling vegetable patch. "During the summertime."

"And which vegetables do you grow?" I ask, picking my way over winding stone pathways between beds.

"These were onions here," Blue tells me, pointing them out. "Potatoes were in those far beds, but we got all of those for the moment. These are beets, carrots, cauliflower, um . . . what was that one, Coll?"

"Kale," Coll says in a whisper, running her fingers over the brilliant purple and green leaves.

"They're Coll's favorite," Blue says. "See how they look like roses?"

"There's heaps more," Sam says. "Herbs all over there. Mint and stuff."

"Mint, ugh," Brin announces, pinching her nose in disgust.

"Do you know how to garden?" Hally asks me.

"A little. Not like you."

"How do you expect to live sustainably if you can't garden properly?"

I stifle a laugh. "You're right, I should. It's hard when you live on a boat."

"Well, yeah," she agrees. "But when you get home."

I nod.

"We don't eat anything but what we grow ourselves, and the eggs our chickens lay, and what we catch in the sea."

"But we haven't had fish in *ages*." Brin sighs.

"What about other meat?" I ask. "Do you raise livestock?"

"No meat," Hally says. She puffs her chest out a little and looks truly fearsome. "Dad says we don't need it."

Does he now. Samuel's definitely been eating meat on the boat—no wonder he gave me such a sheepish look when I said I was a vegetarian.

"I'm impressed and envious," I tell them, and Hally's bristling gaze loses some of its suspicion.

"We've been taking down the nets, see?" She points to the end of the garden, where there's a metal skeleton over which drapes a length of netting. "Hey, get out of there," she adds to Blue and Brin, who've wrestled their way into a bed of dirt and are now filthy.

"Why?" I ask Hally.

She shrugs. "The birds haven't been trying to eat anything lately."

"That's because there aren't any," Blue says as though it's obvious.

I swallow. "That's sad."

Hally shrugs. "I guess."

"But good for the vegetables!" Ferd pipes up cheerfully from my shoulder.

. . .

Next we spend time in the chicken coop, a great big maze of a space, with wooden houses in which the birds sleep and patches of grass for them to scratch around in. There are twenty-three in total, and they're so used to people that they let us hold and stroke them. Their speckled feathers feel silky to the touch, their soft clucking is almost motherly, and I love it here.

It's nearing dusk as we walk down the hill to the long stretch of sandy beach. Most of the girls bound ahead, but Ferd stays on my back. She grows heavier by the moment but I wouldn't part with her for anything.

Two of the girls disappear to fetch their enormous black horses and lead them onto the beach. They both wave at me and swing themselves up onto the bare backs of the creatures, kicking them into a canter along the shore. Mighty hooves thunder and sand sprays; the girls seem miniature and dwarfed by their mounts, and yet earthily at one with them.

Ferd wriggles down to play with her sisters on the sand, so I sit on a dune and watch the two riders gallop up and down the length of the beach. A golden setting sun streaks the sky pink, the ocean metallic. I bury my feet and hands, feeling the coarse grains against my skin, and I beg myself to live inside this evening, but I am a million miles away. Once I would have lived for the sweetness of this night, I would have devoured it and let it quicken my blood, and now there is nothing. I am separate, and that might as well be death anyway.

Ennis appears silently and sits beside me. He has brought me a glass of wine, and a beer for himself. I'm surprised by his presence, when he has studiously avoided me.

"They're something, huh?" he asks, eyes on the girls.

I nod. "What are your children like?"

I'm not expecting an answer, but he says, "I don't know. I don't know them anymore."

"What are their names?"

"Owen and Hazel."

There's something tight in his voice, so I stop asking about his children.

My curiosity catches hold of something else instead. "So what's this big secret that no one will tell me about how Anik became your first mate?"

"It's not a secret," Ennis says. "It's just not their story to tell. We were on another boat together, before the *Saghani*. There was a storm and she sank, and every man aboard drowned except me and Anik, and the two of us survived because we held on to a bit of the mast and to each other, and we waited in the water for three days to be found. Now we don't sail without each other and that's it, that's all there is to it."

I'm silent. It's far from what I expected, and I turn cold, trying to imagine what it must have been like in that water for so long, knowing the endurance of it must bind you to someone forever.

"Why are you talking to me?" I ask eventually.

Ennis glances at me. "I'm taking pity on you."

I roll my eyes.

The horses thunder by, a storm of sound. Two tails of red hair stream out behind them, tangled with the dark manes of the animals.

"The fish will come back," Ennis says abruptly.

"No, they won't. Not while humans are here."

"There are always cycles—"

"This is mass extinction, Ennis. They're not coming back."

His face twists in denial. I find it astonishing.

"Why do you do this to yourself?" I ask him. "It's like punishment. Why?"

"Because there's nothing else. There's nothing else for me. There's this, and there's my children, and they're not even mine anymore unless I can keep going, unless I can make something of myself."

"Correct me if I'm wrong, but what does money have to do with getting custody?"

"I'll never get them back unemployed and penniless."

"So go back, drive taxis, clean buildings, pour beers, whatever. You can't be a father if you're not there."

He shakes his head. I don't think he can hear me, not really. I stare at him, and something sinks slowly in through my pores. Recognition.

Ennis and I are the same.

He told me I judged him, that I thought him scum, and the truth is I did. But how can I judge his destructive compulsion when I bear the same?

"I can't fucking stop," Ennis admits. He gulps his beer, I think to calm himself. "It's a sickness."

I said the same thing to Niall once about my wandering feet, about leaving him and hurting him over and over, but hearing it said now, it sounds more like an excuse than anything. It sounds selfish.

Ennis goes on, purging himself, maybe seeking some kind of absolution, but he's come to the wrong person—I have none to give. "Fishing's been in my family for hundreds of years. Generation after generation of fishermen. There was nothing else. Only thing I was raised on was the need to find the Golden Catch, to be the first one to do it in a long line of men obsessed."

He's quiet awhile, and then he adds more softly, "It's the only thing I'm *good* at. There has to be some way to be a father and a good man, and still be me."

I don't have an answer for that. I never worked out how to be relied upon and also free.

Ennis's hand on the glass trembles. "If I have to give it all up to be there for them, then I will, but I have to end it well. I have to . . . *achieve* something."

"Even if it puts people in danger."

"Yes." His voice cracks. "Even then."

We are silent as the girls go up and down, up and down. There's a heaviness between us and it's made of shame, but there's also a new understanding.

"What if you set the others free?" I ask.

"I can't do it on my own."

"Could you do it with me?"

Ennis looks at me. "Just the two of us?"

I nod.

Slowly he shakes his head. "No. I don't think so." But something in his gaze has shifted; I've the feeling I've struck a match.

"Dinner!"

We both turn to see Basil bellowing from the house. Ennis rises. The gray in his beard turns silver in the light.

"I'll wait for the girls," I say, wanting to be alone.

The white fetlocks of the horses are thick and heavy; love pulses through their muscles and the small bodies atop. The littlest, Ferd, is six. My daughter would be that age now, her hair jet-black like mine, like her father's.

13

NEWFOUNDLAND, CANADA

MIGRATION SEASON

"Why are you crying?"

I open my eyes to find Ferd sitting on the sand in front of me. The other girls are walking the horses back up the hill. The sun has sunk completely now, the stars a glittering blanket above.

"I'm always crying," I say, dashing the tears from my face.

"Hally's always crying, too. Mom says it's because she had a past life and it keeps sneaking back in."

I smile. "That's nice."

"And it's probably true, if Mom says."

"Yeah, probably."

"Come on. Aren't you hungry, Franny Panny?" She laughs at the name, making me laugh, too.

"Aye, I'm famished." She leads me by the hand up to the house. The beam from the lighthouse circles, inexorable as the tide, there and then gone, there and then gone.

A card table is added to the end of the large dining table, but it's still a squeeze to get all fourteen of us seated. Gammy doesn't banish her kids to another area, and they're all impeccably behaved at dinner.

"To Dad," Coll says in her dreamy whisper. We all raise our glasses to Samuel.

Dinner is served, a delicious winter vegetable stew. Basil has refrained from his usual ridiculousness, except to walk around the table ensuring everyone has a stalk of rosemary and a slice of lemon atop their bowl, and that the grown-ups all have a glass full of wine. I'm surprised to find myself enjoying his particularities, his passion, his attention to detail. He catches me staring at him and winks, ruining the moment.

"I haven't gotten to the bottom of who your new girl is," Gammy says, and all eyes turn to me.

"She's our ornithologist," Mal says. "Her birds are gonna lead us to the fish."

"There's no more birds left," Ferd protests.

"There are some," I tell her. "They're only hiding."

"Which ones?" Hally asks.

"The Arctic terns," I say. And all of a sudden I am back in my husband's lab the first time he told me of them. I'm with him as he sheds real tears, the first I'd ever seen him shed, describing the journey of these little birds, the courage of them. "They have the longest migration of any animal in the world, from the Arctic to the Antarctic and back again."

"And you follow them, Franny?" Gammy asks. "To study them?"

I nod. "I have trackers on three." I swallow. "Two, sorry."

"Then why do the trip yourself?"

"It's part of the methodology."

"Don't you have a team? You do this on your own, you track them all that way?" She shakes her head slowly, not taking her eyes from me. "What would possess someone to choose such a lonely life?"

There is silence as they wait.

I fold my hands in my lap and feel the question. "Life's always lonely. Less so with the birds. They led me to my husband, once."

It sounds mad.

The silence lengthens.

"Fucking mental," Basil says abruptly.

"Language, Bas," Dae says as the girls dissolve into giggles.

After dinner the girls decide to sing, which I gather they do a lot. They argue for a good five minutes about what the first song will be, until finally Hally declares they will sing only Irish songs for me, so I might feel less homesick.

But it's raw, and suddenly it's Kilfenora, my family in their kitchen as they played for me, it's my mother's cottage by the sea, and it's missing her, it's my husband and the distance between our bodies and it's my daughter, the child I never wanted, the child I fought a battle to be rid of, the one I fell deeply, devastatingly in love with, the one I lost. It's the littlest one, Ferd, her fingers around my neck and her hot breath against my ear, she has cracked me open and now my own littlest one is in my arms once more, a too-still thing, a most precious thing, breathless and without warmth, and no matter how often I try to leave it behind there will never be an end to this ache, this pain, the feel of her unbearable weightlessness in my hands.

I can hardly feel my body as I move for the door. It's cold outside and I hardly know it, and before I close the door behind me I hear Blue ask, "Did we upset her?" and Anik's voice replying, "Something darker did that," and I'm walking for the hills and shore and sea. I take off all my clothes and wade out into the icy water and the pain is immense and also nothing nothing nothing.

I lie in the sea and feel more lost than ever, because I'm not meant to be homesick, I'm not meant to long for the things I have always been so desperate to leave.

It isn't fair to be the kind of creature who is able to love but unable to stay.

It is Léa and Gammy and Hally who finally find me. They wrap me in a blanket on the seashore and I hear someone saying, "Let me die," over and over and then as Gammy kisses my forehead and Hally strokes my hair and they hold me so tight we tremble, I realize it is me.

"Stay," Hally whispers in my ear.

But I can't.

TRONDHEIM, NORWAY

EIGHT YEARS AGO

"Hello?"

"Hi." I listen to his breathing a long while.

"Where are you?" he asks, and he sounds very tired.

"Trondheim."

A moment for him to take that in, to readjust. I ask so much of him. I wear him down. "Why Trondheim?"

"Because I was in Oslo but the city lights made it impossible to see the Aurora."

"But you've found it? How is it?"

"I'm watching from the balcony. It's the most gorgeous thing, Niall . . . You'd love it."

"Whose balcony is it?"

"A friend's."

"Are you safe?"

"Aye."

"Whose balcony is it? Can you text me their name and address?"

"A couple I met at dinner, Ann and Kai, I'll text in a bit."

"Do you have enough money?"

"Aye."

"When are you coming home?"

"Soon."

He pauses awhile. I slide down onto the floor with my back to the wall. The brilliant greens and purples dance across the sky. I can feel him through the phone, it is such a potent thing, like I could touch him, feel his breath on my cheek, smell him. I'm dizzy with it, with his nearness and his terrible absence.

"It's lonely here, darling," I say, tears spilling onto my face.

"It's lonely here, darlin'," Niall says.

"Don't hang up."

"I won't."

And we don't, not for a long time.

NEWFOUNDLAND, CANADA

MIGRATION SEASON

They leave me in bed with hot water bottles piled about my feet. A distant part of me is embarrassed, but the current creature I am just wants quiet.

Only quiet is a different beast when it finds you. A perfect kind of thing until you have it and it turns on you.

My joints ache as I rise; there is screaming in my head and I hurry down the hallway to the stairs, and then I find my way back outside despite the cold, I feel none of it anyway, and I walk up to the headland and I sit where I can watch the wild Atlantic and I return to those first days with you, my darling, as I always find myself doing.

PART TWO

It starts as a tickle that creeps its way deeper, into a scratch, a scrape, a choke, until all I can do is cough up feather after feather, born of my very body and I can't get any air, not one breath—

"Franny!"

There's something atop me, pressing me into the ground, oh god, it's a body—

My husband is pinning me to the bed. I jackknife, repulsed at the sudden confinement of limbs and the powerlessness.

Niall immediately scrambles back, raising his hands. "Easy. It's okay."

"What are you *doing*?"

"Franny—I woke up and you were strangling me."

I stare at him, trying to catch my breath. "No . . . I was choking . . ."

His eyes are wide. "You were strangling me."

Dread curls inside. I have never slept a night beside someone, never woken beside another body. Last night we were married. This morning I have tried to kill him.

I stumble, caught in the sheets, then run for the toilet in time to vomit.

He follows me, tries to hold my hair but I shrug him off, not wanting to be touched, too ashamed to be touched. When I'm done I rinse my mouth. Can hardly look at him.

"I'm sorry. I sleepwalk. And other things, sometimes. I should have said."

He takes this in. "Right. Okay. Fuck." He laughs a bit. "I'm kinda relieved."

"Relieved?"

"I thought you might have been *really* regretting last night."

There's something so wry in his voice that I too find myself with a slightly unhinged laugh on my lips. "I was asleep."

"Must have been one hell of a nightmare."

"I can't even remember now."

"You said you were choking."

Scratching in my mouth and lungs—I shiver, block the memory as best I can.

"Do you often dream of choking?"

"No," I lie, moving past him for the kitchen. With the contents of my stomach flushed down a drain I'm starving. His apartment is simple and too modern for my taste, but we talked about finding a new place last night, somewhere that can be ours.

I raid his fridge but all he has are ultra-healthy grains and seeds and right now I need something greasy to sponge up all the alcohol we consumed last night. "Can we go get a fry-up?"

"Is this really not a big deal to you?" he asks. "Should I expect to get strangled every night? What else happens? Do you leave the house? Is it dangerous?"

For the first time since I woke I force myself to look him in the face. *There he is again, pinning me to the bed, stronger in every muscle than I am, something shocked and determined in his eyes and is this how I looked when he woke to the same thing?* "It won't happen again," I say. "I promise. I have medication I can take." Another lie. There are no meds that work. But I don't want him to be scared—for me or *of* me. I don't want that look in his eyes, for him to feel the way I felt, waking to his hands pressing me small.

. . .

Three more nights of the same—not strangling, exactly, but thrashing or walking about the apartment and tearing through kitchen cupboards. Niall is terrified I'll hurt myself. I don't admit that it's happening more than usual because I have never been so dislodged from reality as I am in this strange apartment with this unknown man. Instead I ask him to help me remove all the sharp things from his bedroom, and any extra furniture, and I ask him to have a lock placed on the inside, the key to which he will keep somewhere I cannot find.

I don't tell him that this makes me very nervous.

I don't tell him that as I try to sleep tonight the walls are shrinking and the ceiling is falling and that I want to kick down the door or smash through the window and get the fuck out of this apartment and this town and even this goddamn country, I don't tell him any of that, I just tie my wrists to the bedposts because I don't want to strangle my poor husband as we sleep.

"What are we doing today?"

Niall unties my wrists so I can roll over to face him.

"Don't you have to work?"

"What's the point?" he asks. "Nothing ever changes."

I am surprised to hear this from him but I suppose I shouldn't be; the other side of passion is melancholy, after all. Instead of reminding him that there is always a point to educating people I kiss him. We make love in the morning light, but I am tense with the memory of feathers and my wrists are sore, and I don't feel close to him, I feel in bed with a man who recognizes none of the monstrousness I keep hidden.

Afterward he asks again what we're doing.

"Anything you want," I say.

"Really? You don't have anything planned?"

"I'm off today."

"I know, but there's nothing outside work you planned?"

I look at him, frowning.

He laughs. "I heard you on the phone yesterday, arranging to visit some-one in Doolin."

"Were you eavesdropping? You creep!"

"It's a small apartment."

I make a face.

"So do you want to drive or will I?" he asks.

"What if I want to go on my own?"

"Then go on your own."

I consider him, looking for a trap. He seems genuine, so I shrug and feign disinterest. "Come if you want, but you'll probably be bored."

He heads for the shower. "Boredom's for the boring."

Most of the trip to Doolin is without music or talk, with only stretches of quiet that feel comfortable in one moment, awkward the next. The car is airless, so I have the windows down even though outside it's freezing.

The closer we draw, the more unraveled I feel. I become convinced that this is wrong and I must turn back, that this door leads only to something harmful: it's why Mam never led me here herself.

"So tell me about this accent of yours," Niall says into the quiet, I think because he senses my unease.

"What about it?" I ask, keeping my eyes fixed on the stretch of sea to our right.

"I can't work out what it is," he admits. "Sometimes I think it might be English, other times you sound American. Then it'll be pure Irish."

"You married me without knowing where I come from."

"Aye," he says. Then, "Do you know it?"

"Where I come from?" I turn to him with a mouth open to answer, but stop. "I . . . Maybe not."

"Is that what this is about?" Niall asks, nodding at the road unspooling itself before us.

I nod.

"All right, then. Grand."

The small house sits on a ridge in the hillside and from its driveway we can see all the way down the sloping green to the sea. Rocky, uneven pad-docks crisscross the expanse between, with a scattering of goats here and there.

Niall knocks because I'm unable to. The man who answers is a thousand years old and wind-bitten and hard-faced. He squints to make us out.

"Afternoon, sir," Niall greets him. "We're looking for John Torpey?"

"That'll be me. Unless this is about the land and then old Jackey ain't here."

Niall smiles. "It's not about the land."

I clear my throat—Niall can't do any more of this himself, for he knows no more about why I'm here. "I'm wondering if you might have ever known an Iris Stone."

John stares at me, squinting until it seems his eyes are closed. "This a joke?"

"No."

"You'll be the wee daughter, then. I'd heard you were about in the world. Look at you now, all grown." He sighs deeply and invites us in.

I am tense all the way through, unsure what to expect but feeling nearer the truth than ever.

The house is simple, with remnants of a woman's touch here and there, a life left over from someone else. Old lace curtains, their edges dirty now. Once-cheerful porcelain figurines on a bookshelf, most chipped. A thick layer of dust covers every surface, and the windows are so dirty they let only streaks of light through. I feel instantly sad, gazing at the loneliness of the place. There's a single photo on the mantelpiece of the fireplace. It's a much younger John with a shock of incredibly orange hair, a dark-haired woman beside him, presumably his wife, Maire, and a little girl between, one with an inky swath of locks just like her mam's. I don't get much of a look at it before John is beckoning me to sit.

"What are you wanting, dear? If this is about the land after all then we've things to discuss."

I frown, confused. "No, sir. I'm just here to ask after my mother. I was told by Margaret Bowen in Kilfenora that you might know her."

He laughs then, the sound turning quickly to a wheezing cough. "Ah, now I see. Margaret's losing her senses, can't remember a thing about who belongs where."

He goes into the kitchen and Niall and I listen to him shuffling around.

"Can I help you, John?" Niall asks, but John only grunts and returns with a floral tray, on top of which he's placed a plate of digestive biscuits and two glasses of water.

"Thank you," I say, taking a glass and noticing the smears of dirt on it. John must be close to blind.

"I'll give it to you straight, lass, 'cause it seems you know very little."

"I'd appreciate that."

"Iris is my daughter."

My fidgeting hands fall still. Everything of me falls still.

"I haven't seen her now in many years but that's her there." He points to the photo on the mantel.

I rise on weak legs and reach for it. Shock steals the breath from me. Up close, the little girl looks just like me. I had no idea—I've never seen a photo of my mother at this age. I return to my seat, cradling the photo in my lap, leaving fingertips pressed to her face, to her dark mane and the little red dress she wears.

"That was taken down at the shore," John says, and it's the shore we can see now, all the way down at the base of this sprawling hillside.

I clear my throat. "But then if . . . If you're my grandfather why wasn't I sent here to be with you?"

"Now why would that have happened?"

"Well . . . when Mam left."

"She left?"

I nod blankly. "When I was ten."

John's shoulders sag. His face gentles a moment, loses some of its creases, and I'm able to see a flash of true grief in his small, liquid eyes.

"Ah, now. That's a burden of mine, and it's part of a dark time."

"Could you tell me? Please? I don't know anything about my family."

Niall takes my hand and squeezes it. It startles me; I had forgotten he was here.

John folds his old, gnarled fingers in his lap. They are shaking a little with age. "Maire, my wife there, she was a wanderer. Her feet ne'er touched the ground. But she swam in that ocean each day, and had all the lads admiring her, and I couldn't be easy with it. She'd go missing, you see, for days at a time, and I told myself it didn't matter, she was still mine, the strange, lovely lass, the one everyone wanted for himself. But when wee Iris was born I took it into my head that she'd come of some other man."

I study the photo again. It's true, the little girl looks nothing like the man.

"Maire swore black and blue she was mine, and that was all right for a while. But it ate at me, and one day I couldn't stand it anymore, and I told Maire to take the girl back to where she belonged, wherever it may be, to whoever it may be. I'd had done with them both.

"So Maire divorced me and changed her name back to Stone. She gave Iris her name, too. And they wanted nothing to do with me and that was the way it stayed for twenty-odd years until I had a letter from Iris telling me Maire had passed."

He looks away from me now, to the window. "You hadn't been born yet, lass," he tells me softly, and then he falls silent a long while.

I'm glad of it, of the break. And I'm so glad of Niall's grip, the warmth of it, when there has never before been a hand to hold mine.

"You say she left, child?" John asks me eventually.

I nod again.

"I was hoping that curse wouldn't pass from mother to daughter."

"I think it did." And on again, to granddaughter.

"It makes sense Iris didn't want you left with me," John eventually says. "I was no father to her. Only . . . I wake some nights and there's no surer thing in me except that I was all wrong, that she was mine after all."

I can't keep the tears from slipping down my cheeks. One of them drops onto the photo, distorting my grandmother's face, drowning her. I wipe it off so she can breathe again.

"Where did you go?" John asks.

But I don't want to tell him. I don't want this man knowing anything about me, this man who throws away his family as though they aren't precious.

"To my father," I lie.

"And he was a good man? She found a good man to love her?"

"He's a good man and he waits for her." This is absolute nonsense but the sheer falseness of it coats me like armor.

The sky is beginning to darken. Night will soon fall.

"How is she?" John asks abruptly, and I hear the pain in him and the longing, and I feel the same in myself, the pain and the longing, and a small ugly part of me hates him for it, for not being able to help me find her, for knowing less than I do, and another part of me loves him for it, and it is all too much and too swift and so I get to my feet.

"She's well," I say, and then for no reason I can name, simply because it feels warm to say so, I add, "She speaks highly of you. I mean, of her memories of her father . . ."

John covers his face with a shaking hand. It is too terrible, all the wasted years. I have to get out of here.

"Thank you for having us," I say stiffly. "We should go."

"You won't stay for dinner?"

"No, thank you."

I am edging for the door, I can't get there fast enough.

"Will you come back to see me, dear?"

I breathe out, feeling suddenly tired. "I don't think so. But thank you."

It's only when I reach the door that I realize I still have the photo clenched in white-knuckled fingers. It feels a kind of death, to place it back on the mantel.

"Bye, John," I manage. And again, "Thank you."

Then I'm outside in a wind that has blown its way up from the sea. I can hear Niall speaking to John and then he is whisking me back to the car.

He doesn't take me toward Galway, but down the winding road that leads through the bright little town and past it to the shoreline. Pinks and lilacs streak the sky. At the horizon it burns.

The boat to the Aran Islands leaves from here and I wish we could board it but it doesn't run this late; the car park is empty when we pull into it. So instead we climb out and walk down onto the rocks. The ocean roars, steady and ferocious and calling.

"That man up there—he's your family," Niall says.

"He's not."

"He could be."

"Why would I choose someone who never chose me?"

Niall gazes at me. My hair whips over my face and I push it back.

He says, "I hate everyone but you."

I start to smile, thinking he must be making fun of me, but he grabs my arms and holds on to me and there's such a burning thing that my laughter dies and something different comes awake. He throws his head back and *roars*.

A thrill erupts within me, and grief for the years wasted, thrown away by a jealous man. So I let forth a scream of my own, at John and for him, for his loneliness, and I scream for the missing of my mother, and for the never having met my grandmother, and for the madness of this man I have married, who may be just as mad as I am. We scream and scream, and then we laugh, building a world of our own.

Afterward I swim in the ocean awhile, and then I rejoin him and we sit on the rocks to watch dark stain the sky. He keeps an arm about me and I press myself as close to him as I can. It's my least favorite time of day, coming out of the water, but it is better with him waiting for me. Immeasurably better.

"Where's your mam?" he asks.

The lie forms so easily on my tongue. "She's in the wooden house by the sea where I grew up."

He considers this. "Then why does it feel like you're looking for her?"

I don't reply.

"Do you know where she is, Franny?"

My throat thickens as I shake my head.

"You haven't spoken to her since you were a kid?"

"I've been trying to find her."

He absorbs this silently. Then, "What of your da?"

"I don't have a da."

"What happened to him?"

"No idea."

I wonder if I will ever tell Niall the truth of my dad, or if I will keep it buried in the dark, rotting place within.

"Then why'd she send you to live with him?"

"She sent me to the only place there was left, to his mother in New South Wales."

"Australia? Shit." He scratches the early growth of his beard. "Accent seems obvious now. Hybrid thing that it is. How long did you live with your grandmam?"

"Why are you asking so many questions?"

"Because I want to know the answers."

"You didn't before."

"Yes, I did."

"Then why didn't you ask? Why now?"

He doesn't answer.

"Why didn't either of us ask a single question?" I press. "We were so stupid."

"Regretting it already?" he asks. The wedding, if it can be called that.

And for one long moment I think the answer will be yes, it seems obviously yes, only when I open my mouth it's to say the other word, and I'm astonished to feel it as truth.

We both catch sight of an egret carried by an eddy. "Too windy for you, my love," Niall murmurs to it. The bird is flung about and stolen from view.

"I was with her a few years," I say. "Edith. But I came and went a lot, and in the end I didn't spend much time with her before she died."

"What was she like?"

I try to find the right word, my mind reluctant to go back there, to that farm and all its hard edges, all its loneliness. "Unforgiving," I say.

Niall strokes my hair off my face and kisses my temple.

"Mam wasn't like that," I murmur. "She was warm and sweet, and lost. I loved her so much. She had the wandering thing but she was terrified of it, too. She begged me not to leave her. She was fine being on her own until I came along and then the thought of being without me made her want to die. That's what she said. But there was a boy I liked. I wanted to go to the beach with him and I didn't fucking tell her, I just went. Why did I do that? I stayed away two whole days—or it might have even been three. So by the time I got back it was too late and she was gone. Like she warned me she'd be."

"She just left?"

I shake my head. He isn't listening. "*I* left." I look at him and brace myself for a truth, the worst one of all. "I always leave."

He is quiet a long while, and then he asks, "But do you come back?"

I rest my head on his shoulder; I rest myself in his hands. It seems a safe place to be kept, even to belong. But where does he get to belong? What crueler fate is there than to belong in the arms of a woman who dies each night?

For years I thought of that evening in Doolin warmly, the evening I first knew I was his. It was only when he seemed bewildered by this recollection that something long since cast aside returned.

"I thought you hated dead things," Niall said.

And I remembered how we walked along the rocks until we found the seabird settled among them, its neck broken and wings twisted at violent angles. It had gone simply from my mind, that image, like a light winking out.

15

I have waited for a rare moment alone to drag the crudely sharpened end of my toothbrush through my wrist. It hurts more than I'd thought. I drag it again, trying to deepen the wound. I know I've done it right when the blood is born dark as night. It's slippery and I lose my grip on the toothbrush, only to find it again and go for my other wrist, wanting it over—

She smells of sweet, cheap sugar as she kneels and gathers my arm strongly in her grip. The makeshift weapon is flung from my reach and she is calling for help and I am sobbing for her to let me go, please just let me go—

Her name is Beth. My cellmate. We don't speak to each other, not after those first days when I tried to end it. I don't think she will ever speak to me again, and that is fine. She and I don't cry at night, not like the women in other cells. We don't shout like they do, nasty lewd comments for the benefit of the guards or to rile each other up. I think they shout and cry to give voice to the fury and the fear of being so reduced. No, Beth ignores me and I lie shivering in horror, the horror of walls and of what I've done. I am unmade.

After only a month or so I was moved from the relatively comfortable single bedrooms of the women's prison, with its bedspreads and kitchens and sweet-smelling bodywash, to Limerick Prison, which is a different world and far more fitting. Here the cells are small and gray and concrete. Beth and I share a metal toilet and the window is opaque.

There are women here who've been violent because of drugs or alcohol. Women with addiction problems. Women who steal or commit vandalism. Abusive mothers. Homeless women. There are men, too. It is a mixed prison, after all, and not much keeping us apart. One door, to be specific. To be terrifying.

There are all kinds here. But I am the only woman who has killed two people.

I've been here nearly four months when it first happens. It takes them that long to realize that the murderess is harmless, catatonic, even. I don't speak, I hardly eat, don't manage to move much, except to clean and walk when they let me outside. But even without a voice I manage to offend Lally Shaye—it's something in my eyes—and she beats me black and blue. It happens again a month later, and then in another three weeks. It's becoming a habit of hers. I'm an easy target.

After the third attack I'm sent back from the infirmary with broken ribs and a broken jaw and all the blood vessels in one eye burst. I feel like hell. But Beth looks at me and stands up. It is the longest she's regarded me since that bad day near the start.

"Get up," she says in her Belfast accent.

I don't, because I can't.

She takes my wrist and wrenches me to my feet; it hurts less to surrender to it.

"You don't stop this now, it'll never stop."

I shake my head, listless. I don't care about being beaten.

Then Beth says, "Don't die in here. Not in a cage. Get free and die, if you have to."

It stills me. An idea forming.

"Lift your hands." She lifts hers, making fists like a boxer. It seems absurd. I'm not this, I can't fight. She yanks my arms up for me, positioning them. Ribs hurt. Lungs wheeze. Spine sags.

She punches me. I gasp in pain, cupping my cheek.

And Beth sees it. The flash of anger in my eyes. A remnant of *willpower*, not completely dead after all. She stokes it, calling it back to life, and all right, then, why not, I set my mind to a plan: die free.

16

NEWFOUNDLAND, CANADA

MIGRATION SEASON

I walk over grass wet with dew and through a blanket of dawn fog. After a mostly sleepless night I should be at my lowest, but instead I find myself bolstered this morning, determined to continue on our way. I never expected this journey to be easy, so what right do I have to give up at the first hurdle?

Despite the early hour, when I push through the back door and into the warm kitchen the lighthouse is already flush with agitation.

They're watching the news, crew members and children alike crowded into the living room. The coals of the fire have been forgotten and are just about out, I see, and it's this that makes me think something must be wrong.

Daeshim glances at me—all other eyes are glued to the screen—and murmurs, "Commercial fishing vessels recalled."

It doesn't register. "What? What does that mean?"

"They've made it illegal to fish for money."

"Where?"

"Anywhere."

"Hang on—*all* fishing vessels?"

"Every damn one," Basil says. "Shackled to land for the foreseeable future, and if you don't do as you're told they seize ownership of the boat. Cunts."

"Language," Gammy snaps. None of her children laugh this time.

"So we're stuck here," Léa says.

I look at Ennis. He hasn't said a word, but there's no color in his face.

This has been a long time coming. It's terrible for the economy and the people whose livelihoods come from the ocean. It's disastrous for my plan, and for poor Ennis's ability to get his kids back. But even so, I can't help smiling inside. Because it's not bad at all, not really—it's wonderful. It's an enormous turning point, a step forward, at long last, by those in power, and as I stand here what feels a million miles from him, I know exactly what Niall's smile will look like.

The St. John's hotel room is claustrophobic with four men and two women crammed inside it. I'm sitting with my head poked out the open window, smoking a cigarette. Basil, to whom the cigarette belonged, sits opposite me; I've gone through three in the time it's taken him to smoke one. Ennis didn't want to impose on Gammy, so we're back in town, waiting to hear how Samuel is, and trying, listlessly, to figure out what to do with ourselves. Our captain hasn't appeared all afternoon. Anik said Ennis had taken himself off to mourn the *Saghani* privately.

A trip to the coast guard yielded an information packet about the new laws that are coming into effect and what to do with our vessel. If we're not docked in our home port then the vessel is to be frozen for thirty days before being released, and Ennis can then take it straight to his Alaskan mooring, without detour and under the supervision of a maritime police officer.

I'm the only one who has nowhere to go. If I go back to Ireland the garda will grab me for breaking my parole.

So my only option is to find another way to follow the two remaining tracked terns.

"Are you okay?" Basil asks, voice low.

I ignore him, my mind busy turning the problem over. "Can I have another?"

He passes it to me, groping at my fingers before I pull them away.

"What's with you?"

"Nothing." I just don't want to be touched, especially by you.

Basil frowns, leering at me in a way that is so over the top I want to shove his face away. "Franny. I'm into you. You don't have to worry."

My mouth opens and I nearly laugh. "That's what you think I'm worried about?"

"Well, then what?"

His presumption and arrogance are hardly fathomable; I actually do laugh this time, and see him blush. We sit in silence and smoke, the cigarette leaving a foul taste in my mouth and not making me feel relaxed at all.

"I'm going for a walk," I announce.

"Do you want any company?" Mal asks, but I shake my head.

"I have some stuff to figure out."

I go down to the docks and share a few ciggies with some of the beached sailors. There'd been rumors circling that this could happen, but none of them thought it'd be so soon, in that way that nobody ever thinks the things they love will end. I ask them what their plans are and most say they'll head home, sell their boats to be repurposed, find some other way to make a living. Some of them already have backup plans in place. One of them, an older man with deep wind grooves lining his face, sheds a few tears, but when I try to console him he shakes his head and says, "It's not for the job. It's for the violence we brought to the earth."

I walk past a couple of tourist charter businesses and wonder if I could ever afford to charter a private boat to take me the distance. Doubtful. How the hell do you make a huge amount of cash in a hurry, without resorting to theft?

There's a pub on the corner that I saw when we came in—I head for it and order a Guinness and a whiskey. They have the fireplace raging so I sit in front of it, next to a young man with a beagle called Daisy. Daisy sniffs my hands and then parks herself at my feet to let me pat her. The owner, whose name I've already forgotten, tries to talk to me but when I don't have much to say he grows bored and finds new conversationalists.

Léa sits and hands me another Guinness.

"I don't need a minder," I say.

"Sure you do. You walk into oceans when you're not being minded."

I finish my whiskey and move on to the stout. Daisy's ears are silky soft to touch. Her bottomless chocolate eyes gaze lovingly up at me, and then drift shut as I stroke her ears.

"Do you think we could de-commercialize the *Saghani*?" I ask her.

"How?"

"I don't know. Remove the power block? The netting, the freezer . . . all the fishing gear."

She looks at me with pity, and it's irritating. "You really are desperate, huh? Why?"

"I have a job to do."

"Why does it matter where they die, those birds? Because they'll die one way or another, no? And what does it even matter if they do? Makes no difference to us."

The question leaves me breathless. I don't have any response to it, to the apathy.

It occurs to me that Léa is so tense I can almost see the grinding of her teeth through her jaw. She's dealing with her own crisis.

"There'll still be boats for you to work on," I tell her softly. "It's gonna be okay."

"Why'd you fuck Basil?" Léa asks abruptly. "He's such an asshole."

I stare at her. "I didn't fuck Basil."

"Not what he said."

My mouth falls open. But really, why am I even surprised?

"What are you punishing yourself for?" Léa asks.

"What does it matter?"

"It matters to me. I'd say it probably matters to your husband, too."

"My husband left me."

It's her turn to be speechless a moment. "Oh. Sorry. Why?"

I shake my head slowly. "I'm bad for him."

"You're in a dark place," she says impatiently. "I get it. I've been there. But you have to keep your shit together. It's dangerous at sea and I can't be looking out for you all the time."

"I don't need you to. We're not going back to sea, remember?" Not together, in any case.

She drops her eyes.

When I get to my feet she follows suit, so I have to say, "I just need a minute alone, okay? Sorry. I'll be fine after a walk. See you back there."

To get out of the pub I have to go past the gambling area, and there, sitting at a slot machine, is Ennis. I hesitate, then walk over to him.

"Hey."

He presses the button, over and over, like he's a machine himself.

Malachai mentioned Ennis has a gambling problem. I can see it now. "Want to get some fresh air?" I ask.

He grunts something like a no and finishes his rum and Coke in one go.

"How long have you been here, Ennis?"

"Not long enough." He sounds very drunk.

"Have you . . . won anything?"

No response.

"I think you should come back to the hotel with me—"

"Fuck off, Franny," he says flatly. "Just fuck off out of my life."

I oblige.

Outside it's grown colder. I head for the sea, but I've only made it half a block when I register unease and stop. I have no idea what's changed between now and two seconds ago, but suddenly this doesn't feel right and I need to get back to the hotel, I can't get there fast enough. I can see its light in the distance as I pick up my pace.

Instinct, always. The body knows.

A man steps into my path.

"Riley Loach?"

I recognize him. The protester who was wearing the striped beanie and looking inside me. I don't say anything but my heart thunders because how did he get that name?

"You part of the *Saghani*'s crew?"

"No."

"Fuck off."

"Okay." I make to walk past him but his hand lands on my arm. It sets my hairs on end.

"You know what you and your friends are doing to the world?"

"I agree with you," I say quickly. "It's wrong. But the sanctions have put an end to it."

"You think that's enough? To let the lot of you get away with what you've done? It's bullshit!" He's *so* angry. I don't know what to do, how to defuse this.

"Look, I'm not one of them. I'm trying to—"

"I saw you, bitch. So tell me where your captain is. I can't let this go unpunished."

The animal rears within me. "No fuckin' idea."

He is a large man, at least double my size, so when he pushes me back into the wall I feel the presence of his strength. I feel it in those same ancient instincts, given to me by generations of women, the adrenaline I inherited flooding my system, I feel it in the punch kick fight fuck kill of my body and I want to hit him right now, I do, but instead I hold myself very still, sensing it all, knowing I could be a hair's breadth from a great deal of pain or worse, some violation of my body or even death and without warning I snap my teeth at him, so fucking furious I could goddamn burn the world down.

He jerks back, surprised by my strangeness. Then he laughs and presses me by the throat to the wall, blocking my air, slamming my skull. Pain lances down my spine.

"Just tell me where they are."

But I don't, and so he drags me painfully around the corner and into a darker street, and whatever noble quest he's set himself on has been poisoned by hate; I see it the second before he does it, the way in which he'll make me pay for his hatred. His hand gropes my crotch, going for the buttons of my jeans, but by then I've well and truly had enough.

I scream at the top of my lungs and with a silent prayer of thanks to Beth I send a left jab to his guts, and a second and a third, and as he loosens his grip in surprise I slam a right cross to his throat, another to his jaw. Hard, harder than any punches I've thrown, hardened by fear and rage and *how dare you touch me*—a cross to the bridge of his nose, a hook to his ribs, I have to land as many as I can before he gathers himself, and he isn't expecting any of them but in his pain he manages to fling out his own fist and I try to block it but I'm not strong enough and it takes my forearm and head at once. The world spins. I sink to one knee and go for his groin, but he's expecting it now and he blocks me, grabs my right hand and twists it up until I scream in pain. No one is coming I can't believe no one is coming I've made so much damn noise. I'm alone here, and he's about to break my arm and I can feel the breathless throbbing rage of refusal and as it fills my body I reach with my left hand for the pocketknife I keep tucked into my boot and I think, *Fuck this: I refuse*, and so I twist and rise and stab the blade up into his neck.

He gasps in shock. His hands loosen.

Blood is a cascade upon us both.

People arrive, I think. There is movement around us.

"Holy fucking shit—" someone is saying and someone else is demanding the police be called and someone is telling them all to shut the fuck up and arms are holding me upright. The knife drops from my hand. "It's all right," someone says against my ear. But the man is still looking at me, looking and looking, and clutching at his neck, trying to stop the bleeding and sinking to his knees, and I think he's hardly in his body anymore and I think I'm hardly in mine.

"Easy," the voice says, and it's Ennis holding me upright.

He walk-drag-carries me somewhere. Back to the hotel? I am dull with shock.

The others are here now, pulling us faster and it's not the hotel at all but the boat we're rushing toward, and I think it's because there are people following us. We run, an adrenaline-fueled blur, feet slapping on boards and low voices giving urgent commands. I blink and I'm on the boat and the guys are working like madmen to get it moving. I blink and the *Saghani* is smoothly away from the shore and out into the ocean. I blink and I am in a room I don't know, some part of me thinks it must be Ennis's cabin, maybe, I don't care, and from far away he is speaking.

"You're not alone, love," he is saying. "Be easy. You're not alone."

Does he think that's true?

"Is he dead? Did I kill him?"

"I don't know."

I give in. A dam breaks and weariness floods in. It's all I can do not to pass out. I blink and I'm in a bed.

"Are we leaving?" I ask.

"We're already gone," Ennis says. "Sleep."

"Did I mess things up for us?"

"No, love," he says. "You got us free."

But I'll never be free. I wonder if this was how my father felt the day he killed a person.

17

SOUTH COAST OF NSW, AUSTRALIA

NINETEEN YEARS AGO

Edith is out with the lambs tonight, hunkered down with her rifle to watch
for the reflective eyes of hungry foxes. She makes me do this some nights,
despite my protests—I've told her a thousand times I refuse to kill any animal, even to protect our livelihood, and anyway protecting the lambs is what
Finnegan is for, but still she sends me out into the cold on watch duty, the
rifle awkward in my unwilling hands. "When it comes time, you'll do what
you have to," she says in that way of hers, the way that brooks no argument,
and I've yet to spot one of the predators so I don't know if she's right.

In any case, tonight is my chance. I've scoped out the locked box of
treasures she keeps under her bed, and I've taken pains to steal her key
and make a copy of it because I just know she's the type of woman who
would notice if it was gone for too long. Copying a key is actually no easy
task when you're stuck on a farm way out of town and you won't get even
your learner's license until you turn sixteen and that's an entire year away.
I had to pay Skinny Matt to do it for me, and he's the most stoned kid at
our school, so he wasn't exactly reliable. Next it was a matter of waiting
for lambing season, when the first little ones drop messily from their mother's

bodies and then need protecting from all manner of hunter—not only the foxes but eagles, too, and wild dogs sometimes. They're hungrier and hungrier now that their wild prey grows scarcer. These are the only nights I can be certain Edith won't catch me: she'd lie in wait out there until her body wasted away and her bones turned to dust, if she had to. Determined and silent.

It's possible I'm being a bit paranoid about the level of protection Edith has over this box. But anyway. It's interested me ever since I got to this bastard of a farm. My grandmother is a hard kind of woman, see. She doesn't tell me anything about my parents—she doesn't talk much to me at all, really, except to bark orders, and if I don't complete her slave labor to the required degree of perfection she doesn't let me go to surf rescue training, which is just about the only thing I like doing in this country, and since I just got my bronze medallion I'm now responsible for lifesaving patrols and she doesn't seem to get the importance of that—but she has this box and I'm convinced there are secrets hiding in it. Instead of turning her bedroom light on, which she might see from the paddock, I creep through the dark and lie flat on my tummy to root around until I can feel the cold of the box's edge. I drag its heavy weight free—heavier than I'd expected—and dart into my room to open it.

The weight of the box comes from several military medals that belong, I'm surprised to see, to my grandfather, who was apparently in a regiment of Light Horse infantry. I read the inscriptions on them and run my fingers over the metal, trying to put pieces of a puzzle together. Why doesn't she speak of him, or keep any pictures around the house? What's so private about her marriage that she has to keep all remnants of it locked away from curious eyes?

I move on from the medals, lifting free a pile of various papers. Some are business documents—the deed to the farm, mortgage statements, and the like—which I put aside without reading. I don't know what I'm looking for, really, just some sign that I didn't get sent to the wrong farm, the farm of a woman who has no son and therefore can't be my grandmother. She doesn't speak of him, or of my mother. I don't know where he is or what he does for a living—I don't even know his name.

A pile of photos slips free and spills all over the carpet. I gasp at the faces staring up at me, a rush of heat filling my cheeks. It's him, I know it is, because there's Edith as a younger woman holding a baby, or walking on the beach with a little boy, or chopping vegetables at the kitchen bench with a teenager, or sitting around a campfire with a young man. He has long blond hippie hair in a few, in others it's been cut very short. His face is handsome and dark-eyed, his mouth wide as though made only to smile.

And there he is with my very pregnant mother. He has his arm around her and she's laughing at him, and they look *so* happy, and there is the front paddock behind them, the one I walk through every day to catch the school bus. I don't realize I'm crying until my parents are wet. On the back in messy handwriting are their names. *Dom and Iris, Xmas.*

Dom.

I put the precious photo under my pillow and then keep going through the rest of the box. It's right down the bottom, what I'm looking for, I guess. The explanation, or at least a chunk of it.

Dominic Stewart, twenty-five years old at the age of incarceration.

I stop and stare at the word.

There are other words smattered over the legal documents. My frantic eyes catch and transfer them to my echoing mind, my scattered mind. *Long Bay Correctional Complex, Sydney. Life sentence. Standard non-parole period of twenty years. Plea of guilty. Intent to kill. Convicted of murder.*

Crack!

I lurch upright. The papers fall from my hands and I scramble to refill the box. That was a gunshot. It doesn't mean she'll be back any time soon but I am done with this, with the contents of this box that I should never have opened. I want nothing to do with it, I've wasted so much time on it—

"Franny!" Edith shouts and then she has opened my bedroom door and is staring down at the mess I've made. We are both silent a few beats, and her eyes are the coldest I've ever seen them, the most frightening and the most frightened, I think, and then she says, "I've shot Finnegan."

It takes too long for me to process that. "What?"

"Damn beast was chasing away the fox and I didn't see him in the dark."

"What? No."

I peel past her and run outside into the dark. The lambs and their mothers are in the closest paddock, the one between us and the sea. I sprint to the fence post and then stop, breathing heavily. I can't see much except a dark shape in the distance.

"Thought you might like to be with him when I put him out," Edith says.

"He's still alive?"

"Not for long. Bullet went straight through his neck."

"Can't we call the vet? Or we could take him there now! Let's get him in the truck, quickly!"

"There's nothing to be done, Franny. Come with me or not, up to you."

"He's mine, though!" I plead. I'm the one who leads him round and feeds him apples and clips his hoofs and scratches inside his ears even though it makes my hands all black. I'm the one who loves him.

"That's why I've called for you," she says, and she is so calm and so cold and she doesn't care about what she's done, she doesn't give a shit that she's just murdered our beautiful old donkey who does nothing but bravely try to protect the little ones in the night.

"You're a bitch," I say clearly, and it shocks us both, for I've never uttered a bad word to anyone in my life, let alone my terrifying grandmother. "You're a fucking bitch," I go on, fueled by rage and grief and impotence. "You did this on purpose. Just like you never told me about Dominic."

Edith goes through the metal gate, leaving it open for me. She has the rifle in her hand. "Do you want to be with him or not?" she asks as she walks across the grass and down toward the still-breathing body.

But I can't, I can't go near him, I'm too frightened of what he will be when he's gone, what he will look like, what will be left.

"Shut the gate, then," Edith says.

And I do, and she shoots Finnegan in the head, and it's so loud, so horrible, that I turn and go to the truck, taking the key from the dash and turning on the engine. I am getting the hell out of here. I've driven this truck for the last few years; Edith made me learn, and it doesn't matter that I don't have a license or any money or belongings, it doesn't matter that the photo is still beneath my pillow: I hope it stays there forever, fading and curling and turning to dust before anyone ever sees it again.

A strong hand snakes through the window and snatches the key from the ignition, killing the engine. "Hey!" I snarl. But Edith is already walking back to the house.

I run after her and try to get the key from her hand, panicked and urgent and doesn't she understand that I have to get out of here, I don't belong here, I'm suffocating here.

"You want to leave, that's just fine," she says, "but you don't get to take my truck."

I let out a gasp of frustration, tears flooding my throat. "Please."

"Things don't always take the shape you want them to, kid, and we gotta learn to endure that with a bit of grace."

It humiliates me. I hate her.

She goes inside and I sit on the front porch, sobbing. For my Finnegan, my only friend, and for wishing my mother was here. Edith doesn't care about me. I think the day I got sent here ruined her life. At least I know now why she hates me so much: I'm a reminder of her rotten son.

Hours have passed by the time I head back in. I've waited until I'm sure she's asleep, unable to face her again tonight. But as I'm moving toward my room I hear a soft sound coming from the back door, and I can't help it, I am compelled to creep to the window and see her there, sitting on the back step in an orb of lamplight, alone and holding the tag from Finnegan's ear, weeping softly.

I sag against the wall, resting my head.

"Sorry, Grandma," I whisper, but she can't hear me through the glass.

Breakfast is a silent affair, but that isn't unusual. Edith didn't reclaim her box of secrets last night, so I locked it and placed it back under her bed, regret heavy upon me. I didn't touch the photo under my pillow—I couldn't bring myself to give it back to her even though I can't imagine ever wanting to look at it again. I'm tired now with a night of tossing and turning behind me. It takes me the entire bowl of porridge to drum up the courage to ask. "Did he really kill someone?"

Edith nods, not looking up from the newspaper.

"Who?"

"Ray Young."

"Who's Ray Young?"

"Just a boy who grew up nearby."

"Do you know why he did it?"

"He never said."

I stare at her, stunned by the cavalier way she shrugs.

"How did he and my mother meet?"

"No idea. In Ireland, somewhere."

"You never asked him?"

"None of my business."

"Did they seem . . . in love? When he brought her back here?"

Edith looks up from the paper, gazing at me over her reading glasses. "What does that have to do with anything?"

I don't know.

"It had nothing to do with him killing that man, that's for damn certain. Or with him getting sentenced the very same day you came screaming out of Iris on that couch over there. I pulled you out and stopped her bleeding. She was crying with loneliness and whatever love there was between them, it didn't stop her taking you away."

She folds up her paper and takes her bowl to the sink.

"I'll need your help digging a hole for Finnegan," Edith says, and I nod. "Yes, Grandma."

As she pulls on her boots I ask, "How did he do it?"

"Strangled him to death," my grandmother replies.

18

DUBLIN, IRELAND

TWELVE YEARS AGO

The raindrops are fat and cold on my face. I don't have a raincoat or umbrella, so I make my peace with getting wet. Dublin is a dreary place when the sky is gray and yet there's something moody about it, mysterious, something you could get caught up and lost in. I am headed for the library, which is down near the quay.

Most mornings I wake to a kiss as he leaves for work. This morning it was so early there was barely any dawn light peeking through the shutters and in the dark his lips could have been a dream. I didn't have a shift today so I was determined to try to make Niall's apartment feel more like home, with some color, plants, art, anything. But within those walls I felt my feet begin to tap and my fingers begin to fidget and as I ignored those things there came a tightening around my throat.

I remembered then that I have wanted to visit the Dublin Library for some time and so I hopped on a train from Galway and here I am, hurrying to beat the downpour and breathing with ease. I duck inside the large building, over the mosaic floor and beneath the high ceiling, into the dome-like reading room I remember enjoying when I first returned to Ireland. I'm not sure what I'm looking for, maybe something on genealogy, but first I stand a moment and enjoy the space. Then I immerse myself in the pages.

Sometime later I feel a vibration in my bag.

I miss the call, and as I catch sight of my phone screen my heart lurches and I am flooded with the realization of having done the wrong thing, though I'm not quick enough to quite identify what that is. Eight missed calls from Niall. Three text messages asking me where I am. Dark has fallen outside; the entire day has passed while I lost myself in reading. Shit.

I call him immediately.

He answers with, "Are you all right?"

I try to keep my voice light. "I'm fine, sorry I missed your calls, I'm in Dublin."

There is a long pause. "Why?"

"I wanted to come to the library."

"Just . . . randomly?"

"I guess so."

"And you didn't think to mention it."

"I . . ." The horrible truth is that it didn't even occur to me. I haven't done this before, not since we married, haven't let my feet lead me where they will. I don't say that this is nothing, that I'm only a couple of hours away, that I could have gone much farther and that I can go where I want because some instinct tells me that would be callous.

"I came home to see you at lunch and you weren't here, and I've come home now to bring you dinner and you still weren't here. I thought maybe you'd . . . I just didn't know where you were."

Abruptly I'm having trouble breathing again. "I'm sorry. I should have said. I didn't think."

Another pause. There is hurt within it. "Do you plan on coming home any time soon?"

"Aye. I hadn't thought that far ahead, but maybe a night or two?"

"Right. Grand. See you then." He hangs up.

I stare at my phone. Then I walk back out into the rain, which is really falling now, and I walk all the way to the train station and I buy a ticket for the next train back to Galway.

. . .

The biology faculty is abuzz with life, which is strange for a Tuesday night. Or any night. All the lights are on and there must be at least thirty people in the department kitchen. I edge my way inside, keeping my back to the wall and looking for Niall. He wasn't at home, which meant he'd be at work, only I didn't realize I'd be arriving in the middle of a staff party. I have come straight from the train, my shoes squelchy, hair damp.

I spot him in the center of a group of men and women, and edge closer, wanting to know what he's saying that has them so enthralled. There is a dark cloud over him that I can see from here.

"Humanity is a fucking plague upon the world," Niall says.

That's when he looks up and spots me. Our eyes meet across the space. I see relief in him, which creates the same in me, and then I see something cooler.

He moves to kiss my cheek. "You're here."

I nod, all the words I rehearsed on the train having evaporated.

"There's a riot going on because some piece-of-shit poachers snuck into a sanctuary and carved off the tusks of the last elephants," he says heavily.

My heart hurts. I can't bear to hear it. Because we keep hearing it. And nothing changes. I could weep but for Niall the pain is much colder. I think he is really starting to lose hope.

Before I can think what to say, he shakes his head. Exhales long and slow, then pours me a mug of wine from a nearby table. "Come on," he murmurs, leading me over to his colleagues. "Friends, meet my wife, Franny."

There are two male professors whose names I forget immediately, a lab assistant called Hannah, and the blond lecturer who shoved a dirty plate at me—Professor Shannon Byrne. I meet her shocked eyes—she thinks she must have misheard. "Wife?"

"Wife," Niall confirms.

"Nice to meet you," I say.

"Lovely," Shannon manages, shaking my hand briefly. "When did this happen, Niall?"

"Six weeks ago."

"You're kidding. Why weren't we invited?"

"No one was invited."

"You certainly kept that quiet! How long have you been together?" she presses.

Niall smiles a sharp kind of smile. "Six weeks."

There is an awkward silence among the group.

"Madness," I say. The tension breaks and they all make noises of amusement or understanding.

"All of love," one of the men says, "madness."

"My wife calls it a fever dream," says the other. I decide to like them both.

I look at Niall and nod. "That sounds right," and I think I can hardly recognize this person I am married to.

"I never imagined Niall could be interested in anything other than his job," Shannon says.

"Neither did I," Niall says.

"It's fearless, isn't it," Hannah says, cheeks flushed pink.

I meet her shy gaze in gratitude. "It's something."

"Shannon's head of biology," Niall tells me. "You should sit down with her. Shannon, I'm telling you—Franny has a staggering passion for ornithology, and she's very smart."

Shannon's eyes flick down to my muddy jeans. She's wearing a navy woolen dress and heels. Her blond hair is elegantly tousled. My black mane is in a sweaty, messy braid that makes me look twelve years old. I don't have the inclination to care, but I dart a look at Niall's face to see if he's noticing the discrepancy. He's not.

Without warning he says, "A flock of crows fell in love with her as a child."

Heat floods me.

"What do you mean?" Shannon demands.

When it's clear I'm not about to reply, Niall explains. "She fed them every day and they started following her, bringing her gifts. It went on for years. They adored her."

"Not every day," Shannon says. "Not during winter."

I look up at her. Nod.

"Not true," she says simply. "Crows migrate."

"Birds go where the food is," Niall says. "Birds of the Corvidae family have the ability to recognize individual human faces. Franny became their food source so they had no need to migrate."

Shannon shakes her head as though the very idea offends her.

Don't, I wish, sending it out as loudly and silently as I can. *Don't take the magic from it*. I feel dirty, like something precious has been sullied, like I want to get the fuck out of here, or throw my mug of wine in her face, and maybe Niall's, too.

"It's why I wanted you to meet with her," Niall goes on.

"Do you have an undergrad?" Shannon asks me.

"No."

"You haven't studied at all? How old are you?"

"Twenty-two."

Her eyebrows arch. "What's that—a ten-year age gap?"

Niall and I glance at each other. Nod.

Shannon shrugs. "Well, you're young, you have plenty of time. Give me a call and we'll sit down and talk about what you'll need to apply."

Instead of explaining that I have no interest in doing that I just say thanks. They are all too happy to move the conversation back to things they're comfortable with—currently the paper Shannon is about to publish on interspecies breeding programs—so I use the moment to edge out of the circle, place my untouched wine back on the table, and head for the door. It swings shut behind me and the sound from within is muted almost to silence. I take a breath of relief. The lift button turns yellow for down.

The door behind me opens and the sound of voices floods out once more. I don't turn, but a hand takes mine and pulls me sideways into another room, a dark one, an office space, I think.

"Too pompous for you?" my husband asks. I can't see him very well in the dark. I think he might be a wee bit drunk. "What are you doing here?"

"I came to find you."

He spreads his hands: here I am.

"Was that payback?" I ask.

"What?"

"The crows. Giving away something precious."

He is silent, and then he sighs. "No. Not consciously."

"I don't know how to do this," I say, and my voice breaks.

"Nor do I."

I move through the dark, wanting to distance myself from him. There are tall windows along one wall, and I peer through them to the grounds below. The park looks ghoulish in the darkness, its trees casting strange moving shadows. A car drives slowly past, flashing its headlights into my face and then disappearing. Something uncomfortable lives in the moment, waiting. I'm crawling out of my skin because I have never had to be responsible to another person, never had to tell anyone where I'm going. It is a kind of binding. "I warned you," I say, and then hate myself for it.

"You did," he says, moving closer. "And I still wasn't . . . expecting it. Just tell me, darlin', that's all. Just let me know you're off somewhere, and that you plan on coming back."

I turn around. "You didn't think I'd gone for good?"

"It crossed my mind, aye," he admits. "You gave me a fright, Franny."

The unease seeps out of me. "I'm sorry," I say. "I'd never leave you for good." With the words I realize it's true, and a different kind of binding takes hold, a deeper, more ruinous one.

Niall moves close and holds me, his mouth to the crook of my neck. "I hate myself for the crows, for giving them away. I knew I was doing it. I think sometimes I'm conditioned for destruction."

We don't move, but outside the world is still shifting and breathing and living. The moon lopes her path over our heads. I live in his words, and in the vastness of his contradictions.

"But you're holding me so tenderly," I say.

"Does it feel like a cage?"

My eyes prickle. "No," I say, and I feel that deep and terrible binding for what it is, I know its face and its name, and it's not a binding at all, but love, and maybe that's the same kind of thing after all.

"Will you go somewhere with me?" I ask him.

"Where?"

"Anywhere."

Niall's arms tighten. He says, "Aye. Anywhere."

The *Saghani*, NORTH ATLANTIC OCEAN
MIGRATION SEASON

I wake from my delirious sleep feeling blurry. It takes good long minutes for me to work out where I am (Ennis's cabin, his bed) and what happened last night (I stabbed a man). I don't remember it well.

Niall, why haven't you come to find me?

The crew's in the galley, perched on various benches and leaning against walls, watching Basil stir a huge pot of oats on the stove and talking in hushed tones. All but Ennis. He's never here, always apart.

There is fear in them as they spot me. I can sense it, just the flicker of it. An animal thing. A wariness of the unhinged woman they now share a small space with.

"How are you feeling?" Anik asks me.

"Fine." I can't access what I feel about last night. It's already gone to live elsewhere. "So we're on the boat. And it's moving."

Nobody replies to that. Their gazes say it all.

"Well, shit," I mutter.

Basil hands me a bowl of porridge with a sprinkle of cinnamon and lemon rind on top. He doesn't meet my eyes. I go out to the mess and sink into the leather booth. They follow me with their own bowls, sitting around me as though everything is normal. I miss Samuel's big smiling presence.

Nobody speaks until Ennis strides in, folds his arms, and says, "Right, here it is. We've illegally left port. I've had a radio call from the maritime police telling us to immediately turn around and they'll look leniently on us because the announcement's only just gone out and we could argue we hadn't clearly understood the new laws."

I put my spoon down.

"There'll be another giant reason the cops want to chat with us now," Dae points out, and all eyes turn to me.

"Yeah, and maybe we should help them out with that," Basil says. When nobody replies he speaks more loudly. "A woman we hardly know murdered a man last night. And instead of staying to report what happened, we just ran."

"He was one of those protesters—" Mal starts.

"So? So fucking what? This isn't The goddamn *Godfather*. We don't *kill* people. She killed a man in cold blood."

"Cold blood?" I say.

"She might not have killed him," Léa says. "We don't know."

"How did you even do it?" Dae asks me, confused.

"She had a blade," Anik says.

"Why would she carry that?" Basil demands, still not looking at me.

"Maybe because women get attacked," Léa snaps.

"Oh, here we go—"

"I've carried the pocketknife since the day I was stabbed in prison," I say. The crew falls silent.

"I spent four years in a cell in Limerick. It was violent. I learned to fight. I learned to fear other people. When I got out I started carrying the knife."

The air is thick with shock.

Ennis is searching me. I can't read his expression and I don't think he can read mine. The others are trying to process.

"Oh, my days," Mal says faintly.

"What the fuck." Basil is staring at me now and there's something hard in his gaze. "So we have a violent criminal on board who stabbed some poor guy to death. Why's that okay?"

"Poor guy?" I say.

"What—did he touch you a bit so you had to murder him?"

"You chauvinist piece of shit," Léa snarls but I barely hear her.

"You know what?" Basil asks. "I'm so sick of feminism being the excuse every time a woman behaves badly. A chick is violent and she blames it on men. It's pathetic."

I should be angry. There is a resounding surge of it from those who surround me. But instead I feel only contempt for Basil, and a kind of pity that he has let himself be formed into such a small man. He sees it on my face, I think, because he flushes with humiliation and his rage is kindled even further.

It's Ennis who rounds on him. "He attacked her," the captain says and I am startled by his fervor. "He attacked her because of us and she didn't say anything about where we were, so he fucking assaulted her and you don't think she should have defended herself?"

Basil makes an angry helpless sound. "What did you go to prison for?"

"I killed two people."

"Jesus," he snaps. "This is *fucked*."

"Calm down, Bas," Dae says.

"No! We need to radio the police! If we turn back right now—"

"Go cool off," Ennis orders.

Basil starts to protest until—

"*Go!*"

The cook storms off, swearing angrily under his breath. Ennis turns back to us. His eyes find mine, gray as dawn.

"I apologize," he says.

I don't know what to say.

Mal asks softly, "Is that why you didn't want to go ashore?"

I nod. "I broke my parole to come here. Wasn't supposed to leave Ireland for another five years. My passport's false. And—" Here I go, why not all of the truth and be damned? "I'm not an ornithologist. Or any kind of scientist."

They stare at me.

"I beg your pardon?" Mal says.

"I never studied. I don't have a degree. I just read lots."

There is another long silence as they try to work out what to do with that.

"Fucking hell, Franny," Léa says eventually.

"Let's *not* tell Basil that bit," Mal suggests.

"How'd you get the tracking stuff?" Dae asks.

"It's my husband's."

"But why are you doing all of this if you're not involved in it?" Anik asks.

"I am involved. We all are."

Then, "It doesn't matter," Ennis says, and he's calm, and something about it makes the thought enter my mind that he must have known, but that's silly. "There are two birds still tracked. I can intercept them. Follow them to fish."

I breathe out, feeling my eyes prickle. I have an urge to hug him.

"They're way out west," Léa argues. "And headed south fast. You don't know those waters, Skip."

"I can find them," Ennis repeats, and he sounds sure enough to believe.

"What does it matter if we're just gonna get arrested the second we land with a freezer full of fish?" Dae asks.

"I know a guy," Anik says. "Could move the catch under the radar, if we needed him to. If we can find a catch."

"Oh, Lord," Malachai breathes, then can't help laughing in disbelief. It is ludicrous enough to make anyone laugh, this criminal world in which we've found ourselves. Léa's head is shaking continuously, while Dae keeps rubbing his eyes as though to wake himself from a dream.

"So let's take a vote," our captain says. "Anyone for turning back and handing over the boat?" *And handing over Franny*, is what he doesn't need to add.

I hold my breath.

Nobody raises a hand.

"All those for carrying on, come what may?"

Silence.

Then Anik's lone hand, lifting into the air. "We're in it now," he murmurs. "So let's finish it."

One by one the other hands follow suit. I dash tears from my cheeks, hands shaking with exhilaration.

Last night it was over, all of this. Today we are deeper within the wilderness than we've ever been.

"So we head south," Ennis says, "and hope our fuel lasts, 'cause they've put out an alert about the *Saghani* so we won't be able to dock until it's done."

"And we hope our engines hold," Léa says.

"And we pray for fish," Dae says.

"And birds," Anik says.

I nod.

And birds.

I take my bedroll onto the deck to sleep. I won't stay in that cabin, despite Léa's protests. As a concession I tie my wrist to the railing, which prevents me from going overboard in bad weather or during sleepwalking. It's cold and lovely out here. A clear sky full of stars.

Later Ennis comes down from the helm and sits on the wooden boards beside my sleeping bag. He doesn't say anything, as is his wont.

So I speak.

"Why did they vote to keep going?" I ask, because I've been asking myself the question all evening. The others aren't bound as Ennis and I are.

"You're one of us," Ennis says. "We don't hand our people over."

It hurts to hear that, hurts in that way that feels frightening and good at the same time. I rest my head on my knees and look up at the moon. She's nearly full tonight, and more golden than white.

"I didn't mean to kill him," I murmur. Then, "That's not true. I did. I meant to kill him very much. And I think that's why I shouldn't have stabbed him."

Ennis doesn't move or speak for a long time. Night turns above.

It's been an age when he says, "Maybe not. But I'm glad you did."

GALWAY, IRELAND

TWELVE YEARS AGO

"The world was a different place, once," Niall says into the microphone. "Once there were creatures in the sea so miraculous they seemed straight out of fantasy. There were things that loped across plains or slithered through tall grass, things that leaped from the boughs of trees, which were plentiful, too. Once there were glorious winged beasts that roamed the sky-world, and now they are going." He stops and looks for my face in the lecture hall. "They aren't going," he corrects himself. "They are being violently and indiscriminately slaughtered by our indifference. It has been decided by our leaders that economic growth is more important. That the extinction crisis is an acceptable trade for their greed."

He said it's hard, sometimes, to finish. The bile rises in his throat and he could break the lectern beneath his hands, overcome with a profound sense of loathing for what we are, all of us, and the poison of our species. He called himself a hypocrite for always talking, never doing, and he said he hates himself as much as anyone, he's as much a perpetrator, a consumer living in wealth and privilege and wanting more and more and more. He said he's fascinated by the simplicity with which I live, and envious, and I thought it curious because I've never thought of it that way. When he asked me what I really want, deep down, all I could think of was to walk and swim, so I guess he's right.

I can see him struggling to continue with the lecture today. It's been months since I've attended one of his classes, and I'm concerned to see the level of despair that leaks into his voice, the anger patent in his deliberateness, his pointed accusations and need to make us understand. I can hear in his voice the rage he experiences at his own futility, and I wish I could ease it for him somehow, smooth it away with the touch of my fingers or the whisper of my lips, but it's bigger than I am, it's an anger to swallow the world.

After the class I wait for him in his lab. I make myself look at the gull carcass, stretched and pinned still, though I don't know why. Maybe because it returns me to the moment we first touched, the intimacy and the fear of it.

"The world'd be a better place if it was humans we could stuff and pin up and study," Niall says as he enters.

I can't help smiling a little. "No, it wouldn't."

"Can I show you something?"

I follow him to a projector screen. He turns down the lights but without showing me anything he looks at my face, at my eyes, and murmurs, "You look so tired, darlin'."

Less sleepwalking lately, more nightmares. It's usually one or the other. I'm a little frightened of sleep, a little frightened of my body and what it will do. But it's not what's worrying me now.

"You look so hopeless," I tell him. "Are you okay?"

He kisses my eyelids tenderly. I breathe out and lean into him, knowing he's not okay at all.

The video runs, thrown large onto the screen. There is no sound. Only a sudden expanse of white that blinds us both. When we look again, there are hundreds of snowy breasts and crimson beaks and the movement of elegant, sharp wings.

I move closer to the screen, hypnotized.

"Arctic terns," Niall says. And then he tells me of their longest of all journeys, he speaks of the survival of them, the *defiance* of them, and finishes with, "I want to follow them."

"On their migration?"

"Aye. It's never been done before. We'd learn so much—and not just about the birds themselves but about climate change, too."

I smile, excitement throbbing to life within. "Let's."

"You'd come with me?"

"How soon can we go?"

He laughs. "I don't know. I have work . . ."

"This is your work."

"I'd have to get funding. It'll take a lot of effort."

I swallow my disappointment and turn back to the screen.

"We'll go, Franny. One day. I promise."

But he's said this before and we never go anywhere.

"Tell me where they fly," I murmur, and he does, he takes me over oceans and onto foreign continents, he takes me to the other end of the earth, farther than anyone has yet followed. In his voice I hear tears. I turn to him.

"I went to your house this morning," he says.

"What house?"

"The wooden one by the sea."

"Where Mam and I lived."

He nods. "No one has lived there in a long time. I went inside. It was so cold, darlin'. The wind cuts straight through it and all I could see was your little body huddled into the bed with your mam trying to stay warm."

I hold him, I wrap myself about him. If I make of myself a thick enough shell then I will keep him safe; if I fuse myself to his skin, if I am *needed*, then surely we can't be parted.

Cutlery scrapes against plates and echoes off the high ceiling. It's practically a cathedral in here.

We are staying the weekend at Niall's parents' place, so I can meet them. Niall wanted to do a half-hour coffee; it was me who suggested the whole weekend when I heard his dad's longing on the phone. Arthur Lynch is a quiet, cheerful fellow who misses his son a lot. Penny Lynch is a different story. I should have opted for the coffee.

"What do you do for work, Franny?" she asks me, even though Niall's already told her. I'm just grateful someone is speaking.

"I'm a cleaner at NUI."

"And what drew you to that vocation?" Penny asks. She's wearing a cashmere sweater and ruby earrings. The fireplace in the corner is the size of Dublin, and the wine we're drinking has been in the cellar as long as Niall's been alive.

"It's not a vocation," I say with a smile. I don't know if she meant it as a joke but it's pretty funny to me. "It's just a job I could get with no skills or qualifications. It's easy enough to come and go, and you can do it anywhere in the world." I pause with the fork halfway to my mouth. "Actually to be honest, I don't mind it. It's meditative."

"Happy days," Arthur says. His cheeks are very red from the wine and he seems chuffed to have us here. His accent is more Belfast than Galway.

"And what do your parents do?"

Niall exhales loudly as though he's about to lose his shit. He must have briefed them before we arrived, and his mother isn't following the script.

"I don't know," I tell her. "I haven't seen either of them in a long time."

"Then they're unaware of your marriage to Niall?"

"They are."

"What a shame. You've done so well for yourself, I'm sure they would be proud."

I meet her hazel eyes, the same exact color as her son's. I'm not playing whatever game this is. "I'm sure they would be," I agree. "Your son's very special."

"How's the new gardener going, Dad?" Niall asks loudly.

"Very well indeed—"

"How did you two meet?" Penny asks me.

I put my wineglass down. "I sat in on his class."

"Only person in the history of my teaching career to leave in the middle of a lecture," Niall says.

"I bruised his ego."

"What a meet cute," Arthur says.

Penny's gaze is precise; everything about her is careful and poised. She says, very deliberately, "I suppose working on the university campus might allow one access to a successful young professor's schedule."

"Jesus, Mother——" Niall starts to say but I squeeze his knee under the table.

"Sadly the faculty isn't so transparent with their lecturers," I tell her. "No matter how hard I looked, I couldn't find any information about the professors' net worths or their marriage statuses. Made it really hard to know which classes to sit in on."

It takes a moment, and then Niall dissolves into laughter. Even Arthur has a chortle, while Penny keeps her eyes trained on me and offers a magnanimous smile.

"I just like birds, Penny," I tell her. "I promise."

"Of course," she murmurs, signaling for one of her staff to take our plates.

"I don't think I've ever been so happy," Niall says, still grinning with glee. I roll my eyes and hide a smile of my own. I don't want to condone making fun of his mother—he's lucky to have one who still wants to be around him, and now that the moment's passed I regret the jab.

"She was just being protective," I say.

"She was being an enormous bitch, and what's worse—she didn't even have the wit to be subtle about it."

We're in the guest wing because Niall didn't want me sleeping in his childhood bedroom. That bedroom was a haven for him but it was also his prison; Penny used to punish him for the smallest things by locking him in there to think about his behavior, and as this occurred daily it offers him a cold childhood to remember. Venturing into that bedroom is stepping back into his inadequacies, his loneliness, the feeling of being responsible for his mother's happiness and also an utter failure at it.

"Here you are, darlin'." He's run me a bath, so I cross to the en suite, undressing as I go and letting clothes fall where they may, as you do when you're on holiday. I sink into the hot water and Niall sits on the edge of the tub, peering around at his parents' ornate bathroom tiles and gilding as though the sight of it all bewilders him.

"I'm glad I married a girl who can hold her own," he says.

"Did you marry me to annoy your mother?"

"No."

"Not even partially? Because I wouldn't mind if it were partially."

"No, darlin'. I stopped trying to get reactions out of my mother a long time ago."

"You're still so angry with her."

I'm surprised at how quickly his response comes. "Because she's not good at love," he says.

I wake from a dream of trapped moths, throwing themselves repeatedly into a pane of glass as they try to reach the light of the moon. Niall's gone from the bed so he doesn't see what I see: that my feet are covered in dirt, and have smeared it all over the sheets. I pause. Oh no. I must have gone roaming in my sleep.

At breakfast something is wrong. Penny is striding around the house giving terse instructions to her staff, while Arthur buries his face in a newspaper, hoping for invisibility. Niall pours me a cup of coffee and steers me to a window seat overlooking the gardens.

"What's wrong?" I ask.

"Penny's greenhouse cages got left open last night. Her birds escaped."

"Oh shit . . ." I try to make out her cutting words in the next room, and hear something about reimbursement and pays being docked. I gulp my coffee and tell Niall I'll be back in a moment.

Sunlight turns the surface of the pond molten. Long grass brushes my calves as I walk to the greenhouse. It's quiet and cool inside; I can already see the huge cages at the end are no longer alive with color and movement and sound, but empty like a skeleton. I inspect the lock on the door and my heart sinks—there is no key or combination, simply a deadbolt that can be easily opened from the outside. I wonder if they hesitated before their escape, wary of what lay beyond the cage, or if they surged free, a vibrant bursting of joy.

"I had over twenty species," says a voice and I turn to see Penny. She looks out of place in this earthy cave.

"Niall showed them to me once. They were wonderful." And trapped. Even if I hadn't seen the dirt on my feet, or the type of lock, I would know what happened. There was an ache in my chest from the first moment I saw them in here, hidden from true sky. More than anything I wanted to set them free. But only my other half, the savage half, would actually do such a thing.

"Penny, I . . ." I clear my throat. "I'm so sorry, I think it might have been me."

"I beg your pardon?" She walks into a shaft of sunlight and I'm startled to see a sheen of moisture brighten her eyes.

"I was outside last night, sleepwalking. It seems . . . I mean it must have been me." I take a step toward her, resisting the urge to reach out. She's very still. "I'm so sorry."

"Nonsense," Penny says faintly. "You can't be blamed for something you had no control over."

There is a long silence and I will myself to think of some way to fix this. I see now how much she loved the birds, and it's so painful to realize how I've hurt her.

"How can I make it up to you?"

She shakes her head slowly. Instead of pride and steel she is abruptly small, and old, and scared. "It was a contradiction. I felt sad every time I looked at them."

My own eyes feel hot.

Penny gathers her poise and drapes it upon herself once more. "Franny, please forgive my rudeness last night. I deal with many patients who suffer a quality that can damage their lives and those of the people around them. I thought I might have recognized that quality in you, but it was unfair of me to make that judgment, and inappropriate to diagnose someone I'm not treating. It's a failing of mine."

"Oh . . ." I'm not sure what to say to this. "What's the quality?"

"I thought you might be fickle."

In the crisp silence I recognize her apology for what it is: a politely veiled barb.

"Have something to eat," she tells me coldly. "You've had a busy night. And you might want to consider letting me prescribe you something for the sleepwalking." She leaves me alone in the greenhouse, and she's right: I'm impulsive and changeable and restless, but those are kind words for a more brutal truth.

The *Saghani*, MID-ATLANTIC OCEAN
MIGRATION SEASON

It has taken us a month to reach the equator. No birds, no fish, and no other boats for quite some time. We are utterly alone out here, but crossing the equator, according to the crew, graduates me from landlubber to shellback. "You're a real sailor now, Franny," they say.

Ennis has been hugging the American coasts—he says we'd never catch up to the birds by turning east. Crossing the Atlantic would take too long, when instead we can set a more gradual course to intercept the birds somewhere much farther south.

Brazil is now to our right, so close we can see her. To our left is Africa. My feet itch to touch land in those places, to explore them, but there isn't time.

Basil doesn't look at or speak to me, which suits me fine. He spends most of his time snarling about his status as little more than a prisoner on this ship, since he wasn't given the opportunity to vote for turning back. He's still cooking obsessively but there's only so much he can do now that our food stores have run down to mostly tins. I'll be happy never to eat another variation of beans. Most of my time is spent with Léa, Dae, and Mal, learning the ropes. Even now, after so long at sea, I still seem to know next to nothing, and Mal makes an effort to teach me incorrect terms so that when I use them everyone giggles.

Out here it's easy enough to pretend we aren't fugitives. I can pretend I'm not wanted for murder—again.

This afternoon I am belowdecks in the belly of the boat, relegated to the engine room with Léa. It's my least favorite task, it being hot and stuffy down here. Léa's got me checking the gauges for things like hydraulic fluid, air pressure, and oxygen, which has to be done regularly. She's working on something greasy, as usual getting it smeared all over hands and face, but stops abruptly with a string of curses.

"It's stuffed."

"What is?" I ask.

"Our backup generator."

"Can you fix it?"

"Nuh."

"So what does that mean?"

"Means we're fucked, Franny," she snaps, wiping sweaty hair off her face. "Without a backup, if the mains go down at any point all the power stops running and there's nothing we can do about it."

"What do we use power for?"

She snorts. "Everything, dumbass. Temp regulation, navigation, the power block, all our hot water, everything in the kitchen, and not to mention goddamn *drinking* water."

"Right. Shit. Is it likely the mains will go down?"

"Yeah, it's likely, happens all the time."

"Only we never notice it because the generator kicks in?"

"You got it, Sherlock."

She stomps up the ladder—I was warned never to call them stairs—and I hurry to follow her. "Where're you going?"

"To tell Skip."

We find Ennis on the bridge and I listen as Léa explains the problem with a lot more patience than she did with me. Ennis doesn't react except to let out a long breath, and I think his shoulders look less square. He turns back to the helm, gazing out at the empty sea before us.

"Thanks, Léa."

"I think we have to go ashore."

There is a long silence before he says, "Not for a while yet."

"Captain, we can't carry on without a backup. The risk is huge, it's madness. Second something happens—"

"I understand, Léa."

She swallows and straightens up, and I can see her gathering courage. "And do you also understand that you're putting us in danger?"

"Yes," he says simply.

She glances at me. Her gaze softens a little. "Okay, but we can't keep on like this forever, Skip. We need a real plan to keep Franny out of trouble. Sooner or later we have to refuel and resupply—it's not fucking *Love in the Time of Cholera*. Let's just pray the old girl's still above water by the time these imaginary fish come along."

Once Léa has stomped out, Ennis and I share a quiet look.

"I'll find another boat," I offer.

Ennis ignores me. "Still on the same course?" He can see the on-screen chart as well as I can, but he makes me go over it again. We've been marking the terns' route clearly so we can see the patterns of movement, which are appearing more unpredictable by the day. They're currently flying away from the coast of Angola toward us.

"Still south-southwest," I say. "We'll intercept them if they hold their course, but Ennis, they might not. Depends on the wind and the food."

Ennis nods once. He doesn't care. Like Anik said, we're in it now.

"They'll hold firm, and so will we," he says.

Léa always switches her bed light out first, while I read for longer. But tonight she doesn't nod off instantly, as she normally does. She rolls over to face the wall and asks, muffled, "How'd you lose your toes?"

"Frostbite."

"How'd you get frostbite?"

"I just . . . went walking around in the snow without shoes on."

"That was pretty fuckin' dumb, wasn't it?"

"Yep."

"What do you imagine is gonna happen when we find these birds?"

"What do you mean?"

"We get a good haul, all right, and that's sweet for us, but what happens to you? Do you plan on ever going home again? Or will you be on the run for the rest of your life?"

"You don't have to worry about that."

"I'm worrying about it. You get picked up, you go back to jail, right? For breaking your parole? And when they identify you for what happened in St. John's . . ."

I close my book.

"They'll work out whose passport you've been using," she warns me as if I'm unaware.

"How?"

"I don't know! How do police do anything?" She sits up angrily, swinging her legs to the floor. "What aren't you telling me? 'Cause you sure as shit don't seem like a woman on the run."

"I'm not on the run."

"You should be! You should be *scared*, Franny! I don't want you going back to jail."

I hear the tears in her voice and realize with horror that she's started crying. "Jesus, don't do that," I try. "It's not worth *that*."

"Oh, fuck you," she snaps, covering her face.

Reluctantly I climb out of bed and move to sit beside her. "Léa, come on."

"You don't care, do you?"

"Not really." Hard to care when the plan is to die long before anyone catches me.

Léa looks at me, and there's something about the pain in her eyes, there's a seduction in it, and before I can look away she is kissing me.

"Léa, hey, we can't."

"Why not?" she asks against my lips.

"I'm married."

"Didn't stop you with Basil."

"That was destruction, it didn't mean anything. This would."

She sighs a little; she has turned languid and knowing. "So let it."

We kiss again and I want to, I want to sink into it and let it overwhelm everything, let the intimacy salve my wounds, and I think it would, it might, but what a betrayal that would be, not only to Niall but to my own sense of certainty, to this migration I've begun. The only person I'm intent on destroying is myself, with no more collateral damage along the way.

So I end the kiss as gently as I can, and I go back to my bed and turn out the light. She watches me, wordless and wanting and unsure in the dark. Then she, too, sets herself to sleeping.

We are a plague on the world, my husband often says.

Today there is a huge landmass to our left, and it surprises me because there is no land on the chart I've been studying. As we draw close enough to see, I realize that it's an enormous island of plastic, and there are fish and seabirds and seals dead upon its shore.

I write to Niall; the pile of letters to send him grows fat with the weight of my thoughts. I try to come to terms with our relationship, with the mistakes I made and the twisting paths we chose to take. I ponder the way things could have been different but try not to dwell there; only regret lives in what-ifs and I have an ocean of that already. Instead I spend most of my time in the sweetness, the moments hidden between words or looks, the lines he wrote me while I was away, always generous and tender despite my abandonments. I live in the nights we spent in bed, reading to each other, or the weekend mornings we ran each other baths, or the endless bird-watching trips we took, silent and perfect and breathing each other in. I try to pretend we will have more of these moments.

. . .

Down along the coast of Brazil we travel. Each day begins with hope, is spent straining upward, gazing, searching, frightened of blinking, and ends breathless with despair. Only two wear trackers, but there should be many more of you, and you should be near. Where are you? Are your little wings still flapping? Are you still struggling against winds and tides and exhaustion? What if you aren't there when I reach Antarctica? What if you die on this journey, like the others? My meager attempts to find meaning in the end of my life will come to nothing.

I wonder if this matters.

I wonder if there is meaning in any death, ever. There has been meaning in the deaths of the animals, but I am no animal. If only I were.

I wonder if Niall will be able to forgive me for failing.

The power to the radio goes first. Léa and Dae manage to get it back up again, but this causes an outage to the kitchen, meaning the fridge, microwave, kettle, and oven all go. We eat our way through the cold food as quickly as we can, but most of what we have left goes to waste.

Things fail by the day; Léa explains it's because the boat is automatically rerouting the power to the autopilot system, which uses the most energy and will always be the most important thing aboard—apart from the navigation system. We lose our television, and our ability to refrigerate the stores. We are lucky to have made it to warmer weather before we lose the heating. The hot water goes in and out—someone is usually testing it to see when we might steal a quick shower or a cup of tea. Soon the autopilot fails; the battery is too low to be able to sustain it. Followed, a day later, by navigation.

Nobody says a word about any of it. There are tireless efforts to fix what has gone. Léa and Dae work night and day on the equipment, sometimes getting things up and running again, mostly not. The rest of us work around the clock to keep the boat moving, scooping water out of the engine room and off the deck, trying to keep everything dry. Ennis rarely sleeps now that there is no autopilot, and he spends his days with charts, compass, and sextant, navigating the way sailors of old once did. It is terrifying, all of it, and I can feel fear coming off the sailors in waves, yet I can see in the captain a quiet kernel of passion sputtering to life, a return to the way the world once was. He doesn't know this ocean and yet I think some ancient heart of him knows all oceans, the way some ancient heart of me does.

It's not only Ennis and me who now take comfort in the red dots of the terns but the whole crew. One by one they have made their way to the bridge to ease their trepidation and check that the little beacons of hope are steering us true.

"It's time to stop," I overhear Anik say to him one day. "We had grand plans, and we made it a long way, but it's over now, brother. The birds are too far ahead, and the ship's failing."

I think this will be it. We can't limp on this way forever.

But all Ennis says is, "Not yet."

I watch the captain return for the bridge, leaving Anik to stare after his friend. I know what Ennis must be thinking: we've come too far to stop now. He hasn't reached whatever line it is he won't cross. I don't know where mine lies, but I haven't reached it yet either.

I approach the first mate carefully, trying to offer support. "He'll find us a way through this," I say softly. "He's strong."

Without looking at me Anik flashes a bitter smile. "The stronger you are, the more dangerous the world."

GALWAY, IRELAND

ELEVEN YEARS AGO

On our one-year anniversary the thing I feel most is astonishment. Niall isn't surprised in the least, but a part of me has always quietly thought this a frivolous adventure that would lead, ultimately, nowhere. We would discover too many qualities we didn't like in each other, I would panic, leave, he would grow bored of me. Sometimes when I'm cleaning I imagine Niall and I are playing a monumental game of chicken, and I wonder who will be the first to admit how silly we are, to back down or laugh or throw in the towel, this was all good fun, wasn't it, darling, but now back to our real lives, to the business of finding proper husbands and wives. Cohabiting with a stranger has been a terrifying, embarrassing nakedness.

But today, as with every day, I am astonished by how deeply we are falling in love.

What luck. What willpower.

To celebrate the anniversary we go to a couple of sessions in town, making our way from one pub to the next and listening to the circle of musicians in each. It is one of my favorite things to do because the fiddles always fill me with an inexplicable familiarity. The musicians gather, the music swells, and the shared pleasure is tangible.

After some time the songs shift, turning slow and melancholic. I know the tune from somewhere . . . Without warning it comes, the answer. My grandmother used to play it and hum along while she did the washing up. "Raglan Road."

Niall reaches for my hand. "What's wrong?"

"Nothing, sorry." I shake my head. "Have you ever felt born in the wrong body?"

He squeezes my fingers.

I ask, "Who are you, do you think?"

Niall takes a sip of his wine. Probably trying not to roll his eyes. "Dunno."

"We've spent every day together for a year and you're still a stranger to me."

We consider each other.

"You know me," he says firmly, "where it matters."

Which must be true because it *feels* true.

"But who am I?" Niall echoes. "What does it matter? How should I answer? How would you?"

Who am I?

"You're right, I have no idea," I say. "But I think it might live somewhere in the day Mam left. Why else would I keep going back there? Why else can't I stop looking for her?"

Niall kisses my hand, which is also his hand, my mouth which is also his.

"Maybe mine lives in all the days my mother stayed," he murmurs.

"Did she try, at least?"

He shrugs, takes some more drink. "We can only give what we have."

"Do you want children?"

"Yes. Do you?"

This will change things. I almost lie to protect what we have, but even to me this lie feels too cruel, too damaging. "No," I say. "I'm sorry. I don't."

Niall's eyes shift. Something in him is so startled I don't know if he will be able to settle back into place. The equilibrium of his certainty is thrown off balance.

"Why not?"

Because what if I left that child like my mother left me? What if my darkest fears are real and I truly have no control? How could I do that to a child?

"I don't know," I say, because my cowardice would choke me if I tried to give it voice. "I just don't."

"All right," he says eventually, though this will not be the end of it. He says without warning, "I don't think you should go tomorrow."

"Why not?" I have a train ticket to Belfast, on the hunt for a lead.

"Because I don't think you should keep looking."

I'm thrown. "I will find her eventually—"

"She doesn't want to be found, Franny. Why else make it so difficult for you?"

I shake my head, my chest tight and swollen.

"If she wanted to see you, she'd reach out."

"Niall, listen to me," I say as calmly as I'm able. "This restless thing . . . it can take over." I will him to hear me. "If I ever leave you—if I have to go—I want you to promise that you'll wait for me to come back, you'll wait for me, and if that's taking too long and you can't wait any more, you have to come and find me and make me remember."

He doesn't say anything.

"Do you promise?"

Slowly he nods. "Yes. I promise."

"You'll wait?"

"Always."

"And you'll find me, if that's what it takes?"

"Even had you not asked, darlin'."

The song ends and that heavy weight shifts off my chest. The nameless ache. In its place is bone-deep relief, and love. We stay for another drink, and we don't talk of anything, and I could listen for hours but Niall has something else planned. We ride our bikes down to one of the docks to where a small, motorized dinghy is waiting. My eyes widen as he gestures for me to climb in. I wonder if he has hired this boat, or if we're stealing it.

I don't mind either way. A shiver of delight finds me as we set out into the dark water. We hug the coast, traveling north by the ceaseless circling light of the lighthouse. The salty smell of the sea and the sound of its crash, the sway of the waves and the black abyss of its depths, the reaching dark of it, up to where it meets the inky velvet sky pricked through with glitter. With the stars reflected in the water we could be sailing through the sky itself; there is no end to it, no end to the sea or the sky but a gentle joining together.

Too soon Niall turns us inland. We climb out onto a stretch of rocks and he hauls the boat up behind us. With a finger to his lips he gestures for me to be silent and we creep along the shore until the gaping mouth of a cave opens. I can hear something over the crash of the night-ocean. Many somethings. It's a purring and then trills, hundreds of them, an echoing song. My heart starts pounding as we edge our way into the cave. The smell drapes itself upon me, a pungent musty warmth. Niall's hand finds mine and he pulls me to the ground, whispers for me to lie flat on my stomach. The rocks are crooked and cold but above the noise is swelling, and there are shapes in the dark, shadows. I think briefly of bats—the movement is the same sort of fluttering.

"What are they?" I whisper.

"Wait."

Eventually the clouds in the sky move so that the light of the almost-full moon shines into the cave, casting them in silver. Hundreds of nesting birds, flying and flitting and calling to each other, a sea of black feathers and curved beaks and shining eyes, a world of them.

"Storm petrels," Niall whispers. He lifts my hand to his lips. "Happy anniversary."

And I understand that we will never need the word, for this is a greater proclamation, this is the immensity of love and its furthest-reaching depths. I kiss him and hold him and we stay here, watching and listening to the beautiful creatures, for these few dark hours able to pretend we are the same.

. . .

It's almost dawn when he takes this night and destroys it with naught but a handful of words, as most things are destroyed.

Back on the shore, wading from the dinghy to the rocks. Seawater about my ankles. Gray draped upon us.

"Franny," he says, and I turn, smiling. The water reaches his knees. He holds the boat's edge. His skin looks ashen.

"I've been searching, too," Niall says.

"For what?"

"Only I went a different way about it. I could never work out why you didn't want to go through the police."

My smile falls away.

"You never found her because she took your father's name. She was legally called Stewart, then, not Stone."

He moves a little closer but still leaves space between us, unable, somehow, to close that last gap.

"Darlin'," he says, and *so* gently. "You know what happened. Do you remember?"

Do I remember?

No.

But I could go back, couldn't I? Really go back this time, to the secret places.

I could walk back into the wooden house by the sea all over again. Call her name all over again. See her body hanging by its neck all over again.

"Oh." I take a breath and the world blurs.

"She didn't leave you," Niall says, but he's wrong. "She died."

I nod once. Yes. I know this now. I have always known it, somewhere. As I know the shape of her swollen face and the red of her burst eyes and the blue of her bruised skin. I know how dirty her feet looked, hanging there without shoes or socks. I wanted to cover them to keep them from the chill. It was so cold in that house.

My legs wobble, sitting me gracelessly in the water.

How funny, that such a thing should drop so delicately from my mind. A falling, fluttering leaf.

What else have I lost that has fallen free?

"Franny," Niall says. I see him kneeling before me. His face is blurry and handsome and no longer a stranger's.

"I remember now," I say, and he presses his warmth to my cold and his mouth to my eyes and I feel it so strongly, the knowing. Whether I leave now or in ten years, I am done here, in this place.

23

The *Saghani*, MID-ATLANTIC OCEAN
MIGRATION SEASON

"Before you go," I say.

The crew turns back to look at me. We've just finished breakfast in the mess, all but our inimical captain.

I clear my throat, not wanting to say it.

"Get on with it, will you?" Basil says. "Boat's falling apart, or'd you forget?"

"The laptop battery's died again, and this time there's no power to re-charge it."

Pain crackles upon the air. This was bound to happen, but by saying it aloud I've killed what little hope the crew had left.

"It's not like last time—it doesn't mean the birds have drowned," I try to convince them, try to convince myself, "it just means we can't see them anymore."

Dae puts his arm around his boyfriend—Malachai's struggling not to openly lose it.

"Ennis says it doesn't matter," I say more softly. "He says we know where they're going."

"Ennis has lost his goddamn mind," Basil says. "He can't sail seas he doesn't know. None of us can."

This is not the first time it's been said. The crew are wound tight with anxiety, thrown off their game by unfamiliar waters and failing machinery.

I look to Anik for guidance but his eyes are focused somewhere far away.

"It gets worse," Léa says. "The water pumps have failed, which means we can't run the desalinator, so we have a couple of days left of drinking water, max."

"Oh my god." Dae slumps his head onto the table.

"That does it, then," Basil says. "We're stuffed."

"What do we do?" Mal asks. "Birds or no birds, we need water."

Basil rises to pace the room, full of aggressive energy. "Are we really too scared of mutiny to save our lives?"

"What are you talking about, Basil?" Léa asks.

"We've tried. Nik's tried, and if *he* can't get through to him, then the old man's cooked." Basil quivers with frustration. "We should land. We'll do it ourselves."

"Skip's the only one who can do that."

"Any one of us knows how."

"That's not the point—"

"We could lock him in his cabin."

"No one is locking him anywhere!" Léa says. "He's our captain!"

Basil shakes his head. "Same as what happens when he gambles, he can't see when it's time to surrender."

"Have you tried?" Daeshim asks and it takes me a second to realize he's addressing me.

"Me?" I ask. "Why would he listen to me?"

Nobody answers.

"I'm not dying for this boat," Basil says quietly, and he's been deflated of air, of anger. "I'm not dying for fish or birds or any fucking thing."

"Real sailors don't board vessels without knowing they could—" Léa starts, but Basil says, "Be quiet," and she stops.

I get to my feet. On the main deck I am rocked by a gust of wind. White streaks in the sky, pulled along like the sea spray we leave in our wake. I pause to think, to seize a single thought, but they are as wispy as the clouds, as insubstantial. I don't know what to do, how to argue for an end to all of this, for land and police and a cell I swore I'd never return to. And yet how can I not? It is madness to continue on until the *Saghani* is in pieces and all seven of us have drowned or, more likely, died of thirst.

I look up at the man on the bridge. His untrimmed beard and bloodshot eyes. His conviction. His children. He's phantom-like. A pursuit only, and no edges left at all. If we go ashore we'll never leave again. Beached forever. A rearing thing inside me says no. My will makes a monster of me, time and again. Eyes fix on something off to starboard. A couple of kilometers away, maybe less. Shapes in the water, not far off the coast.

"What are those?" I ask Dae, who's returned to his work on the rigging.

He squints against the sun. "Fisheries. Salmon, probably."

There is a boat alongside the nets.

I hurry back to the mess. "Anik," I say. "I need you to take me somewhere."

The first mate's eyes narrow.

It happens quickly. Anik and I climb down into the skiff and set off over the water. We don't tell Ennis; Léa has said that if we slow to a stop we might not get going again, and I don't want him to have to make that decision. So we need to be quick. As we approach the salmon vessel I can make out people on the deck, watching us. It's smaller than the *Saghani*, but not by much.

"Ola," a man calls. *"O que o traz para fora?"*

"Do you speak English?" I ask.

"A little, yes," comes the reply.

"We need water," I say. "Our generator is down and the pumps have gone. We need drinking water. Could you help us?"

He points to land. "A port, very close."

"We can't go there."

The sailor looks confused. "It is very close. There is water on land." He says something to his crew members and they return to their duties. The man strides away and that's the end of the conversation.

"Fuck."

"Now what?" Anik asks.

"What if we snuck on board?"

"See him?"

I follow Anik's pointed finger to the man in the crow's nest, watching us. "Are storerooms generally in the same place on all boats?"

Anik studies the boat and shrugs. "Near enough."

"You go back to the *Saghani*. I'll meet you there."

"What?"

"I'll bring the water."

He snorts with laughter. "It's nearly two miles away. More by the time you're swimming. And how will you carry the water?"

There's rope in the storage box. I haul it over my shoulder, wait for the lookout to turn away for a moment and then I slide quietly into the sea. I stay under as long as I can, resurfacing closer to the hull of the salmon boat. When I circle around, I find that there are multiple ladders extending down to the fisheries—most of the sailors have used them to disembark their boat and spread out around the circular farms, checking their fish.

I don't wait around to make sure it's safe—the *Saghani* is getting farther away every minute—I haul my waterlogged body and coil of rope out of the water and up the ladder. It's quiet on board, at least. The fisheries look like seething pink tentacles curled into orbs. I pad, dripping, to the ladder and follow it down onto the mess deck. There's no one in the galley, and no one in the storeroom, so I'm easily able to find the water containers—five-gallon carriers lined up along the wall. I also spot a store of batteries, and shove several into my sports bra. I can only carry two of the water containers, so I grab them and struggle out, straight into the approaching captain.

He stares at me, a salty thief dripping wet and shivering. Two of his men look equally astonished to see me.

I take a breath, heart jackhammering, and when no other words come to mind I say, "Please."

The captain looks as lost for words as I am.

There is a long, painful moment and in it the *Saghani* travels farther away, it grows steadily more impossible that I will reach it again, but in his face I can also see an understanding settle, for he knows of the sanctions at play, everyone does, and then the captain steps aside with a gesture for me to pass. I sag in relief.

"*Thank you.*"

I haul the water up the ladder and my feet slap loudly on the deck. Tie one end of the rope around my waist with a bowline, link the other through the two container handles and finish them with the same. The bowline, I think, is my favorite knot. It doesn't slip. Then step to the edge of the railing. This could be the stupidest thing I have ever done, *anyone* has ever done. I could be about to sink myself to the bottom of the ocean.

I almost laugh, almost stop breathing. But panic is an enemy. Any emotion at all can be an undoing. Slow your breaths, deepen them, time them to a metronome. Make your limbs calm and your mind quiet and in you go.

I don't try to dive, as the containers would wrench me out of it. Instead I go straight down, hitting the water smoothly and kicking upward before the containers have even hit the surface behind me. They sink and drag me down with them and for one horrible moment I'm done, I'm dead and this is too soon, it's unforgivably soon and all that will be left is a bloated floating thing tethered to the sea's floor by her own chains and then I am kicking with all the power I can muster, dragging myself up to the surface with arms and feet. But I needn't have worried about being weighed down: the containers of fresh water float. I settle into a rhythm, ignoring the shouts of the sailors who are watching this madwoman, ignoring everything except the feel of the water around me.

Mam always said it was only a fool who didn't fear the sea, and I've tried to live by that. But there's no way to conjure fear if it doesn't exist. And here is the undeniable truth: I have never feared the sea. I have loved it with every breath of me, every beat of me.

It honors me now, lifting my limbs, making them light and strong. It carries me with it, embracing me as I embrace it. I can't fight it. I wouldn't know how.

From a letter Niall once wrote me:

I am only the second love of your life. But what kind of moron would be jealous of the sea?

· · ·

Anik drags me into the dinghy with a lot of cursing and takes us the last few hundred meters, where we are met by the entire crew, including Ennis.

My arms and legs are useless, and I have to be lifted onto the boat. They wrap me in a blanket and carry me below, and they kiss my cheeks, each one of them, making me smile, and they thank me and I think they are shocked and it's unnerving me.

"That's enough, then. Leave me in peace."

The sailors file out, all except Ennis, who stays.

I reach to take his fist, smoothing it into an ordinary hand once more. It is a thick, rough hand, with chipped and dirty nails, with scars.

His eyes meet mine.

"The batteries will help. But the water's only enough for a week," I say softly. "I'm with you. I'm with you to the end, as far as we can go, but if you have a plan, Ennis, then now is the time for it."

He squeezes my hands, dwarfing them inside his own. "Franny," he murmurs, "you frightened me," and then he kisses my forehead.

24

The *Saghani*, THE COAST OF ARGENTINA
MATING SEASON

Once it was mild here, even in summer. Now it's much warmer than it should be. The climate has always been ruled by the Antarctic, who stretched her cool fingers north to stroke this fertile coast. Now her reach is much shorter, for she is much smaller. We're a long way south when we turn into a cove and let our engine rumble to a halt. Not far from us lies "the city at the bottom of the world," as Ushuaia is known. No fishermen come to this cove, Ennis says, only luxury holiday yachts and sometimes locals who want to swim. Fishing has been banned here for centuries. It is where our captain always meant to reach before surrendering to his failing vessel, the only place he knew of that is private and hidden and maybe, just maybe, will allow us to remain undetected while Léa and Dae get what they need to fix the boat. Turns out he did indeed have a plan, and the extra water got us here.

Anik delivers the crew to shore in his skiff, while Ennis and I wait on the *Saghani* a long way out, far enough to watch for any approach. Rearing above is a dying forest and the magnificent Martial Mountains, once covered in snow, but I can't turn my eyes from the ocean, not now, not when we are so close.

It's my thirty-fifth birthday today. I don't tell Ennis. Instead I pull free the bottle of French wine Basil has stowed in his cabin.

"Let's drink this," I say, returning to the deck.

Ennis glances at it and laughs. "He would murder you."

"I'll buy him another."

"That's a Domaine Leroy Musigny pinot noir."

I stare blankly.

"It's worth five thousand dollars. He's been saving it for twenty years."

My mouth drops open. "Now I really want to drink it."

Ennis grins, while I put the wine back.

We play cards to while away the time, and we don't drink five-thousand-dollar wine but we do drink forty-dollar gin and it goes down a treat. The sun only begins to set at 10:00 p.m., tracing the remarkably blue sea with delicate threads of gold. The little boats lining the shore light up, winking on one by one and turning the world fairy.

"My in-laws drink that sort of wine every night," I say with my third double warm in my mouth.

Ennis whistles long and slow. "You must have had a few nice drops in your time then."

"They bring out cheaper stuff for us. We wouldn't appreciate it." He grimaces and I laugh softly. "The funny thing is that we probably wouldn't. At least I wouldn't."

"Niall might?"

"Yeah, he might. He'd pretend not to, though."

"I think I like Niall," Ennis says.

"He'd like you, too." That is a lie. Niall hates fishermen, unreservedly. "He'll be jealous when he hears about all of this." Another lie. Niall has never wanted to adventure for the sake of it—he only wants to save the animals.

"Haven't you been writing him?"

"Yeah, but . . ." I shrug.

"There are other things to write first."

"Guess so."

"Apologies?"

I hesitate, then nod.

"Don't apologize too much, kid. It'll bleed you dry."

"What if you've a lot to apologize for?"

"Once is enough for anything."

I suppose that's true. It's impossible to control someone else's capacity for forgiveness.

"Why did you name her *Raven*, Ennis?" I ask.

He runs his hand over the wood of the railing, rough against smooth. "Because she flies."

As soon as the others are back with the parts, we work through the night and all of the following day, helping Léa and Dae as much as we're able. There are so many bits and pieces to fix that it seems never ending. I grow more anxious by the minute, eyes always darting back to the water, waiting for the approach of maritime police. If anyone reports the commercial vessel for putting down anchor somewhere it shouldn't . . .

I have taken on Ennis's desperation to be apart from land, to be only adrift, always.

By the second night there's no more to be done. Léa has ordered a part from a mechanic on land and all we can do now is wait for it. So we drink. Malachai's nervous energy is so heightened he can barely sit still. Basil is crueler than normal. Léa is surlier. Ennis more silent. Anik is exactly the same as he always is, while Dae is left to muster what positivity remains and enough of a shred of cheer to make us play cards.

I don't know what I am.

Hours pass. I am counting them, almost, even though there is no point in it whatsoever. We don't turn on any lights, but sit on the deck lit only by moonlight. And to Dae's credit, he gets everyone involved and he relaxes us enough to laugh at his bad card tricks. Even Malachai calms down and tells us a story about the pranks he used to play on his sisters. As we laugh it comes to me without source or explanation that I feel one with them. Against all odds, I feel *happy* with them, and I know I could belong here, on the *Saghani*, if only in another life.

They make it harder to think of dying. They make me entertain the shadow of an idea, one that has something to do with life after this migration, and that's dangerous.

I asked Niall once what he thought happened to us after we die, and he said nothing, only decomposition, only evaporation. I asked him what he thought it meant for our lives, for how we spend them, for what they mean. He said our lives mean nothing except as a cycle of regeneration, that we are incomprehensibly brief sparks, just as the animals are, that we are no more important than they are, no more worthy of life than any living creature. That in our self-importance, in our search for *meaning*, we have forgotten how to share the planet that gave us life.

Tonight I write him a letter telling him I think he was right. But that also I think there *is* meaning, and it lives in nurturing, in making life sweeter for ourselves, and for those around us.

"Don't you ever stop?" Léa asks, sitting beside me. A splash of wine from her glass slops onto my paper, smearing my untidy words. "You're obsessed. What do you write to him?" she demands. "Do you tell him about us?"

"Sometimes."

"What do you say about me?"

I look at her. She's a little drunk, a little needy. "I say you are unforgiving and superstitious and suspicious. I say you're wonderful."

She takes a gulp. "Bullshit. Tell him he's a fool. Tell him you don't need him. You don't need him, Franny." And then, blearily, "*Stupide créature solitaire.*"

"What do you think happens to us when we die?" I ask her.

She snorts with laughter. "What's wrong with you? Why does it matter?"

"It doesn't."

There's a silence, and then she gives a great heaving sigh. "I think we go where we deserve to go and that is only for God to decide."

She's quiet after that, and so am I.

Later, when she nose-dives drunkenly into bed, I get her a glass of water (from our once-more working water tap) and leave it beside her. The others all retreat to sleep, too, but I stay up awhile, returning to the empty main deck. It's Basil's turn on watch duty, and I can see him smoking in the bow, eyes trained to the shoreline in case of approach. I have no desire to go anywhere near him and suffer another stream of vitriol, so, on a whim, I climb all the way up into the crow's nest. I'm not meant to come up here—it's too easy to slip and fall if you haven't spent your life on boats—but there's no one around, and tonight I want to see as far as I'm able, I want away from other breathing bodies, I want sky. The pretty lights of the other boats wink and glow below me and I wish they'd flick off and leave the world in darkness. All these humans have left no space for anything else. I learned this love of darkness not from my husband, though I learned so much from him, but in our bottom paddock in the deep, witching hour of the morning, with true night draped above in a sky full of stars and a sea roaring gently in the distance and my silent grandma beside. All those nights we spent down there in that pitch-black paddock, and never a word between us, only an occasional sigh from me because I'd rather have been in bed.

Sitting here now, in the uppermost part of this boat, I would give anything, any part of me—my flesh or my blood or my very heart itself—to be back inside one of those nights, standing beside her in the dark, she who infuriated and confused me, she who was unknowable and unreachable, she who loved me when no one else did, only I was too intent on loneliness to see it.

It's late when I hear something. I must have fallen asleep in the crow's nest because I stir awake at the distant sound of a boat engine.

I stand slowly. Keep a firm hold on the railing. Squint in the darkness. The lights that are drawing closer are white and blue, and approaching from the mouth of the cove, from sea.

Fuck.

Why hasn't Basil seen them yet? Has he fallen asleep? I look around for him and see him standing at the railing, silently watching the boat's approach. He's wearing a backpack. He is leaving, he has done something. I go dark inside with knowing and with no disbelief, it makes too much sense for disbelief. A part of me thinks I should have tried harder, I should have reached out to him and maybe that would have stopped this. But what use is that now? It's done.

It's not for the faint of heart, the crow's nest of a boat. It is very high, and though climbing up can seem simple enough, descending again is nauseating. One rung after another, down down down, keep moving, don't lose your balance, look only at the rungs. The boat spins below me as vertigo hits and I must pause, slam my eyes shut, and breathe quickly through my nose. Wait for the world to right itself, for my stomach to readjust. Then down once more, stepping rhythmically on and on until feet hit wood.

I don't bother confronting Basil, but hurry into the belly of the boat.

I go to Ennis first, alone in his captain's cabin. He must be a light sleeper for he wakes the instant I open his door. "Police," I say, and he's up.

That's when the siren sounds. Jesus, it's like a bomb alarm, it makes me think the sky is falling, that this is the end and that I can't go back to prison, I can't.

The others are up now, too, all of us panicked and half dressed in the mess. All except Basil.

"I'm going to kill him," Anik says in this disturbing way that's a little too convincing.

"What do we do?" Malachai asks in a voice three octaves higher than normal. He's vibrating with fear. Dae puts a hand on his arm to try to steady him.

I climb the ladder onto the main deck and the others follow me. It's different here now, it's flashing lights and a deafening siren, does it really have to be that loud?

Basil looks at us and we look at him. No one says anything but I could suffocate on this silence and I could tear the stubborn look from his face and I think the others feel the same because Anik spits at his feet and Basil finally has the grace to look at least a little ashamed.

It's Léa who takes my hand and tugs me back, out of the light-drenched sphere and into the dark. Ennis is lowering the rope ladder over the hull and into the water. I realize what they're doing and do I have the energy for this, to keep running, to find myself lost in a foreign land and scrambling for a new way south? As it turns out, I do. All it takes is the flicker of a prison cell in my mind to make me hurry over the side and down that rope ladder into the dark.

"Go," Léa says from above and I realize she is talking to Ennis. Ennis who has become as mad as I am. Ennis who thinks he can't possibly return to his life having failed.

"We'll meet up with you after we sort this mess," she tells him. "Go and finish what you started."

He's thinking about it. I can see him up there, paused on the precipice.

"Stay," I argue. "Go home to your children, Ennis."

But the police are boarding starboard and Ennis moves with instinct, lowering himself down above me. He's too deep in it to give up now.

Basil's arguing about something, and so are Daeshim and Anik, too, and then a police voice, louder than the rest, asking for everyone to be quiet, the boat is going to be impounded and will Riley Loach please step forward, she's a person of interest.

A female voice speaks up, hoping, I suppose, that they haven't been given a picture. "That's me."

Léa.

Shit, that wasn't part of the deal. Even if this is just her way of giving us a head start, even if they'll soon work out that she isn't Riley Loach, and she didn't stab a guy in the neck, I find that I can't just leave. I scramble back up the ladder, wriggling up beside Ennis, sure on these ropes after having spent months working with them. Ennis holds on to my waist to stop me from climbing any higher, but it's all right, from here I can see.

There are several cops. There's animosity, I think, I don't know why, but one of them grabs Léa by the arms and pulls her toward the gangplank to their police vessel. "Hey, don't grab her like that," Basil says, and Daeshim is trying to help Léa, everyone is sort of reaching for her and she says something, snarls it in French and wrenches her arms out of the cops' and it's chaotic then, the policeman shoves at her, trying to force her down the gangway but there's so much anger in the shove that she stumbles, unprepared for it. Someone tries to catch her, but her head connects dully with the railing. Her body sinks to the deck. She tries to sit up, reaches for something I can't see, and then she stops moving.

Shouting erupts. Shock and disbelief and her name being said over and over and her body being shaken but it's still not moving, it's not waking and I think, No, not again, please not again.

Ennis tries to drag me down but I hold on tight. I must keep my eyes on her because I must make sure she moves, must see her open her eyes.

"Franny," Ennis says. "Climb."

It is quiet and still inside me.

"Franny."

I don't move. I can't, how could I?

"Please," Ennis says.

I look down at him in the shadows of the hull. He says it again, *please*, and so I climb. Into the water we go, the two of us, sinking down and entangled as though in an embrace, holding each other for the space between heartbeats and then he slips through my hands and I'm alone.

The world above is fierce movement and color and sound. Underneath is calm.

Weightless.

Flight.

A diving cormorant, I strike out for the shore, wings back, feet kicking. Smoothly I carve through the water, breath held to stay beneath, guided by the dark shape in front. Good lungs, he told me once, and it's true, he stays under a long time, and I have no choice but to try to match him because I will not be the reason we are spotted from above. Too soon we're up and breathing again but it's all right; we've swum quite a distance and they aren't looking for us yet, they think we're on that boat, they think I'm lying motionless on the boards of that deck.

We keep swimming, almost to the shore now. We're abreast of the scattering of moored boats, unsure where we're going but knowing we have to get away from here—

I stop.

It is called the *Sterna Paradisaea*. That's how I know what to do. *Look for the clues, they're hidden everywhere.* This isn't a clue, it's a goddamn neon sign.

"Ennis," I say, and he stops, waits for me to reach him in the dark. He's panting hard, not used to swimming this far. His eyes look crazed.

There are no lights on in the forty-foot steel yacht. We climb up onto its deck and straight to the covered hull. No keys, either, but we go below and Ennis finds a set. "Always a spare in the pantry," he grunts.

I go into the cramped bathroom and don't turn on the light. I look at the silhouette of my reflection, and I slap my cheek, once, twice, wanting it to hurt, wanting it to bleed, and when it doesn't, when it's not enough I almost go to smash my forehead against the glass, but Ennis is pulling me away, constricting me, ignoring my struggles and my sobs until I give up, and collapse and weep against him. The second he lets me go I pull away from any comfort because what if she's dead.

We wait until dawn. Until the *Saghani* is empty, the police gone.

Ennis stops the yacht beside her and waits for me to board her once more. "You're coming, aren't you?" I asked him, but he said he couldn't. Instead he waits for me to run through the ransacked boat, stripped by the police of most belongings, of anything of interest, including my laptop. But my paranoia about my pack, about the preciousness of the letters it holds, has meant that I always keep it stashed under my bed and with a great stroke of luck I find it still hidden there, waiting for me.

I check the bridge just in case, but as Ennis warned, the steering wheel has been locked in place so even if the boat were seaworthy we wouldn't be able to sail it anywhere. With a last farewell I climb back down to the yacht and then together Ennis and I sail on past her, a ghost ship in the gray dawn and I think what might have happened to Léa, I think of where she is now, in some hospital room or a morgue and I want to *scream*, but I hold it inside, I hold it where it burns, because where we're going I may need it yet.

As we leave the mouth of the cove Ennis meets my eyes and there is a thing unspoken now, something I know he understands. *There may be no end to this we can survive.* Not with only the two of us, setting out on a stolen boat this small, leaving behind the tracking software and the little red dots, discarding a trail of destruction in our wake like the delicate film of a snake's shed skin. We didn't get goodbyes or parting glances. We didn't get guarantees any of them will find a safe way home, if home exists for them beyond what has been burned to ash with the slip of a foot, the crack of a skull.

We watch the *Saghani* for as long as we can. As he navigates south into the most perilous stretch of ocean left on this planet the captain weeps unashamedly.

I am too numb for any more tears. Too animal now.

PART THREE

25

When my daughter is born without breath, drowned by my body, part of me goes to sleep.

I go in search of something to wake it.

YELLOWSTONE NATIONAL PARK, UNITED STATES
SIX YEARS AGO

I waited for him at the airport. There is that. I always ask him to come with me, but he is a different kind of creature. He has his own grief to bear and his own strength to gather, and he finds his in work, not in freedom from responsibility, not in journeys or movement or turning resolutely forward and not looking back. So I've left him once more, when I promised I never would again.

I will stop making that promise now. It demeans us both.

I've found my way to Yellowstone, to one of the last pine forests. It is an empty place now, not as it once was. The deer have all died. The bears and wolves went long ago, already too few to survive the inevitable. Nothing will survive this, Niall says. Not at the current rate of change. There is no birdsong as I walk among the trees and it is catastrophically wrong. I regret coming here, to where it should be more alive than anywhere. Instead it is a graveyard.

As my boots crunch on the carpet of dead bark and leaves I can hear her crying as she should have done when she was born. I must be going mad. Panic sets in, silver eddies over my skin as light moves upon the iridescent scales of a fish.

It's been many months since I've seen Niall, though we write religiously, always. Right now a letter is not enough. I need to hear his voice. My eyes are blurry as I hike my way to the nearest lodge. I am shaking as I rent a room and close its door and switch on my phone. The walls spin a little and I can't get this pain out of my chest, out of my insides, I have to leave here.

The phone dings as dozens of missed calls and messages flood in. They are all from Niall, and I turn cold with fear because this isn't normal, he doesn't call me unless there's something wrong.

He answers on the second ring. "Hello, darlin'."

"Are you all right?"

He is quiet a moment. Then, "They've declared the crow extinct."

The air leaves me in a rush. Like that, all panic is gone. All this self-absorption dissolves and what I have left is the memory of twelve friends offering me gifts from their perches in the willow tree. I have an enormous sadness—and I have concern for my husband to outweigh it all. I know what this will do to him, what it *has been* doing to him.

"All of the Corvidae family have gone," Niall says. "The kestrel was the only raptor left, and the last one of them died in captivity last month . . ." I can hear him shaking his head, losing his voice. I can hear him gathering what's left of him. "Eighty percent of all wild animal life has died. They say most of the rest will go in the next decade or two. We'll keep farmed creatures. Those will survive because we must keep our bellies full of their flesh. And domesticated pets will be fine because they let us forget about the rest, the ones dying. Rats and cockroaches will survive, no doubt, but humans will still cringe when they see them and try to exterminate them as though they are worth nothing, even though they are fucking miracles." There are tears in his throat. "But the rest, Franny. Everything else. What happens when the last of the terns die? Nothing will ever be as brave again."

I wait to be sure he is finished, and then I ask, "What can we do?"

He breathes in and out, in and out. "I don't know."

He has spoken before of a tipping point. A point where the extinction crisis would pick up speed and things would begin to change in ways that directly impact humans. I can hear in his voice that we have reached that tipping point. "There's something to be done," I say. "You know it better than the rest of us. So what do we do, Niall?"

"There's a conservation society in Scotland. They've been predicting this for decades, breeding more resistance into some of their creatures, trying to grow new habitats, rescuing wildlife."

"Then we'll go to Scotland."

"You'll come with me?"

"I'm already on my way."

"What happened to Yellowstone?"

"It's too lonely without you."

He doesn't say it back. He always says it back, but not this time. Instead he says, "I don't think I can do this again."

And I believe him.

"I'm coming home," I promise. "Wait for me."

LIMERICK PRISON, IRELAND

TWO YEARS AGO

"Hey, Stone, wake up."

I don't want to. I've been dreaming myself a seal, watching sunlight move through water. When I open my eyes it's to see Beth and our cell and everything warm slips away.

"Come on. They spotted one."

"One what?" I ask, but she's already moving.

I rise grumpily from bed and follow her into the rec room. All the women are crowded around the television this morning, and the guards, too, even them.

It's a news bulletin.

A lone gray wolf has been discovered and captured in Alaska, amazing scientists who believed them extinct. Authorities were alerted to its existence after it killed a flock of livestock south of the Gates of the Arctic National Park and Preserve. Experts say this behavior only occurred because its own natural habitat and food sources have all perished, but they fail to understand how this solitary creature— a female—could have survived so long undetected and alone.

I move closer to see the footage, everything tightening and hurried inside me. She is thin and scrawny and magnificent. They have her in a cage and together we watch her prowl back and forth, gazing out at us with eyes of such cool wisdom I shiver.

The farmer whose livestock was slaughtered has called to have the creature destroyed but the public outcry over this has been loud and unrelenting, so much so that state government has stepped in to forbid the harming of the gray wolf— speculated to be the last of any wolves in the world. She will be moved to and cared for by the wildlife conservation team Mass Extinction Reserve, based in Edinburgh. People from all over the world are reportedly flocking to Scotland to see the gray wolf, the very last of her kind.

Which brings us to our final reminder that if you or anyone you know wishes to visit the remaining forests of the world, you need to join the waiting lists immediately, for it is becoming more likely that the lists will outgrow the life spans of the forests.

I barely hear the reporter, locked in the black eyes of the wolf. I imagine her at MER, with its eager, heartbroken volunteers and scientists, and know she will be beloved. But given there is no way for her to reproduce even in captivity, I can't help but wonder if she should have been left to live out her solitary life in the wild. I can't help but think no animal, ever, should live in a cage. It's only humans who deserve that fate.

MER BASE, CAIRNGORMS NATIONAL PARK, SCOTLAND
SIX YEARS AGO

The people who live and work at the Mass Extinction Reserve conservation base are all one of two breeds. The first: earnestly, irritatingly optimistic. The second: outraged, and not interested in being anything otherwise.

Niall is the only one of them who seems to exist somewhere in between. I say "them" because there is no one on this base who would pretend for a second that I belong here. I can't contribute anything except to cook and clean, and to the scientists this means very little. They are profoundly single-minded. As they should be. They are in a battle to stop the turning of the world.

We were greeted at the airport in Edinburgh by a young couple who acted as though Niall was the second coming. Everyone on the base has read his work and knows it intimately—they refer to it in meetings. (I only know this because Niall sometimes invites me to sit in on them, and I do so swollen with pride.) We stayed a week at the headquarters there, and then were driven north to the Cairngorms National Park, which is where their wildlife sanctuaries are located and has blessedly clean air. What I have gathered here is that the conservationists have made amazing progress for certain species and no progress for the rest. It was always going to be this way, Niall tells me. They had to choose the more important animals, the ones we need and those with a chance of survival, letting the no-hopers fade into extinction. Interestingly, insects are high on their list—bees, wasps, butterflies, moths, ants, and some types of beetles, even flies. As are hummingbirds, monkeys, possums, and bats. All these animals are pollinators; without plant life we are truly fucked.

This was where Niall and I felt our hearts sink in unison. Saving specific animals purely on the basis of what they offer humanity may be practical, but wasn't this attitude the problem to begin with? Our overwhelming, annihilating selfishness? What of the animals that exist purely to exist, because millions of years of evolution have carved them into miraculous being?

This is what I ask today, after a month of holding my tongue on the matter, and what causes all the heads in the room to swivel my way. Niall is beside me, holding my hand under the table. They afford me a lot of patience because I am married to Professor Lynch.

James Calloway, a professor of genetics in his seventies, says simply, "We are only so many. Prioritizing is life."

There is no arguing with that.

Niall squeezes my hand, which is nice. We don't touch much anymore, not since Iris was stillborn. It's been over a year since we made love, and maybe that's due to the fact that most of that year has been spent apart, but even now, reunited, I sometimes can't imagine how we ever will again. There is a universe between our bodies.

Then again, today he has taken my hand and held it tightly, and that is no small thing.

Talk turns to future migrations and how much of a problem these pose to the remaining breeding pairs of bird species. They are genetically engineered to go in search of food but when no food can be found the journey becomes fatal. The birds die of exhaustion.

"Professor Lynch has written about human involvement in migration patterns as a possible source of species prolonging," James, who chairs the meetings, says.

"It's a theory," Niall murmurs.

"We can't be following birds around the world," Harriet Kaska says, ever contrary. "The scale of that would be completely unfeasible. We need to be containing the birds so there is no need for migration. Simplify and prevent." Harriet is a professor of biology from Prague with a Ph.D. in climate change and another in ornithology. She is obsessed with arguing with Niall, and I think it's because he challenges her professionally in a way none of the others do. Her notion to prevent migrations is one they have argued about at length. My opinion on the matter, not that it's required, is obvious.

"Migration is inherent to their nature," Niall says.

"But it doesn't have to be," Harriet says. "We live now in a state of necessary adaptation. This is what's required of them—it is the only means of survival, as it has always been."

"Haven't we forced them to adapt to our devastation enough?"

This is what they seem to do in this room: argue for the same things, round and round in circles.

Talk moves to the Arctic terns, for Niall has written often of them, predicting they will be the last birds to survive because of their practice in flying farther than others.

"It doesn't matter," another biologist, Olsen Dalgaard from Denmark, says. "Give it five to ten years and they won't make the distance. With zero sustenance along the way, they can't."

"You're mad if you think carnivorous seabirds will be the last standing," Harriet tells Niall as though she is about to start taking bets. "It will be the herbivorous marshland species. Only ones with sustained ecology. Fish are gone, Niall."

"They're not, actually," he says calmly, always calm as though he doesn't care, when I know for a fact that he rarely sleeps due to the force of his terror.

"As good as," Harriet says.

Niall doesn't continue arguing, but I know him. He believes the terns will keep flying as long as they must; if there is food anywhere on this planet they will find it.

I excuse myself, tired and wanting fresh air. My snow boots and parka are waiting for me by the door. I slip into them and step out into the wintry world. My feet lead me to the largest enclosure. I'm pretty sure I heard someone say it was half the size of the entire 4,500-square-kilometer park, and all of it with one enormous fence around it. There are wonderful animals here, and not only those native to Scotland but many that have been rescued and introduced to the park in an effort to stop their extinction. Foxes and hares abound, deer and wildcats and lynx, rare red squirrels, elusive little pine martens, hedgehogs, badgers, bears, moose, even wolves lived here once, before the last died. A sanctuary unrivaled by the rest of the world, but only capable of so much. The balance of predator and prey is a delicate one, and these are the last of their kinds.

I wish I could walk through this chain-link fence. The far side of it interests me so much more than this side, but even I wouldn't be that stupid. Instead I go down to the beach of the loch, which is no ocean but still a great relief to the lungs. I'm not supposed to swim in it, but I do. Just a quick dip into the icy water and out again, scrambling to pull my clothes back on, so much more alive than before. I saw an otter here one day, and melted.

It is a privilege I lucked into when I married Niall. To live here, in this rarest part of the world, where dwell most of the last wild animals. I don't deserve to be here—I offer nothing except love for a man who offers a great deal. And true love for the creatures. There is that, little may it matter.

I take my time walking back to the dining hall where everyone eats together, except that Niall is still working so I eat on my own and then go to bed in our little cabin. I'm asleep before he returns, as is the way most nights. He tends to be up and gone before I wake, too. The kisses he once left me to dream of dried up some time ago.

Sleep is difficult tonight. I must be getting a cold because I can't stop coughing. There is a tickle in my throat and no matter how much water I drink I cannot ease it. Not wanting to wake Niall, I rise and pull on thick socks and a wool sweater. I head to our bathroom. It's just next to the bedroom but in the dark it feels much farther away than I expect. My feet keep moving, shuffling and colder than they should be. Finally my hand finds the light switch but when I flick it the power is out. It's cold in the dark bathroom. The air here has grown frigid—perhaps a window was left open. There's enough light from the red of Niall's electric razor for me to see the outline of my reflection, and the glow of eyes. I blink, frowning at the way the red bounces off my irises, like an animal in the dark.

The cough comes again, worse this time. My raw throat scrapes and hacks and there's something there, something scraping at me. I stick my fingers into my mouth, reach right back and feel the brush of a soft, itchy thing. I pull, coughing and spluttering as it cuts free of my throat. I can't see what it is, but in the sink it feels like a feath—

"Franny," someone whispers.

I whirl in the dark but it's only Niall.

Still, my frightened heart doesn't do as it's told. It thunders on, knowing something I don't. He reaches for my neck, a caress, and then a tightening, and my air is gone. In a moment the eerie stillness of the bathroom dissolves and there is a violent twist of limbs as I surge forward and he swings my head into the mirror—

"*Wake up!*"

I blink and the pain is gone from my throat, gone from my skull, moved to live inside my feet, which are burning. It's brighter here, wherever I am, silver and no longer red. It's the forest in deep night, with moonlit snow and stars and my hands are around Niall's throat.

I gasp in horror and he wrenches himself free, coughing once, twice, then taking my hand and yanking me through the trees.

"Quickly," he says, softly as though frightened of being overheard.

"Where are we?"

"Inside the enclosure."

My bare feet falter. *Is this a dream?*

"Franny, come on."

"How did we get here?"

"You were asleep. I followed your footprints." Like a tracker in the night.

I gaze around at the place I've longed to enter. Then at Niall, ghostly in the light. "Did I hurt you?" I ask.

His expression softens. "No. But there are hungry animals in here."

I nod and we hurry. I can see the footprints he followed. They don't belong to me, but to the woman who lives inside, the one who wants the wild so much that come nightfall she steals her way into my skin. If she can't have wild, I sometimes think she's intent on my death instead. Whatever sets her free will do.

We reach a decline and slow our pace to ensure we don't slip down its edge. At the bottom is a shoulder of the loch, with no beach to protect it, only a steep jutting of hillside. I can see Niall's intended course—he's headed close around the loch, as it will bring us more quickly to the fence, but I pull him to a stop.

"I don't think we should skirt too closely."

"If we go up and around the ridge it'll take too long."

"Come on, we're fine. Don't be dramatic."

"We're not meant to be in here, Franny. It could get us kicked out."

"Oh, please, they're not gonna send *you* away."

"*Stop*," he snaps suddenly, startling me. "This isn't an adventure. It's serious."

"I know that—"

"I don't think you do. Nothing is serious for you. You don't commit to anything."

We stare at each other in the moonlight.

"I'm committed to you," I say.

He doesn't reply, not in words, but the air feels thick. "Come on," is all he says in the end. "Your feet'll be frozen already, aye?"

They are indeed, protected by no more than the drenched woolly socks I dreamed of pulling on.

"Put my boots on," he offers, but I shake my head and take his path, angling down to the water's edge.

It's not me who falls, but Niall.

He slips almost soundlessly onto the frozen edge of the loch and then straight through the ice. It must be deep here, for he disappears instantly under the surface.

I step into the water behind him, a knife edge to my spine. The cold, *my god*. It's rendered him immobile. But I've spent my life in cold water and my body knows how to move, how to reach for him and pull him to the edge. It doesn't yet know how it'll get us out; there's nothing to grip on to but slippery snow. The shore of the lake is like a wall.

"Niall," I say through chattering teeth.

He doesn't speak, so I shake him hard until he nods and lets out a grunt. I scrabble for a hold and painstakingly drag us, hand by hand, around the shoreline until we reach a spot shallow enough to climb out.

"Hold on to the edge," I order him, then pull myself up onto the snow. It's so fucking cold. I'm having trouble making my limbs obey. "Niall," I say, "I can't pull you out, you have to climb."

"Can't."

"You can—I just did it."

I can see him trying, but he's waterlogged and frozen.

"Niall," I say, "try harder. Do not leave me alone."

He struggles out of the water and with my arms dragging him, manages to lift his body free. For a moment he slumps on the snow, but I pull at his hands roughly. "Come on, quickly."

We stumble around the loch, keeping a wider berth this time. Things rustle in the underbrush but we don't see them, no reflective eyes or shadows in the night. I lock the gate behind us and support him along the path that leads to our cabin. No one has noticed our presence in the enclosure; it will be like tonight never happened.

Except for the cold we have smuggled out with us, deep in our bones.

I run a shower, not too hot, then help Niall out of his clothes. He's shivering so hard, but once I get him under the running water he starts to calm. I undress and climb in with him, wrapping my arms about his body, pressing what warmth I have into him.

A time later. "Are you all right?"

He nods, reaching to cradle my head. Our lips are against each other's shoulders. "Just a night dip, aye? You do them all the time."

I smile. "Aye."

"Must be your selkie blood," he murmurs.

"It must."

"I've missed you, darlin'."

"I've missed you."

"Why do you go?"

I don't answer at first. "I'm not sure."

"Can you try to think?"

I turn my mouth to his neck and press it there. Trying. "When I stay," I whisper, "I think it does harm."

"I think you're frightened."

It brings a kind of relief to admit it. "I am. I always am."

"That won't do forever, my love."

I swallow, remembering the feel of the feather in my throat. "No, it won't."

There is a long silence, but for the fall of water.

"My father strangled a man to death," I tell him softly. "My mother hung herself with a rope about her neck. Edith drowned on the fluid in her lungs. And my body suffocated our daughter.

"I dream of choking, and I wake to find myself trying to steal the air from you. There's something broken in my family. It's most broken in me."

Niall strokes my hair for a long time. Then he says, very clearly, "Your body did not suffocate our daughter. She died, because sometimes babies die before they're born, and that's all." Then, once more, "*I've missed you.*"

And I am done with the universe between us. It is so perilous, this love, but he's right, I will have no cowardice in my life, not anymore, and I will be no small thing, and I will have no small life, and so I find his mouth with mine and we are awake at last, returned to a land long abandoned, the land of each other's bodies.

It feels an age since I've had him, and I am clutching at him as he pulls me tighter, moves callously inside me as though to destroy whatever civilized parts of me still exist, to push me through them into something uncivilized, something barbarous, and as I feel that liberation from my own shame I come with a leap, a bound into the air, a tugging away of something into the wild and lush and out of control, a place where I don't run or leave, somewhere I am still.

26

MER BASE, CAIRNGORMS NATIONAL PARK, SCOTLAND
FOUR YEARS AGO

Niall and I watch her, holding our breaths. When she extends her wings up and back like the *Winged Victory* I feel my pulse quicken. Her beak, usually orange to match her legs but now sooty for the winter cold, darts upward and then down into the bush. She eats one, two, three grass seeds.

The indrawn breath of the collective viewers is exhaled.

"Good girl," I whisper.

"See!" Harriet cries. "I knew it. Adaptation."

Niall is expressionless; for once I have no idea what he's thinking. To be fair, he never said the birds wouldn't adapt, only that with a little help from us they might not have to. He's been working on getting permission to fund fisheries in the Antarctic waters but it's been—in his words—"about as successful as pushing shit up a hill." No governments give a rat's ass about feeding birds when the fisheries could be feeding humans. The apathy is staggering.

I gaze at the Little tern, a smaller seabird than her Arctic brothers and sisters. She would normally migrate to the east coast of Australia if we didn't have her caged here, eating grass instead of fish.

I wish I could touch her, but it's strictly forbidden unless absolutely necessary. Not by the base, but by Niall. He says that human touch to an animal is disruptive and cruel. The tern's mate is louder than she is, giving his distinctive, creaking call. He's been eating the seeds longer. The female waited and waited, enduring more in the stubborn hope of freedom. For a while it seemed like we would stand here and watch her starve to death, but today, at last, she's surrendered.

Niall and I head for our cabin. He is silent and introspective.

"What are you thinking?" I ask, but he doesn't answer.

"Today went well," I say, not understanding.

He nods.

"So then what?"

"We should have done better for her," he says. "Harriet thinks it means they'll change their course and their breeding grounds. Start mating on the coast of Australia or South America."

"All of the terns?"

He nods.

"What do you think?" I ask.

"It's smart, finding a species of plant that will withstand inclement weather and grow on most continents. It's smart, seeing if the birds will eat it, when pressed."

"But . . . ?"

"I don't think they're going to fly around the entire world to eat grass."

"Harriet's saying they won't have to fly around the entire world anymore."

He flashes me a look that implies I'm a traitor for listening to Harriet. We're quiet awhile, concentrating on our feet on the slippery ground, on our breath making clouds.

I'm sure we're both thinking of the creature in her cage.

"You think they'll keep flying, don't you," I say.

Niall nods once, slowly.

"Why?"

"Because it's in their nature."

. . .

We leave for Galway in the morning. Christmas with Niall's parents. The car is waiting to drive us to Edinburgh but first Niall and I go to the bird enclosures to say goodbye. Instinctively we both move to the Little terns. The male is eating his grass seeds again, making do, while the female flies around her cage, around and around, her wings brushing futilely against the metal, forever trying to reach the sky.

I turn away, unable to watch her.

But Niall stands witness, even as I know it must break his heart.

Sterna Paradisaea, SOUTH ATLANTIC OCEAN
MATING SEASON

I'm holding the skull of a baby wren. I found it this morning in one of the nests in our yard, right down the back in those willow trees. I think its parents must have left it there when it died. Discarded. Or maybe they waited with it as long as they could. It's like an eggshell, only much tinier, much more delicate. It barely fits on the tip of my pinkie finger. I keep thinking about how easy it would be to crush. It reminds me of her. But not of you. You are made of a different thing. Something far more enduring. I never saw that thing you spoke of, the one that was missing from the stuffed birds in my lab. I see it now, or its absence. Your absence has never felt crueler. I've never hated you until now. I've never loved you more.

The letter smells of him, somehow. I'm holding it to my face when—

"'Scuse me, love."

Ennis is ducking awkwardly beneath the doorframe. I refold Niall's letter and return it carefully to my pack with the rest. That one was from a particularly dark time, not long after Iris died.

"It's about to get rough," Ennis says.

"What should I do?"

"Stay down here. Take your shoes off."

"In case we have to swim." The corner of my mouth curls.

Ennis nods. I think he might be excited about the infamous Drake

Passage. He has nothing else left but this journey, and in this we are the same. I take no excitement in it, only cell-deep weariness, only a need to see its end.

We no longer have anything to follow. No tracked terns. We can only guess at the birds' destination, and it seems an age ago that I even saw them moving. How long has it been since I knew they were alive?

Instead of staying in the small bedroom—there is also a simply stocked kitchen, a cramped bathroom, a dining table, and a set of bunk beds that Ennis graciously offered to take—I go up to the helm and stand by the skipper. There is static in the air. A black sky. I can feel the sea waking slowly, readying itself; I can feel it in my gut.

"Do you know how to do this?" I ask softly.

"Do what?" he asks, but he knows what I mean. After a moment he shrugs. We gaze at the dark churning water and the waves growing steadily before us. There is no land yet in sight. "Not sure anyone knows how to do this," Ennis says.

And then. He turns the wheel hard and steers us sideways up the wall of an oncoming wave, outrunning its hungry crashing teeth, until we reach its lip and sail over its other side, over the steep cliff edge. I let the held breath from my lungs as we plummet down but Ennis is already turning the boat in the opposite direction, sailing up the wall of the next wave and reaching the end just as I think we'll be tipped backward and swallowed. He does this a long time, zigzagging his way between waves, following and outrunning them, turning always for their gentlest slopes and edges. He maneuvers the tiny craft through the enormity of this most perilous sea; it's a dance, and it's quiet, and the sky watches us, and it's as close as I've ever come to feeling utterly at one with an ocean this ferocious.

Rain begins with a rumbling shudder.

The plastic windshield does its best to protect us but soon we are drenched and the waves are sweeping onto us from every side. Ennis has tied us both to the helm, and we do our best to stay upright, exposed and vulnerable.

If they have all died, all the terns, this will have been for nothing. But how on earth could the delicate weight of a little bird, an exhausted little bird who has flown across the entire world with hardly a thing to eat, who has already done so much, survive *this?*

It's asking too much.

I understand, finally. So in my heart I let them go. Nothing should have to struggle so much. If the animals have died it will not have been quietly. It will not have been without a desperate fight. If they've died, all of them, it's because we made the world impossible for them. So—for my own sanity—I release the Arctic terns from the burden of surviving what they shouldn't have to, and I bid them goodbye.

Then I crawl into the bathroom to vomit.

I dream of moths dancing in the beams of car headlights. Maybe it's the nearness of the end that sends me back. Maybe it's my failure.

LIMERICK PRISON, IRELAND

TWELVE MONTHS AGO

The shrink's name is Kate Buckley. She is very small and very intense. I've spent an hour a week with her for over three years.

Today she starts our session with: "I'm not recommending you for parole."

"Why the hell not?" Apart from a few early incidents I've been on good behavior, and she knows it. The self-destructive desire that led me to plead guilty and landed me in this place, and the self-loathing that saw me try to kill myself and then kept me catatonic for the first six months have both been redirected. Now I want out.

"I can't say you've been cooperating in your emotional rehabilitation, can I?"

"Sure you can."

"And how would I do that?"

"You could lie."

She pauses, and then laughs. Lights us both an illicit cigarette. Along with a "more defined sense of ego" she's also cultivated my nicotine habit. Every time I lift one to my lips I can taste Niall.

"I don't get it," I say more calmly. "You said I've been doing well."

"You have been. But you still won't talk about what happened. And the first thing the parole board is going to ask me is whether you've been able to express true remorse."

My eyes drift automatically to the window, my mind turns away from the words and to the slivers of wispy clouds I can make out. Oh, to be on a pocket of air, floating, listless . . .

"Franny."

I force my gaze back to Kate.

"Concentrate," she says. "Use your tools."

Reluctantly I take a deep, slow breath and feel the chair beneath my butt, the floor beneath my feet, focus my eyes on her eyes, then on her mouth, narrowing the world to my physical senses, to this room, to her.

"Willful detachment is a very dangerous state of mind. I want you to stay present."

I nod. I know this; she says it every week.

"Have you agreed to speak with Penny yet?"

"No."

"Why not?"

"She hated me even before all of this."

"Why is that?"

"Because I'm fickle."

"Is that what she said?"

"In a roundabout way. And she's a shrink, so she should know."

"How does that make you feel?"

I shrug. "Transparent."

"You don't strike me as fickle, Franny. Quite the opposite."

"How's that?"

"What have you *ever* changed your mind about?" Kate asks. "I'd call that willful and stubborn," she mutters, making me snort. "Why does it bother you so much? Penny's regard for you. The thought of seeing her."

I look toward the window—

"Focus, please."

And back to her face.

"Do you think it might be because she's going to say things that make it hard for you to maintain your delusion?"

"I don't have a delusion. I told you I let it go."

"And we talked about how they can re-form as a coping method for spikes in emotional distress."

I close my eyes. "I'm fine. I just need to get out of here. I've had enough."

"You were sentenced to nine years."

"Three non-parole. Let me serve the rest outside. I'll do the community service. I'll stay put. Be a model citizen. I can't stand the walls any longer."

"Have you been doing your exercises?"

"They don't work, they don't *get me out*."

"Take a breath."

My teeth clench but I force myself to breathe. Losing my shit in these sessions doesn't help my case.

Kate waits until she deems me calm enough to continue. But she's giving me a funny look now. The one that usually precedes something particularly unpleasant. "Have you heard from Niall?" she asks.

"Since the last time we spoke? No."

"I'm asking if you've heard from him since you've been in here. Any phone calls? Letters? Has he written to you, Franny?"

I don't reply.

"Why not?" Kate asks pointedly.

And she should be proud of me because this time when I lift my eyes to the sky it's with a focus so singular I no longer hear the rest of her words, instead I am weightless and drifting.

"Mrs. Lynch," the judge addresses me at the parole hearing. "It says in your psychiatrist's statement that the only reason you pleaded guilty to the counts of murder was your traumatized state, and that you should have been given proper psychiatric care at the time. This reads to me like your time in prison has offered you some perspective and that you are regretting your honesty at the time of trial. Let me make it clear for you: we do not offer retrials to women who change their minds."

I let my gaze fix on him, despite having been warned not to do this. There is something unsettling about my stare, apparently. "I haven't asked for a retrial," I say clearly. "This is a parole hearing. I've applied for parole."

Beside me, Mara winces. "Your Honor, the application is simple," she says. "Mrs. Lynch hasn't had a single behavioral warning in her entire time in custody. She has been an impeccable inmate, despite multiple attacks on her person for which she was hospitalized. And as I said repeatedly at the time of her trial, this was her first offense. Multiple psychiatrists have deemed her psychiatric state at the time of the incident unstable, carrying on through the trial period. On the basis of the evidence presented against her I strongly recommended to her that she plead not guilty for the counts of murder, but guilty to the lesser charges of manslaughter. She was in no fit state to take my advice, so riddled with guilt and regret for what she had caused that she was intent on seeing herself punished beyond what the crimes deserved."

"You don't consider taking the lives of two people to be an offense worthy of punishment, Miss Gupta?"

"Not when they're accidental, Your Honor. Not to the degree of nine years."

"When asked at the trial about her intent, the accused said she meant to cause both the deaths. I remember specifically because she was quite adamant about it."

"I refer you again to her state of shock."

"And the forensic evidence?" he asks. But before my lawyer can respond, the judge tires. He closes his folder of forms. "We're not here to debate old cases. The issue at hand is whether Mrs. Lynch is a danger to her fellow citizens, or likely to reoffend."

"I'm not," I say. "I'm no danger to anyone."

He considers me. I wonder what it is that he sees standing before him. Eventually he sighs. "Despite what your very assured representation insists, a jury of your peers judged you guilty. But I have here a letter of support from your mother-in-law, Mrs. Penny Lynch. She states that she's willing to accommodate you for the period of your parole, and I'm sure I don't need to express how much of an endorsement this is, given the circumstances. So for this reason alone I'm going to grant your parole. But bear in mind, Mrs. Lynch, that this country has no tolerance for broken paroles and even the slightest misstep will carry with it the weight of your full sentence, and additional time. So I strongly advise you to pay careful attention to the rules laid down by your parole officer."

With that it's finished, I'm free. I feel like giving him the finger and telling him of my plan to skip straight out of this fucking country, this country that has caused me nothing but grief. Instead I thank him politely and hug Mara, and then I'm on my way.

Niall's mother is waiting for me outside the prison. I feel a bit like I'm in a movie, the way she's leaning on her car. Except that she's not the type of woman who leans on cars—that would be far too casual a stance for someone of her stature—so then why I am wary as I approach her. I see it instantly: the toughness has gone out of her edges. The car might be the only thing keeping her upright.

"Hello, Franny," she says.

"Hi, Penny."

There is a long silence. It's sunny for a change, and almost too glaring for us to properly make each other out.

"Why did you do this?" I ask her.

She rounds the car to the driver's side. "It's not for you. It's for my son."

"Can you take me to him?"

Penny nods once.

I get in the car.

27

Sterna Paradisaea, SOUTH ATLANTIC OCEAN
MATING SEASON

Ennis finds me sleeping among the letters, exhausted from throwing up for most of the night. He is much wearier than I am, though—he's been steering us over waves all night, performing miracles. It feels calm now, so he must have laid anchor.

I move over so he can slump onto the hard mattress. It's claustrophobic down here with its low ceiling and narrow walls, but it's nice to have him beside me.

"Where are we?" I ask.

"Think we're about a day or so out. Go take a look."

"You did so well last night. I'm very lucky to have met you, Ennis Malone."

He smiles without opening his eyes. "I'm just looking for the Golden Catch, kid. What are you doing out here?"

I don't answer.

Ennis opens one eye a crack and squints at the letters I'm sprawled atop. "I wonder if your husband knows how deeply you long for him."

My heart flounders. If he doesn't know, then that is my fault and mine alone.

"That's the longing of a parting," Ennis observes.

"Experience?"

He smiles a little. "Yes."

I have never hated you more.

"With your wife . . ." I say, not sure what I'm asking but needing something.

"It was sweet for a long time," he answers. "Simple."

"So then why?"

Ennis rolls onto his back and looks at the ceiling. "Her name's Saoirse," he says. "Thirty-six when she got diagnosed with Huntington's."

Ennis looks at me and something in him reaches out to comfort the shock I feel, the sadness, and I'm aware of the generosity of this.

"It was a wasting thing. She deteriorated quickly, and decided I must leave her."

"Why?"

"Because in her mind we existed somewhere sacred and she couldn't let that be ruined. She didn't want me to see her . . . lessen. It was about dignity, I think. About allowing the thing we had to remain intact. She wanted me to go back to the sea, so at least one of us could live."

"And you left?"

"Not for a long time." I watch him struggle, not wanting to speak. He shakes his head. "I didn't want to go. I fought it. But I had to, I think. It was the only thing she wanted from me. I couldn't fix her and I didn't have anything else to give her . . . She didn't trust me with the children, to be constant for them, she thought it best that I was free and they went to her parents."

"Did she . . . ?"

"She's still alive."

I breathe out slowly, unbalanced. "I don't understand."

Ennis stands up. It feels aggressive in its suddenness. "She begged me. *Begged* me to leave."

It's unbearable, abruptly. The heart of me is cleaved in two. "What are you *doing* here, Ennis?" I demand. "You left your dying wife and your children to come on some fucking fool's errand!"

He looks away. "They're better off without me, those kids. A madman for a father."

"Bullshit. You have to go back," I say. "You have to go back to your family. You don't understand how important it is to be with her when she dies, to be holding her. And when she goes, your children will need you."

"Franny—"

I walk from the cabin. Trying to keep out what has begun to creep back in.

Moths dancing in the headlights.

To the helm and then the stern and *oh*. There are icebergs floating around me, and a crystal sea of blue glass, and an infinite sky of snow. How is it that such beauty still exists? How could it have survived our destruction?

I have never tasted air as clean as this.

Still:

A bag of football uniforms in my hands.

Bare feet in the snow.

The scent of blood in my nose.

GALWAY, IRELAND

FOUR YEARS AGO

It's predictable that I would make this decision tonight, after spending the afternoon at a child's second birthday party. I've watched my husband play with the kids all evening, watched him clean smears of cake off their mouths, watched him kiss them good night as their parents took them off to bed at sundown and the adults' party began. Niall's old colleague, Shannon from NUI, has put on the do for her toddler, which is more like what I'd imagine post-Oscars parties are like, with champagne fountains and floating lights and black-tie formal wear. I have no idea where her money comes from, because an academic's salary is definitely not this lush. Maybe it's family money, like Niall's. Either way, the waste of it all feels gross.

Now that the children are gone I feel tired, and I think Niall does, too, for we find ourselves sitting out back despite the freezing weather, passing between us a bottle of Dom we pinched from the kitchen. Shannon would be horrified if she caught us drinking it without flutes.

"Remember our first Christmas?" he asks.

I smile. "In the cottage."

"You said you wanted to buy it and live there."

"I still do."

"Don't you think we'd go barking, just the two of us out there on our own?"

"No," I say, and he smiles like I answered right.

"Would you like to go home?" Niall asks. "Only interesting humans at this party have been put forcibly to bed."

What I'd like is to have another child, I almost say, but catch myself. "Yeah. Probably. Before Shan brings out the cocaine and goes insane."

"Don't think she's doing it anymore," Niall says after a swig. "Not since having the wee one."

"Oh, right." Of course not. "She's in fine form, anyway. Offending everyone and their dogs."

"Ben told me he has nightmares about her swallowing him whole."

We laugh because it's too easy to picture: Shannon's husband Ben seems utterly terrified of her. Then I notice what Niall's doing and my mouth falls open. "Are you lighting a cigarette?"

Niall grins and nods.

"Why?"

"'Cause it's cold."

"What's temperature got to do with anything?"

"Nothing. Except that it's the reason."

I look at him in the golden light of the outdoor heater.

"I'm tired of fighting," he says, then takes a long drag. "Nothing seems to make any difference."

I exhale. "Don't do that, darling. Don't give up."

There is a lot, right now, for him to be sad about. He's decided to leave MER because his heart is broken and he can't stand it anymore—I know he achieved not half of what he wanted to. Our savings have run out, which means we both have to take paid jobs. And we saw his mother earlier today, who was cold enough to me to rival the snow-covered backyard we sit within. I'm used to it after so many years, but Niall loathes her endless condescension and her refusal to admit she was wrong when she said our marriage wouldn't last a year. I don't know why it means so much to him to be right, but it does. Plus. There's Iris. We never stop being sad about her.

"Smoke if you must," I say. "But don't give up, and don't expect a kiss from me."

He smirks. "I'll give that an hour."

My eyebrows arch.

A gust of cold wind blows in and through me, taking the heater's flame with it. It's darker and colder, suddenly. I reach for Niall's hand and hold it, taken by some unease, some foreboding.

"All right, darlin'?" he murmurs as he stubs out his cigarette and then rises to deal with the heater. I hold on to him, though, staying him, and he sinks back onto the chair to grip my hand. "Franny?"

"Nothing." I shake my head. "Just . . . stay a moment."

So he does, and we sit still and quiet until it passes through me, unknowable and unshakable.

Niall's had about five whiskeys on top of the champagne, so it looks like I'm driving, despite my three drinks. He throws me the keys and I drop them, laughing at his exasperated expression.

"I never promised you I could catch."

"No, you did not, my love."

The funny thing that falls into the silence is a shared thought of how we never really promised each other anything, actually. Not with words. I suppose there were promises made with lips and fingers and gazes. Yes, there were thousands of those.

I put the heater on high and we sit for a minute, warming our hands in front of the vents, urging it to get going.

"Christ almighty," he grunts. "I've had enough of this winter now."

"We're a good long way from its end yet." I start the drive home, windscreen wipers struggling to clear the drifting snow. I drive slowly, unable to see well in the dark, but there are never any cars out here this time of night.

"Did you have a nice night, darling?" I ask.

He reaches for my free hand and squeezes it. "It was tedious as all hell."

"Liar. I saw you laugh so hard champagne came out of your nose."

"Fine." He tries to hide his smile. "It was tolerable. You?"

I nod.

For some reason I decide that I will tell him now. *I would like to have another child. Would you?*

Instead he says, "I do have to go back to MER. And I don't think you should come with me this time."

I'm thrown. "I thought you said you were done with MER."

"I was frustrated, and being childish, but you're right. There's still more to do."

"Good. Of course I'll come. We'll find a way to solve the money problem."

He shakes his head. "I think you should travel."

"I know it's only Scotland, babe, but it still counts."

He doesn't say anything for a long while. Then, very clearly, "I don't want you to come with me."

"Why?"

"We can't come and go from a place like that. If you're there, it means you have to stay."

There is silence in the car. I lick my dry lips. Calmly I ask, "Did I leave, the whole time we were there?"

"No." He pauses, then adds, "But I was waiting for it day and night."

I look at him.

"The road," he reminds me and I reluctantly go back to it.

"Now you're saying I *shouldn't* stay?"

"I'm not saying you should do anything, Franny."

Anger rears inside me. "So how do I win this?" I ask. "Is it some kind of trap? When I stay, you expect me to leave, so I might as well just fucking go."

Niall nods slowly. It is the last thing I expect from him. Heat floods my body, making me nauseous. I breathe deeply until it passes, and then I try to explain. "Something changed that night you fell in the lake. I changed."

He takes my free hand and squeezes it. "No, you didn't, darlin'."

"I know it will take a long time for you to trust me again, but—"

"I trust you implicitly."

"Then why aren't you listening to me?"

"I am."

My pulse is quickening because I don't understand what this conversation is. His calm is starting to derail me—I have none of my own left and my knuckles are white on the steering wheel. Flurries of snow turn the road ahead into a tunnel made by the headlights. "You said I leave because I'm frightened, and that that wouldn't do, and you were right—it wasn't good enough, so I've stayed. For years now."

I dart a look at his face—he is watching me in surprise.

"That's not what I meant," Niall says. "I meant you were frightened of admitting the real reason you wander."

I stare at the road, my mind blank. "The real reason?"

"It's in your nature," Niall says simply. "If you could only let go of all this *shame*, Franny. You should never be ashamed of what you are."

Hot tears. My eyes are flooded with them.

"Have you stayed put since then because I said it would make you brave?"

I don't say anything but the tears slip freely down my cheeks and chin and throat. I am so tired, suddenly, of denying the pull.

"Oh, darlin'," he says, and then I think he might be crying too. "I'm sorry. I'll love you no matter where on this earth you are. I want you to be free to be what you are, to go where you want. I don't want you chained to me."

He isn't John Torpey, frightened of having a wife who was wilder than he was, punishing her for it and living a life of regret. No, Niall is a different kind of man. He reaches to kiss my hand, to press it to his face as though gripping at life itself, or something more ardent, and he says, my husband, changing my life, "There's a difference between wandering and leaving. In truth, you've never once left me."

A gust of air beneath my unfurling wings and I am up, weightless, soaring. I could never love anyone more. And in the same moment comes a terrible awareness. He's opened the cage door I closed on myself and now I'll fly, I'll have to. I see it all laid out before us, how I will wander away again and again, and I won't want to have more children because of it, and no matter what he says, no matter how generous he is, it will ruin us both a little more each time.

"Franny, I think you should pull over."

A snowy white owl flies low over the road, swooping up past the windscreen and into the black night, its plumage moonlit and portentous. I watch it, stunned, frozen. They are extinct, owls. But there one is. Maybe this means there are more hidden away, and maybe there are more of everything and the world is still breathing. My broken heart swells with it, flies away with it, seeks shelter within the night, and then it is gone in a flash of light, a sounding of noise and I see myself instead, myself naked and loathsome and for a split second I want nothing but to destroy myself and so that's what I do—

"Fran—"

Impact.

There are few things more violent than two cars colliding at high speed. Metal screams and glass sprays and rubber smokes. Within it what chance does a human body have? We are liquid and tissue. As fragile a thing as there is. It's like how people describe it, and not. It's slow, and not. The moment stretches out and it doesn't. I have a thought, both simple and complex. In its simplest form: I have killed us. In its most complex it becomes the days I will never have, the children I will never kiss. It lives deep, this thought. It is all of me and somewhere inside it, inside this infinite intimacy, is Niall Lynch.

I wake slowly. Or maybe fast. We are upright, but slanted. I don't feel any pain, and then I do. In my shoulder and my mouth. Then my chest.

"—ny, wake up. Franny. Franny. *Wake up.*"

I open my eyes and for one second I am blinded by the brightness and then in the next second I'm blinded by the blackness. A sound comes from my mouth, something shocked.

"Good girl, you're all right."

I blink until I can see Niall beside me, still in his seat, still holding my hand. "*Fuck*," I say.

"I know."

We're in a paddock. There's a tree growing out of our car. Its trunk and boughs are skeletal for winter, silver in the night. The headlights carve two hollows out of the darkness; I can see moths flickering toward the source, atop a surface of white snow as unmarked as a pane of glass.

I struggle with my seat belt—learning the source of the pain in my chest—then remember to click out of it.

"Do you have any injuries?" Niall asks. "Check your body."

I pat myself down and can't feel anything bad. I've bitten my tongue. A shard of window is in my shoulder. And the bruises across my breasts. But otherwise . . . "I think I'm okay. Do you have any?"

"My foot's a fuckin' mess but that's it," Niall says. "We have to get to the other car."

Oh god. I crane my neck and see it on the road, upside down. "*Shit. Oh, fucking shitting hell.*" My door opens with a creak but Niall isn't following me.

"I'm fine," he assures me, "I just can't get my foot out. Go see if they're all right, I'll work on this. Do you have your phone?"

I search until I find my purse and then drag it free. "Dead."

"Mine has no reception. Get to the other car."

I meet his eyes.

"Easy," he says. "Just breathe. Whatever you find."

I pull myself out of the car. It's freezing outside. My feet sink eight inches into snow and instantly go numb but I'm hauling myself back onto the road.

The car's wheel is still spinning in the air. How much time has passed? Maybe whoever is inside is still . . . I can't move, abruptly. Because I am unimaginably frightened of what I will find. Death, but worse than death, the absence of life within flesh. I cannot move.

"Franny," my husband calls.

I don't turn to him. I stare at the slowly spinning wheel.

"It's only a body," he says.

But doesn't he know? That's the problem.

"What if they're alive?"

Of course. I am moving; the words don't even reach my brain before they reach my body, propelling me to the car. I lie flat on the freezing road so I can see the driver. She's alone in the car. A woman, my age maybe. Short black hair, shaved short.

"She's not . . . awake," I yell. "I can't tell . . . Oh, fucking hell . . ."

"Try to wake her up!"

I shake her gently. "Hey, wake up. You need to wake up."

She doesn't wake. Damn it damn it damn it . . . My fingers are shaking as I reach—I truly, deeply do not want to reach through her body, Jesus, just fucking do it—and feel for a pulse. It takes a moment, a much-too-long moment, and I'm convinced she's gone and I will be touching a rotting thing, a corpse thing, and then at last I feel the softest, flickering beat, like the dart of the moths' wings I saw in the headlights. I imagine the same thing flickering within her, that abrupt defiant hazardous force of life, fainter than it's ever been and yet here, urging. It centers me and I climb in to reach for her seat belt. I can't get it free, I wrench at the thing and—

She wakes.

A muffled whimper. Then a mighty wail, a cataclysmic thing.

"Quiet," I say instinctively, some strange otherworldly creature, and she falls quiet. "You're alive."

A soft, slow moan leaves her and she starts to cry, to panic.

"You're alive," I say again, "and you're upside down in your car, and I'm going to get you out."

The pervasive fog of fear evaporates within me. I hold fast to the facts that will keep us together, the three of us, and these are the facts that I know: she is alive and I'm going to get her out.

"Help," she whispers. "I have to get out. I have to get out."

"I'm getting you out," I tell her and I have never been more certain of anything. I crawl out and run to the other side of the car, climb in feetfirst so that I can smash my foot against the seat belt buckle. The shoes are use-less, heels, for the goddamn first time in my life. I crawl out and fling them off, fling them with all the rage I can afford and then there's calm again, certainty, as I crawl back in and smash my bare foot against the plastic and it hurts, it hurts so much, I can feel the blood in a warm flow over my foot and ankle, but I kick it again and again until I feel the plastic give way, letting the woman free. She falls on her head and I twist around until I can slip a hand beneath her skull. What good it will do I don't know.

She is crying, sobbing, bleeding. It is catastrophic. I have the thought simply and clearly: this is madness.

Our faces are lying close. Turned like lovers.

"I have the uniforms in the boot," she says.

"What's that, my love?"

"For my son's football team. I picked them up today. I was meant to get them a week ago but I kept forgetting and they had to train in their track-suits. He was so annoyed about that. He's such a brat sometimes."

We laugh together, both of us.

I stroke her face. "I think we should try to get out of this car."

"Yes. Can we make sure to get the uniforms?"

"Of course. What's your name?"

"Greta."

"Greta. I'm Franny."

She is shaking, her voice a croak.

"Can you move your body, Greta? I left your door open so you can crawl out, if you can."

"My hair's short because of cancer," she says.

"What?"

"I shaved it. To raise funds. Not because I have cancer. Oh god, I'm sorry, I didn't mean that I have cancer—"

"Shhh, it's okay, I understand." She is panicking again so I say, "It looks fucking badass," and she smiles, bolstered somehow.

"It does," she mutters. "It does look fucking badass." Then, "I really need to get out now."

It occurs to me that I haven't seen her move at all, and maybe that's because she can't, maybe she shouldn't. "It might be better to wait for an ambulance . . ."

"No, I need to get out. I have to get out." She starts to struggle and I'm worried she's going to do herself more damage.

"Okay, hang on," I say. "I'll go round to your side and help you. Wait for me." I crawl out backward and sprint round once more.

"Niall, she's awake!"

"Good," he calls.

"I'm getting her out."

"Is it safe to move her?"

"She's moving herself, I need to help her."

"All right, good girl."

Poor Greta is all contorted in her seat, lying dazed on her head and neck, and I pray she doesn't have spinal damage, I pray we're not about to make anything worse, but if I can get her into our car then maybe, if it's still running, I can drive her to a hospital.

"Can you get the uniforms first?" she asks.

"No, love, we'll get you out first and then I'll get the uniforms, I promise. Come on now, can you move your arms up a bit so I can . . . Yeah, that's the way . . ." I don't know how to drag her out, I can't get a grip anywhere, her body is too slippery with blood . . .

I take another breath and force myself back into the car, my body pressed atop hers so that I can get my arms around her torso. "Wait," she says, terrified, "just wait, wait," but we're past that now, I have her just right so that I can brace myself on my knees and *drag* her out and at first she isn't moving, she's wedged, but I clench my teeth, demanding everything I can, *screaming* with the effort and her body is sliding out over the twisted metal and the rough bitumen of the road and—

I see her eyes fall closed.

All the blood leaves her face. She is waxen, gone. I don't know how I know it so soon, so immediately, but I can see her gone.

"Greta!" I shout.

She's dead.

I stand, recoiling from her. There's so much blood. I see it now. It's spreading around my bare feet. I have pulled her almost in two.

"Niall," I say. "Niall, she . . ."

I turn and stumble back to our car. I open Niall's door and lean over for his seat belt, which he hasn't removed, strangely, and I click it open so that he can get out, and I say, "Come on, we can't stay here—" and then I see.

His eyes are still open.

They are so beautiful, so changeable. I see so many colors hidden within them, the russets of autumn, tawny forests, and even flecks of gold in the right light. They have been deep browns and hazel greens and an endless night black.

They are black now, still.

And monstrous.

I am no longer one but two.

One of me is an old woman who climbs atop his body. Every one of her joints creaks and groans, hardly under her control, but somehow she lays herself upon him, and she cradles his head with its dark, perfectly combed hair, and she presses her mouth to his cold mouth, tasting smoke. "Oh, my darling, no," she whispers. "Please." He gives no warmth but she wills hers into him, she wills it with all she is, he will have every last atom of it. He will have the soul of her. Else she'll leave it here with his.

While one of me remains on the road, frightened of dead things, all.

Hours pass.

I've long since decided to die here with him and Greta when a thought occurs. Standing here like this, grasping at a heat that went long ago, I am freezing to death, my bare feet and hands immovable, my nose aching, ears stinging, eyelashes coated in frozen tears.

The thought is this: the football uniforms. I have to get them out of Greta's boot.

"Niall," I say softly from the road. "Niall."

I want to give him something, something that will part us well, something to let his spirit know I will follow it, and yet I can think of nothing, I am laid bare and empty and stripped of any grace. I am too appalled by the thing that was once him.

How does he die here in the cold with so little ceremony? How does he die without me to look at him as he goes? How did we not deserve last words, last moments, last looks? How could the world be so cruel, *so* cruel as to let him pass alone, unwatched, while I wasted my love on a woman I don't know? It is unbearable.

I stand on the cold ground. I walk to the boot of Greta's car and pull out the bag filled with her son's football uniforms. I walk down the road with one shattered and bleeding foot, back toward a world in which I have never for a moment belonged.

I stop just before the beam from our headlights ends. There is an abyss ahead of me. Not even a star in the sky. I look back at him. I can't leave. I can't leave. I cannot leave him here. Not alone.

My knees give out. I sink to the ground. I rest my face on the bag and I think I won't leave I won't leave I won't leave, and in the end it's something much simpler and older that makes the choice. It urges me to claw to my feet and turn away from that beam of light and walk into the pitch-black night along a road I know will lead only to grief.

It's not love, or fear.

It's the wilderness within that demands I survive.

28

GALWAY, IRELAND
TWELVE MONTHS AGO

"He wanted to be buried?" I ask, staring at the tombstone.

"Yes," Penny says. "You never talked about it?"

"No. For some reason I assumed cremation . . ."

"Because he was a man of science, not religion?"

I shrug. "Guess so."

There is a long silence, and then something in Penny gives way. She moves forward until she is standing beside me in the sunny graveyard. "He wanted his body to offer itself back to the earth, and the creatures in the earth. He wanted the energy of his life to be used for something good. It was in his will."

I breathe out. "Of course."

Niall Lynch, beloved son and husband.

"Thank you," I whisper. "For writing that. You didn't have to."

"It's true, isn't it?"

I swallow tears. "Very much so."

. . .

Afterward, in the mansion that is supposed to be my home for the remainder of my parole, I sequester myself in Niall's childhood bedroom and sleep for nineteen hours. I wake in the middle of the night, disoriented and unable to go back to sleep. I look through his collection of trilobites, touching each one tenderly. Then the pages of a book hiding a treasure trove of delicate pressed flowers. A journal containing endless observations of animal behavior, a photo album of feathers, rocks of all shapes and sizes, beetles and moths frozen forever in hairspray, fragments of speckled eggshells . . . Each tiny thing is more precious than I could imagine, and I realize that even though Niall believed his mother was never really able to love him, here is the proof: keeping all these treasures so perfectly preserved for all these years.

Boxes sit in the corner, labeled *Recent*. Inside I find reams of paper, his publications and teaching notes and journals. I know these things. I have watched him working on them for years. One of the journals is unlike the others, and not one I recognize. It has been titled *Franny*.

I am nervous as I open it. Short, meticulous entries make up a study of a woman who has my name but seems alien at first.

9:15 a.m., she's just thrown a used condom into the hallway outside the men's bathroom, screaming with outrage about the vileness of men.

4:30, she is reading Atwood in the quad again, the essays I quoted.

Roughly 1:00 a.m., she calls her mother's name and I have to shake her awake.

It is a logbook of my life. My actions. As I read, the entries become less scientific, more insightful, more poetic. And as my initial panic fades, I begin to recognize this for what it is. More a study of my husband than it is of me. This is how he teaches himself to know something, to love something.

The last entry I read is this.

Before my wife was my wife, she was a creature I studied.

Now, this very morning, her fingers were splayed over the lump by her belly button, the elbow or fist or foot pressing itself toward us, wriggling to the sound of my voice, reaching to be closer. It moved, this tiny person, and Franny's eyes shone a light so bright as she looked at me, looked in astonishment, in fear and in joy.

She loves this child, and it's her cage. I think she only agreed to keep it because she wanted me to be left with something when she breaks free. The thing that calls to her, whatever it is, will call again. But she has forgotten my promise. I wait, always. Our daughter will wait with me. And maybe one day she too will leave, off on an adventure. And then I will wait for her, too.

After unearthing everything in his room I make my way barefoot into the backyard, around the pond, and into the greenhouse. The cage up the back is empty still—Penny never did replace those birds I freed—but I stand inside it, anyway, and remember so vividly the feel of feathered wings brushing against my face and the taste of his lips.

"Franny?"

I turn to face Penny, realizing that I have been standing frozen in this cage for hours like a lunatic. An uneasy déjà vu drapes over me. We've been here before, she and I, just like this. "Sorry," I say.

"Would you like breakfast?"

I nod and follow her inside. Arthur's spot at the end of the breakfast table is empty and has been now for years. He left after Niall's death, unable to remain in the house where his son was raised. So now Penny is alone here in a hollow mausoleum and anything negative I've ever felt toward her melts away. I want only to shelter her from this impossible loss.

We eat quietly until she asks, "Why did you say you meant to do it?"

I put down my spoon. We haven't spoken since before, I never wanted to face her in the prison, so it makes sense this would be her question, the one that matters most.

"I just . . . wanted to be punished. As harshly as possible." It wasn't hard to convince the court of my guilt, not after the blood alcohol level or the forensics of the car, the tires that didn't swerve or brake, but charged straight for the oncoming vehicle as though seeking annihilation, or even, after, the damage I did to Greta's body.

"What about the tire marks? You veered onto the other side of the road and you didn't brake. Why didn't you *brake*, Franny?"

"There was an owl," I say, and my voice cracks. My head falls to rest on my arms as a tidal wave consumes me.

It feels an age later when a hand gently strokes my hair. "I have something to show you."

Penny takes me into her office and pulls a file from a drawer. She hands it to me and I read *Last Will and Testament*. I'm not ready, but I sink onto the carpet and turn the pages until I see it.

If there are no terns left, I would like to be buried, so that my body can give its energy back to the earth from which it derived so much, so that it might feed something, give something, instead of only taking.

If there are terns left . . .

I close my eyes for a long moment. Preparing myself.

If there are terns left, and it's possible, and not too difficult, I would like my ashes to be scattered where they fly.

The tumbling ocean calms. I rise to my feet, certain at last.

"Can we have his body exhumed?" I ask.

Penny is shocked. "What—But there's no way to . . . They've all *gone*."

"No," I say. "Not yet. And I know where they'll fly."

"How?"

"Niall told me."

Sterna Paradisaea, SOUTH ATLANTIC OCEAN
MATING SEASON

The stretch of ice before us is resplendent and magnificent, overwhelmingly so. It claims command of an entire wintry world, the true heart of its universe. It is imperious and crude and completely impervious, all.

And it is empty.

Even though I let them go, even though I told myself it was over, I must have still somehow been expecting to see a sky filled with birds, or a stretch of ice covered in seals, or something, *anything* alive. Because as the *Sterna Paradisaea* tacks her way slowly toward shore, past great floating chunks of ice, and I cannot make out movement anywhere in the great expanse, my heart breaks anew.

"Do you know where we are?" I ask Ennis. Extraordinary cracks rend the air, the ice breaking off the shelf and falling with a noise greater than any thunder into the ocean. I never expected such sounds.

"Coming up on the Antarctic Peninsula now. We'll make our way east into the Weddell Sea."

I stare at the approaching land.

Something feels wrong, abruptly. The Weddell Sea is where they have always flown. It was always the stretch of Antarctica most filled with wildlife, followed by Wilkes Land on the northeast side, where the terns land if they have cut right across to Australia before turning south, as they sometimes used to.

"Wait," I say. "Can you slow down a bit?"

Ennis gently eases the throttle lever back a little, looking at me quizzically.

I'm not sure how to express the sudden uncertainty. "This is where they've always gone. Weddell or Wilkes."

"We'll never make it round to Wilkes on this much fuel or supplies. That'd take a good couple of months."

I shake my head. That's not what I mean, I don't think. My mind is working swiftly, worrying its way back through all I can remember of Niall's meetings and research and the thousand bloody papers he wrote on this. Weddell and Wilkes have both been closely monitored because it's where the animals migrate to. We know birds haven't been reaching either of these places—any of the species capable of making it so far have died off, except the terns.

Harriet always said there would come a time when they'd stop somewhere closer and eat something different. But Niall believed they would fly to the ice, because it's what they know, and that they'd keep going until they found fish or they died.

"Turn right," I say swiftly. "Starboard."

"What? There's nothing west—"

"Go west, now!"

Ennis curses a storm but he changes direction and rushes about to adjust the mainsail. We carve a path through the ocean that places the peninsula and the South Shetland Islands on our left, and maybe I have lost my mind, maybe to think I could make a punt like this is insanity, maybe I have just killed us both.

People have been lost in the Ross Sea. There is very little shelter, no protection from the elements, and from February onward it freezes over, so there is no way in or out.

It is January third today. We're likely never getting out of here.

Ennis turns to me. For seemingly no reason he grins and gives me a swift salute. I give him one back. Fuck it. Why not?

Because it seems to me, suddenly, that if it's the end, really and truly, if you're making the last migration not just of your life but of your entire species, you don't stop sooner. Even when you're tired and starved and hopeless. You go farther.

Our steel yacht, battered and bruised from the journey, makes its way doggedly along the coast of the Antarctic, and we spend our time staring into the dazzling snow and the stretch of sky, afraid to blink lest we miss anything. The weather turns quickly. Temperatures drop to minus two degrees Celsius. The waves rise. Ennis has his work cut out for him avoiding the dangerous chunks of ice that were once attached to land but now crack and float free. The sound they make as they land in the sea is a mighty *whoomph*. He calls them growlers and any one of them could capsize or sink us.

On day four of our westerly path the wind rises to seventy-five knots, which, according to Ennis, can be fatal in temps this low. I don't understand why, nor do I ask, but I find out soon enough, on day six.

The rigging begins to crust over with ice. Ennis and I dart back and forth trying to hack it off more quickly than it can form, but it's useless, and so Ennis tacks us port toward the shore. We've reached the Amundsen Sea, which has a gentler coastline than the Ross, so maybe it was fate we didn't get as far as we meant to. I go below and start packing what remains of the supplies into my pack. The yacht holds compartments full of thick winter thermals, coats, and boots, which may be the difference between life and death. I am frightened, but what does that matter? If anything, it makes me feel more alive.

"What are you doing?" Ennis asks me. He's at the helm, setting off the EPIRB—some sort of emergency radio signal to identify our position to rescuers. The boat's done. It won't carry us any farther.

"I'll keep going on foot," I say. "Wait here. I'll come back."

He ignores me and packs his own bag.

So we set out together, into the ice.

It is very hard going. It's been some time since I've been able to feel any of my extremities. Yet it is warmer than it used to be. Everything is warmer, and melting, and changing, and dying. This may be the only reason we haven't frozen already.

We rest in the day, buried under the surface of the snow, and we walk at night to stay warm. Keeping the sea to our right always, so we can find our way back. We hold hands sometimes, because it helps to feel less alone. I think of all my lost ones, of my mother and my daughter, of Greta, of Léa, hoping against hope that she is not among them, and Niall, of course, almost with each step.

On the third day of walking I'm pretty sure Ennis is done. His steps have slowed dramatically and he's struggling to hold a conversation. We stop and sink onto the cold ground. I pass him a tin of baked beans from my pack, and we share it in silence, watching the still world around us. I don't think I will be able to keep walking without him. Not if all I'm going to find is more ice.

"Why are you here, Ennis?" I ask.

He doesn't answer, just eats his beans, concentrating on the effort it takes to swallow.

But after such a long time, he says, "I didn't want you to have to do it alone."

It takes hold of my chest. The generosity of this, and the love. We've shared love, the two of us, that cannot be denied. I'm so grateful for it, and for not having to be alone. It's how I come to know that whatever pretense I've been clinging to is done now. There's no point, not now we've reached the end.

"He died," I say softly. "My husband."

And Ennis says, "I know, love."

A slow turning of the world.

"We're alone out here," I murmur. "Aren't we?"

He nods.

"They're all gone." I put the empty tin back in my pack, along with our two forks. But I can't yet rise. I don't have the strength. "I was almost there with him," I say. "I was so close by. But I wasn't there, in the end."

"You were there."

"No. I left him and left him. That's what his spirit will take with it."

"Bullshit."

"I should have been with him."

"You were. And he still went alone. We all do. Always."

"It's too far for him to go alone." I press my eyes with trembling fingers. "I can't feel him."

"You can. Why else would you still be walking?"

With that he stands up, and I stand up, and we keep walking.

It only takes another couple of hours. I am trudging up a particularly grueling slope, worrying about Ennis, who has fallen a long way behind, turning back to make sure he's still moving, and then I glance ahead.

And stop.

Because something just flew across the sky.

I break into a run.

More of them appear, swooping and diving and then I am cresting the slope and—

Oh.

Hundreds of Arctic terns cover the ice before me. Squealing and creaking their cries, dancing upon the air with their mates, caterwauling joyously. Sea swallows, they are called, for the grace of their dips through the water, and I see it now as they dive hungrily for fish, in a sea thriving with what must be millions of scales.

I sink awkwardly to the ground and weep.

For the journey they have made. For the loveliness left behind. For you, and for promises, and for a life that was given to fate but could not comprehend your death's inclusion in that.

Ennis reaches me and gives a low rumble of laughter. It's in this moment that a huge whale fin crowns the surface and waves to us from the distance, and we both gasp half out of our bodies and then we are cheering and jumping and it's so beautiful, so desperately profound that I can hardly stand it. What else is hiding in these clean, untouched waters, in this sanctuary?

"I'm sorry the *Saghani* isn't here," I say, wiping my streaming nose. "All those fish and no way to catch them."

He looks at me funny. "I stopped wanting to catch them a long time ago. I've just needed to know they're still out here somewhere, that the ocean is still alive."

I hug him, and we hold each other for a long time, and the sound of the birds echoes all around.

"I wish Niall could have seen this," I say later. God, I wish it so much.

He breathes out deeply. "How long would you like to stay?"

"For always?" I suggest, offering a smile. "We can go. But I have something I need to do first. He wanted his ashes scattered with them."

Ennis squeezes my hand. "I'll go ahead, then, shall I? Leave you to be alone with him."

I nod, but don't let go. "Thank you, Captain. You're a good man and it's a good life you've led after all."

He grins. "It's not over yet, Mrs. Lynch."

"No, it certainly isn't."

I watch him walk down the slope, back the way we came. Then I turn in the other direction, heading for the water's edge. From my pack I draw

Niall's letters, and the small wooden box protecting his ashes. I had meant to let the letters fly free but I find that I can't, Niall would hate the thought of his words littering this untouched environment. So I put them back in my pack, running my fingers only once over his handwriting.

Gently I bring the box to my lips so I can kiss him goodbye as I never did when he was alive.

The wind isn't as fierce as it has been, but it's enough to lift the ashes and carry them through the fluttering white feathers until I can't tell where they end and the birds begin.

I strip off my clothes and wade into the ocean.

29

IRELAND

TEN YEARS AGO

"What have you found?"

"It's an egg."

He moves to my side and we stare down at the little thing nestled in the grass. The most extraordinary shade of electric speckled blue.

"Is it real?" I breathe.

Niall nods. "It's a crow's egg."

I bend to pick it up, but—

"Don't touch it," Niall warns.

"We have to take it back to its nest."

"If you touch it, the mother bird will smell you on it, and reject it."

"So we just . . . leave it there? Won't it die?"

He nods. "Still. The less we touch, the better. All our touching does is destroy."

I take his hand gently. "We could look after it. Hatch it ourselves and set it free."

"It would learn our faces."

I smile. "How lovely."

He looks at me. At first there is a shadow of pity. Of understanding the way of things better than I do. Of his pessimism. But I return the look, and let him see my own certainty, let him see perhaps a hint of how we don't always have to be poison, a plague on the world, of how we can nurture it, too, and slowly something shifts in his eyes.

Niall returns my smile.

THE AMUNDSEN SEA, WEST ANTARCTICA
MATING SEASON

The cold is deep but I am calm. I haven't submerged my head yet. I won't need to, not until the very end. The water will do its work on the rest of my body quickly enough. And I'd like to watch the terns for as long as I can, that I might try to take them with me.

I will take a piece of you with me, Mam. You stole the breath from your own body just as I am doing. You gave me books and poetry and the will to see the world and for that I owe you everything. I'll take the sound of the wind keening through our little wooden hut, and the smell of your salty hair and the warmth of you pressed around me. I will take a piece of you, too, Grandma, for you gave me quiet and you gave me strength, and I'm so sorry I didn't recognize them sooner. I'll take some of you, John, I'll take the photo you kept on your mantel, and all the love you left inside it, waiting there long after they were gone. I'll take each of the gifts the crows brought me, each of the treasures. I'll take the sea with me, deep in my bones, its tides making their way through my soul. And I'll take the feel of my daughter in my belly, I'll take all of her, and keep her always.

But I need take nothing from you, Niall, my love. I'd rather give you something.

The nature of me. The wilderness inside. They are yours.

I sink beneath the surface.

My fingers and toes have gone white as my body furiously pumps blood away from them, trying to keep it at the center of me, where it's still warm, struggling to keep my heart beating.

The sun makes patterns through the water above. I think I dreamed this, once.

The birds are silhouettes now, circling high. I watch them and watch them, and then I close my eyes.

We can nurture it, too.

My eyes snap open. Fish dart past, glittering in the sun. I'm so cold.

What did you say?

You showed me. We can nurture it, if we are brave enough.

But I've nothing left.

There's still the wild.

Quiet.

And then,

Could you wait for me? Just a little longer?

Always.

I surge to the surface, crash to it and burst through it, the air violent in my lungs. I hardly know how it happens but things are moving, bits of me clawing at life, at the sea's floor, dragging free of it yet, dragging free of this endless drowning shame.

I can't move to pull on my clothes except that somehow I do, and I can't stand on two feet except that somehow I do, and I can't walk, there's no way I can walk, except I do. I take step after step after step after step.

We are not here alone, not yet. They haven't all gone and so there isn't time for me to drown. There are things yet to be done.

I don't know how long it takes. It could be hours, or days, or weeks. But eventually I see a vehicle approaching over the ice, and I hear the distant *whoomph whoomph whoomph* of a helicopter's flight, and I allow myself to sink to the ground.

I won't promise you anything. I've given up on promises. I'll just show you.

EPILOGUE

LIMERICK PRISON, IRELAND

SIX YEARS LATER

It's raining the second time I am released from these walls, and this time, unlike the first, I am not empty with the thirst for an ending, I am full to the brim and carrying things with me, things like a degree hard-won and the memory of a vast untouched habitat on the other side of the world.

I am not expecting anyone to be waiting for me.

A dark smudge through the curtain of rain. Leaning against his truck. No umbrella.

I draw closer, thinking it must be Ennis, or maybe Anik—they all know I get out today but I never expected them to come so far . . .

It's none of the *Saghani*'s crew. I haven't met this man before. Perhaps he's not waiting for me at all.

But I walk over to him, anyway.

He is tall and thick and gray, with an oil coat just like the one Edith used to wear when she went out into the paddocks in the rain, and he has dirty boots and lines around his wide mouth and his eyes—and I recognize him.

"Hello," says my father.

. . .

Dominic Stewart's truck smells of old coffee, and I see why when I put my feet down on about thirty old takeaway cups.

"Sorry," he grunts.

I shrug and close the door.

We sit in silence, listening to the fall of rain on the roof.

"Where to?" Dom asks. His Australian accent is broad and fills me, astonishingly, with a sense of home.

I try to think of where he could give me a lift to but come up with nothing. Instead I think of the years I spent hating this man for what he did and where he was sent, and the years I spent ashamed of how like him I turned out to be, and the years I spent simply wishing I had family, even one single member, just one.

"Have you ever been to Scotland?" I ask him.

"No."

"Wanna go?"

He glances at me, then back to the rain. Without a word he starts the car. And I see perfectly the old, faded tattoo of a bird on his hand.

Dom sees me staring at it and smiles shyly. "Iris used to like that one best."

I return the smile.

Mam used to tell me to look for the clues.

"The clues to what?" I asked the first time.

"To life. They're hidden everywhere."

ACKNOWLEDGMENTS

First I'd like to thank my wonderful agent, Sharon Pelletier, for taking a chance on an unknown Australian author and encouraging me to write this book. You were patient and supportive, and without your leap of faith *Migrations* might not exist. It certainly wouldn't have found the perfect home it did, at Flatiron, without your hard work, so thank you so much.

An enormous thank-you to my editor, Caroline Bleeke, who believed in this book from the start and has worked so tirelessly to strengthen the novel immeasurably and then to see it into the hands of readers. You have truly been a dream editor, Caroline, and I can't thank you enough for your kindness, your generosity, and your dedication. Likewise, the whole team at Flatiron have all my gratitude for seeing the potential in this novel and working so hard to see that potential fulfilled, from the gorgeous design, both within the pages and on the cover, to the gutsy sales ideas to the international reach you have achieved. I couldn't have asked for more. Thank you to my extraordinary publicist, Amelia Possanza, and to the rest of the wonderful team at Flatiron, especially Keith Hayes, Nancy Trypuc, Katherine Turro, Marta Fleming, Kerry Nordling, Cristina Gilbert, Amy Einhorn, Flatiron president Bob Miller, and publisher Megan Lynch. Thank you, also, to Matie Argiropoulos and the team at Macmillan Audio for their work on the audio production.

Thank you to my clever UK editor, Charlotte Humphery; publisher Clara Farmer; and their team at Chatto & Windus; and to my lovely Australian publisher, Nikki Christer, and her team at Penguin Random House. It's been a joy to work with you all and I look forward to what's ahead.

Thank you so much to my team of amazing friends. Sarah Houlahan, for sending me those early academic papers about Artic terns and for giving me so many science tips with such enthusiasm, and for listening, always. Kate Selway, for reading the manuscript and doing a "science pass" on it—your details made all the difference. Rhia Parker, for reading the earliest draft of the manuscript, as you always do, and for helping me with such great ideas. Caitlin Collins, Anita Jankovic, and Charlie Cox, for listening to me drone on about the various ups and downs that come with writing a book and for always doing it with a smile!

Thank you to my family, Hughen, Zoe, Nina, and Hamish, for your love and support, and Dad—thanks for teaching me about donkeys! To my grandmother Charmian, and my late grandfather John, for your support, and Pa's insight into how boats move when in a storm. Thank you to my cousin Alice, for showing me around Galway and taking me to Irish sessions; your love of the ocean became a big part of Franny. To my brother, Liam, my grandmother Alex, and most of all my mum, Cathryn (who has diligently read every word I have ever written in endless, endless drafts); the three of you have been so unbelievably wonderful, I could not have written this without you, and I am truly so lucky to have you as my family. And to my partner, Morgan, you have been such a rock throughout this process, believing in me, sharing my excitement, and picking me up when it's hard. Your passionate conviction in your beliefs is continually inspiring, and you've taught me that no one person is ever too small to do their part. Thank you.

Lastly I want to acknowledge the wild creatures of this earth and say that this book was written for them out of sadness and regret for those that have been wiped out and for love of those that remain. I truly, deeply hope that the world without animals depicted in *Migrations* does not come to pass.

PLEASE NOTE: In order to provide reading groups with the most informed and thought-provoking questions possible, it is necessary to reveal important aspects of the plot of this novel—as well as the ending. If you have not finished reading *Migrations* by Charlotte McConaghy, we respectfully suggest that you may want to wait before reviewing this guide.

Migrations

DISCUSSION QUESTIONS

1. The novel's epigraph is taken from a poem by Rumi: "Forget safety. / Live where you fear to live." How does that directive resonate throughout Franny's life? Do you think it's good advice?

2. Discuss the novel's first lines: "The animals are dying. Soon we will be alone here." How does the disappearance of wildlife in mass extinctions shape the characters and plot? What are the similarities and differences between Franny's world and our own? Would you describe this novel as dystopian? Why or why not?

3. Arctic terns have the longest natural migration of any animal, and during their lives they may travel the equivalent distance of going to the moon and back three times. What do Arctic terns symbolize in the novel, and why are Franny and Niall so drawn to them in particular?

4. The first time Franny sees Niall lecture, he quotes Margaret Atwood: "We ate the birds. We ate them. We wanted their songs to flow up through our throats and burst out of our mouths, and so we ate them. We wanted their feathers to bud from our flesh. We wanted their wings, we wanted to fly as they did, soar freely among the treetops and the clouds, and so we ate them. We speared them, we clubbed them, we tangled their feet in glue, we netted them, we spitted them, we threw them onto hot coals, and all for love, because we loved them. We wanted to be one with them." Why does he pick that passage? How do the themes of love and destruction echo throughout the novel?

5. What does Ireland represent for Franny? What does Australia? Discuss the importance of home and belonging in this novel and how Franny's search for it shapes her life.

6. Franny says, "It isn't fair to be the kind of creature who is able to love but unable to stay." Why does she have so much trouble staying, even with the people she most loves? Did you find that aspect of her character sympathetic? Right before their car accident, Niall tells Franny, "There's a difference between wandering and leaving. In truth, you've never once left me." Do you agree?

7. Anik tells Franny, "The stronger you are, the more dangerous the world." What does he mean? Discuss this statement with regard to Franny and Ennis in particular.

8. Franny's conscience is split between protesting destructive fishing practices and depending on a fishing vessel to follow the terns. She and Niall devote much of their lives together to conservation, although their lifestyle sometimes runs counter to that effort (for instance, they still drive, fly, smoke, etc.). Did you sympathize with these contradictions?

9. At the Mass Extinction Reserve (MER) base, the conservationists prioritize saving animals that help humanity, such as pollinators, rather than, in Franny's words, "the animals that exist purely to exist, because millions of years of evolution have carved them into miraculous being." Is that prioritization selfish or justifiably practical? What do we lose in allowing the wild to disappear?

10. Niall and the other scientists at MER argue over the best way to protect birds. Niall believes that migration is inherent to their nature, while Harriet counters that they should learn to survive without migration as a necessary adaptation. Whose argument do you find more convincing?

11. In one of his lectures, Niall says of wildlife, "They are being violently and indiscriminately slaughtered by our indifference. It has been decided by our leaders that economic growth is more important." How does that resonate in our world as leaders debate

the appropriate response to climate change? What is our responsibility to the planet?

12. Franny loves the sea "with every breath of me, every beat of me." What does the sea represent for her? Why is she so drawn to it?

13. Franny describes her life up until she decides to follow the terns as "a migration without a destination." Why do you think she spends so much of her life without ambition or direction? What are the positives and negatives of that sort of existence?

14. When Ennis tells Franny about his wife, Saoirse, asking him to leave so he won't see her Huntington's disease progress, Franny is adamant: "You have to go back to your family. You don't understand how important it is." Do you think Ennis was right to do what his wife asked? Is his inability to stay similar to Franny's?

15. Ennis tells Franny about Point Nemo, "the remotest place in the world, farther from land than anywhere else." When she asks what it's like, he replies, "There's nowhere crueler or lonelier. . . . It's quiet." Why are Ennis and Franny so drawn to Point Nemo? How does it resonate with the rest of the novel?

16. Franny believes "the fear world is worse than death. It is worse than anything." Do you agree? What is she afraid of?

17. Why does Franny take responsibility for the deaths of Niall and Greta? Do you think she is right to blame herself and plead guilty?

18. At a few key moments in the novel, including on the last page, Franny remembers her mother's advice: "Look for the clues to life, they're hidden everywhere." What does she mean? Discuss the role of fate versus free will in these characters' lives.

19. What does Franny hope to accomplish by following the terns on their last migration? What about Ennis? What do you think the future holds for them?

Turn the page for a sneak peek at
Charlotte McConaghy's new novel

"A wildly talented writer."
—EMILY ST JOHN MANDEL, author of *The Glass Hotel*

ONCE THERE WERE WOLVES

A NOVEL

National Bestselling author of *Migrations*

CHARLOTTE McCONAGHY

Available Summer 2021

Copyright © 2021 by Charlotte McConaghy

1

When we were eight, Dad cut me open from throat to stomach.

In a forest in the wilds of British Columbia sat his workshop, dusty and reeking of blood. He had skins hanging to dry and they brushed our foreheads as we crept through them. I shivered, even then, while Aggie grinned devilishly ahead of me, bolder than me by far. After summers spent wishing to know what happened in this shed I was suddenly desperate to be gone from it.

He'd caught a rabbit and though he'd let us stalk the woods with him he'd never shown us the act of killing.

Aggie was eager, and in her haste she kicked a brine barrel, her foot making a deep echoing thud, one I felt on my foot, too. Dad looked up and sighed. "You really want to see?"

Aggie nodded.

"Are you prepared for it?"

Another nod.

I could see the furry rabbit and all the blades. It wasn't moving; dead already.

"Come on over then."

We went to either side of him, our noses peeking over his workbench. From here I could see all the fine colors of its pelt, russet browns and dusky oranges and warm creams and grays and whites and blacks. A kaleidoscope of color, all designed, I supposed, to make it invisible and prevent this exact fate. Poor rabbit.

"Do you understand why I'm doing this?" Dad asked us.

We both nodded. "Subsistence living," Aggie said.

"Which means? Inti?"

"We hunt only what we need and we give back to the ecosystem, we grow food, too, we live as self-sufficiently as we can," I said.

"That's right. So we pay our respects to this creature and thank it for sustaining us."

"Thank you," Aggie and I chimed. I had the feeling the rabbit could have cared less about our gratitude. Silently I bid it a glum apology. But all the while something was tingling in my belly, right down at the bottom of it. I wanted to get out of there. This was Dad's realm, the furs and the blades and the blood, the smell he was always draped in, it had always been his realm and I wished it could stay that way; this felt like the opening of a door to a darker place, a crueler one, an *adult* one, and I didn't know why she wanted this but if she did, if she did want it then I had to stay. Where Aggie went, I followed.

"Before we eat it we have to skin it. I'll cure the pelt so we can use it or trade it, and then we'll eat every part of the carcass so there's no . . . ?"

"Waste," we answered.

"And why's that?"

"Waste is the true enemy of the planet," we said.

"Come on, Dad," Aggie complained.

"All right, first we cut from throat to stomach."

The tip of his blade went to the fur of the rabbit's throat and I knew I had made a mistake. Before I could slam my eyes shut the knife opened my throat and sliced my skin in one long swift motion to my tummy.

I hit the floor hard, cut open and spilling. It felt so real, I was sure there must be blood and I screamed and screamed and Dad was shouting now too and the knife dropped and Aggie dropped and she pulled me tight against her. Her heartbeat pressed to mine. Her fingers drumming a rhythm against my spine. And in her skinny arms I was intact again. Myself, with no blood and never in fact a wound at all.

I had always known there was something different about me, but that was the day I first recognized it to be dangerous. It was also the day, as I stumbled out of the shed into a long violet dusk, that I looked to the trees' edge and saw my first wolf, and it saw me.

Now, in a different part of the world, the dark is heavy and their breathing is all around. The scent has changed. Still warm, earthy, but muskier now, which means there's fear in it, which means one of them is awake.

Her golden eyes find just enough light to reflect.

Easy, I bid her without words.

She is wolf Number Six, the mother, and she watches me from her metal crate. Her pelt is pale as a winter sky. Her paws haven't known the feel of steel until now. I'd take that knowledge from her if I could. It's a cold knowing. Instinct tells me to try to soothe her with soft words or a tender touch but it's my presence that scares her most, so I leave her be.

I move lightly past the other crates to the back of the truck's container. The rolling door's hinges rasp as they let me free. My boots hit the ground with a crunch. An eerie world, this night place. A carpet of snow reaches up for the moon, glowing for her. Naked trees cast in silver. My breath making clouds.

I rap on the driver's side window to wake the others. They've been sleeping in the cabin of the truck and blink blearily at me. Evan has a blanket pulled over him; I can feel the scratchy edge of it against my neck.

"Six is awake," I say, and they know what it means.

"This won't go down well," Evan says.

"They're not gonna find out," I say.

"Anne'll flip, Inti."

"Screw Anne."

There was meant to be press here for this, government officials and heads of departments and armed guards; there was meant to be fanfare. Instead we have been hamstrung by a last-minute motion meant to delay us until the stress of this prolonged journey causes our animals to die. Our enemies would have us keep them caged until their hearts give out. But I won't have it. So we are four—three biologists and one vet—stealing, moonlit, into a forest with our precious cargo. Silent and unseen. Without permission. The way it always should have begun.

There's no more road for the truck so we're on foot. We lift Number Six's container first, Niels and I taking a back corner each while burly Evan carries the front on his own. Amelia, our vet and the only local among us, will remain here with the other two containers to keep watch.

It's a little over half a mile to the pen, and the snow is deep. The only sound Six makes is a soft panting that signals her distress.

A loon calls, distinct and lovely.

I wonder if it stirs her, that lonely cry in the night, a recognition of the same ancient call she makes. But if it does, then she doesn't reply in any way I can interpret.

It seems to take an age to reach the pen, but eventually I make out its chain-link boundary. We place Six's container inside the gate and head back for the other two animals. I don't like leaving her unguarded, but very few know where in the forest these pens have been placed.

Next we carry male wolf Number Nine. He is a massive creature, so this second hike is harder than the first, but he hasn't woken from his sleep so there is that, at least. The third wolf is a yearling female, Number Thirteen. She is Six's daughter, and lighter than either of the adults, and we have Amelia for this last journey. By the time we have carried Thirteen to the pen it's nearly dawn and exhaustion has set into my bones, but there is excitement, too, and worry. Female Number Six and male Number Nine have never met. They are not from the same pack. But we are placing them in a pen together in the hope they will decide they like each other. We need breeding pairs for this to work.

It's just as likely they'll kill each other.

We open the three containers and move out of the pen.

Six, singularly conscious, doesn't move. Not until we retreat as far as we can without losing sight of them. She doesn't like the scent of us. Soon we see her lithe form rise and pad out onto the snow. She is nearly as white as the ground she walks so lightly upon; she, too, glows. A few seconds pass as she lifts her muzzle to smell the air, maybe taking note of the leather radio collar we have placed around her neck, and then, instead of exploring the new world, she lopes quickly to her daughter's container and lies beside it.

It stirs something in me, something warm and fragile I have come to dread. There is danger here for me.

"Let's call her Ash," Evan says.

Dawn burnishes the world from gray to golden and as the sun rises the other two animals stir from their drugged sleep. All three wolves emerge from their containers into their single acre of glittering forest. For now, it's all the space they'll be given and it's not enough, I wish there didn't have to be fences at all.

Turning back for the truck, I say, "No names. She's Number Six."

Not long ago, not in the grand scheme of things, this forest was not small and sparse but strong and bursting with life. Lush with rowan trees, aspen, birch, juniper and oak, it stretched itself across a vast swathe of land, coloring Scotland's now-bare hills, providing food and shelter to all manner of untamed thing.

And within these roots and trunks and canopies, there ran wolves.

Today, wolves once again walk upon this ground, which has not seen their kind in hundreds of years. Does something in their bodies remember this land, as it remembers them? It knows them well, it has been waiting for them to wake it from its long slumber.

We spend all day carrying the remaining wolves to their pens, and return as evening falls to the project base camp, a small stone cabin at the edge of the woods. The others drink sparkling wine in the kitchenette to celebrate our having released all fourteen gray wolves into their three acclimation pens. But they aren't free yet, our wolves, the experiment has barely begun. I sit apart at the computer monitors and watch the feed from the cameras in the pens, wondering what they think of this new home. A forest not dissimilar to the one they came from in British Columbia, though temperate instead of boreal. I too came from that forest, and know it will smell different, sound and look and feel different. If there is any one thing I know best about wolves, though, it's that they adapt. I hold my breath now as big Number Nine approaches delicate Number Six and her daughter. The females have dug a groove into the snow at the very back of the pen and hunker down, wary of Nine's advance. He towers over them, shades of gray and white and black, as glorious a wolf as I've ever seen. He places his head over the back of Six's neck in a sign of dominance and I feel, with exquisite vividness, his muzzle pressing onto the back of my neck. His soft fur tickles my skin, the heat of his breath brings bumps to my flesh. Number Six whines but stays down, showing her deference. I don't move; any sign of defiance and those jaws will close over my throat. He nips her on the ear and teeth sink into my lobe, startling my eyes closed. In the dark, the pain fades almost as quickly as it struck. I return to myself. And when I look again Nine has gone back to ignoring the females, pacing round the perimeter of the fence. If I watch, I will feel the cold of the snow on my bare feet with each of his steps but I don't, I'm already too close, my edges have forgotten themselves. So I look instead at the dark ceiling of the cabin, letting my pulse slow.

I am unlike most people. I move through life in a different way, with an entirely unique understanding of touch. Before I knew its name I knew this. To make sense of it, it is called a neurological condition. Mirror-touch synesthesia. My brain re-creates the sensory experiences of living creatures, of all people and even sometimes animals; if I see it I feel it, and for just a moment I am them, we are one and their pain or pleasure is my own. It can seem like magic and for a long time I thought it was, but really it's not so far removed from how other brains behave: the physiological response to witnessing someone's pain is a cringe, a recoil, a wince. We are hardwired for empathy. Once upon a time I took delight in feeling what others felt. Now the constant stream of sensory information exhausts me. Now I'd give anything to be cut free.

This project isn't going to work if I can't create distance between the wolves and me. I can't get lost in them, or I won't survive. The world is a dangerous place for wolves. Most of them will be dead soon.

It's midnight when I next look at the time. I have been watching the wolves sleep or pace, hoping in vain that they might howl, that one would begin and the rest would follow. But wolves don't howl when they're stressed. The research base cabin is made up of one main room, in which we keep all the computer monitors and equipment, an adjoining kitchen, and a bathroom at the back. Outside is a stable housing three horses. Evan and Niels have clearly already gone home to their rented cottages in the nearest town—I'm so tired I don't even remember saying good-bye to them—while Zoe, our data analyst, is asleep on the couch. I should have left hours ago, and scramble to pull my winter gear back on.

Outside the air is biting. I drive through the forest and onto a snaking road, a couple of miles along the north-west of the Cairngorms, led only by the small orbs of my headlights. I've never liked car travel at night for it turns the thriving world into something empty and gaping. If I stopped and walked into it, it would be a different world altogether, filled with the shivering of life, blinking reflective eyes and the scurry of little feet in the underbrush. I turn the car down a smaller, winding road, one that leads me all the way to the valley in which Blue Cottage sits. Made of grayish blue stone and flanked by a couple of grassy paddocks, during the day its view is twofold: to the south lies thick, beckoning forest, to the north long bare hills that, come spring, will be covered in grazing red deer.

Inside the lights are out, but the fireplace glows orange. I remove all my gear, piece by piece, and then pad through the little living room to a bedroom not mine. She is motionless in the bed, a shape in the dark. I crawl in beside her; if she wakes, she gives no sign of it. I breathe her in, finding comfort in her scent, unchanged even now, even unmade as she's been. My fingers twine within her pale hair and I let myself fall asleep, safe now in the sphere of my sister, who was always meant to be the stronger of us.

2

G*ently,* he says.

Her small hands are gripping so tightly to the reins. She is too tiny up there, so tiny she must surely be flung.

Gently.

He slows her, a palm to her spine to press her flat.

Feel him. Feel his heartbeat inside yours.

The stallion was free not long ago and a part of him remains that way, but when she drapes herself upon him like this, gently, gently, as Dad says, he calms.

I am perched with one leg either side of the training yard fence, watching. There is coarse timber under my hands, a splinter beneath my fingernail. And I am on that horse, too, I am my sister, pressed to the warmth of the trembling, powerful beast, with my father's large, steady hand holding me still, and I am my father's hand, too, and I am the stallion, the light load he carries and the cold metal in his mouth.

All creatures know love, Dad says. I watch Aggie's embrace turn tender and fierce. She won't be flung free.

But the stallion's head lifts in the pink evening light; a scent has been carried to him on the wind and he paws at the earth. I twist on the fence, turning to scan the tree line.

Easy, Dad is saying, calming the horse and his daughter both. But I think it's too late for that. Because I've seen it now. Watching from the forest. Two unblinking eyes.

Our gazes meet and for a moment I am the wolf.

While behind me my sister tumbles from the rearing horse—

I wake disoriented from the dream, dreamt often, also a memory. For a few moments I lie warm in bed, remembering, but the day won't be denied, there is light streaming through the window and I have to get my sister up.

"Good morning, my love," I murmur, stroking Aggie's hair from her face and gently helping her rise. She is guided into the bathroom and allows me to undress her and sit her in the tub. "There's actual, real sun out there," I say, "so we'd better wash this mane in case you want to sit outside and dry it." She loves to do that, as much as she loves anything, but my words are a charade for us both: I know she won't be going outside today.

"The wolves are in their pens. They survived the journey," I say as I massage shampoo into her scalp. "They'll want to run home."

She doesn't respond. It's one of her bad days which means I can talk and talk and she will do nothing but gaze listlessly at something beyond my capacity to see. But I will keep talking, in case she can hear me from that faraway place.

Aggie's hair is thick and long and pale, as mine is, and as I methodically work the conditioner through the tangles I wonder if she was right and we should have cut it all off. She is dispassionate about it now but even despite the effort it takes to care for I couldn't bring myself to get rid of it, this mane she has always been known for, the hair I've spent my life brushing and braiding and trimming for her.

"If we hadn't taken them across an ocean they might have been able to." I help Aggie out of the bath and dry her off, then dress her in warm, comfortable clothes and park her in front of the fireplace while I make breakfast. "There's no love between Six and Nine yet," I say. "But they haven't killed each other, either." The words fall so casually from my mouth that I am startled. Is that the way of all love? That it should carry the risk of death?

But the words haven't reminded Aggie of the same things, she is too far distant to be reached. I want to follow her to wherever she's gone and I also fear that place more than anything. I fear, too, the day she stops returning from it.

She doesn't eat the eggs I leave at her elbow, too tired, too soul-exhausted to manage anything at all. I brush her wet hair slowly, gently, and I speak more of the wolves because they are all I have left that isn't rage.

Blue Cottage isn't far from the project base camp. Both cottage and camp sit on the edge of Abernethy Forest, one of the last remnants of the ancient Caledonian Forest that arrived here after the Ice Age. These old trees belong to an unbroken, 9,000-year evolutionary chain, and it's within them that we placed the closest wolf pen, the one containing wolves Six, Nine, and Thirteen. If they manage to form a pack, we will name them after their new home: Abernethy. There are few houses around here, but behind us sprawls vibrant green pasture for the many sheep farms dividing us from the closest town. This was not where I would have chosen to place a new pack of wolves. But there aren't many places in the Highlands upon which you wouldn't find sheep, and anyway the wolves aren't going to stay put. I only hope they prefer the shelter of forest. Beyond this stretch of wintry pine woods rise the Cairngorm mountains, and there, I'm told, is the wild heart of the Highlands, where no sheep roam and no roads enter. Perhaps this will be where the wolves like it best.

I have the heater on high in the car. The road is slippery with ice, and a light snowfall has begun, a gentle swirl of lace. The drive is beautiful; this is big country, sloping hills and sinuous frozen rivers, stretches of thick forest.

When the black horse blazes onto the road in front of me I think at first I have imagined it. Its tail is a dark comet trailing behind. My foot slams the brakes too hard and my wheels fishtail. The car spins half a circle and comes to a stop backward in the middle of the road, in time for me to watch the horse disappear into the trees.

My chest feels tight as I ease the car onto the side of the road.

A truck rumbles to a stop beside me. "You okay?" a male voice calls from the driver's side window, which is open only a pinch.

I nod.

"See a horse?"

I point in the direction it ran. "Ah shite," says the driver, and then the truck, to my astonishment, promptly heads off-road to follow it. I am horrified as it skids through the snow. I check the time and hop out of the car, following the tire tracks. It's not hard. He's left trenches in his wake.

The snow picks up; the world is falling around me. I'm in a rush now, late for work, but even so. I tilt my head to look up. Flakes upon my lips and eyelashes. My hand reaching to the cool papery bark of a silver birch. The memory of forty thousand aspens breathing around me, their canopy not naked but canary yellow and as vivid as his voice in my ear. *It's dying. We are killing it.*

A shout, from somewhere distant.

I let the memory slip away and start running. Past his truck and into thick snow only disturbed by his footprints and the hoof marks of a frantic horse. I'm sweating by the time I reach the river. A narrow, frozen stretch of ice between steep embankments.

The dark shape of him ahead. Below on the ice stands the horse.

Even at such a distance I feel the cold beneath its hooves. A cutting kind of cold. The man is tall, but I can't see any more of his shape beneath his winter layers. His hair is short, dark like his beard. There's a black-and-white collie sitting calmly next to him. The man turns to me.

"You know this is protected forest?" I ask.

He frowns quizzically.

I gesture to his truck and the mess it's made. "You don't mind breaking the law?"

He considers me and then smiles. "You can report me after I've dealt with the horse." He has a thick Scottish brogue.

We look at the animal on the ice. She's not putting much weight on her front hoof.

"What are you waiting for?" I ask.

"I got a bum leg. I wouldn't get back out. And that ice won't hold forever."

There are tiny cracks on the surface of the river, spreading with each shift of the horse's weight.

"Best get my rifle from the truck."

The horse gives a snort, tosses her head. The black of her coat is broken only by a diamond of white between her wide, darting eyes. I can see the quick rise and fall of her belly.

"What's her name?" I ask.

"No idea."

"She's not yours?"

He shakes his head.

I start climbing down the steep ravine.

"Don't," he says. "I won't be able to get you out."

My eyes stay on the horse as I slip and slide down the jagged edge. My boots hit ice and I edge my way out, watching for cracks. It holds me for now but there are sections thin enough to reveal the dark flow of water beneath. I see how easy it would be to step wrong, for that sheath to split and for me to slip silently through; I see my body dragged and tumbled head over tail until it's gone.

The horse. She is watching me. "Hello," I say, meeting her deep liquid eyes.

She tosses her head and stamps a hoof. She is fierce and defiant; I move closer and she rears, thundering hooves landing with a crack. I wonder if she knows her fury will kill her, if maybe she's fine with that, maybe she would charge toward oblivion rather than return to whatever she fled. A bit and bridle, a saddle. Some horses aren't meant to be ridden.

I lower myself into a crouch, making myself small. She doesn't rear again, keeping her eyes on me.

"You got any rope in your truck?" I ask the man without looking up at him.

I hear him move off to retrieve it.

The horse and I wait. *Who are you,* I ask her silently. She's a strong beast and, if I had to guess, newly broken. It's been a long while since I've ridden a horse and I'm a different kind of thing than I was. I let her see me, wondering what she will make of me.

The man returns with a coil of rope and throws it down. I don't break from her eyes as my hands tie the old familiar knot by rote, I keep her with me and rise to my feet. With a quick motion I loop the lasso over her head and draw it closed about her neck. She rears once more, furious, and the ice will crack, I'm sure of it. I let the rope through my hands so I'm not yanked from my feet but make sure to keep a good hold. When she lands I don't give her the chance to rear again, I pull on the rope to force her head down and then I move in close to lift her foreleg. The two motions cause the horse to bend her other front leg and almost with relief she lowers herself to the ice and tilts heavily onto her side. I drape myself over her body, stroking her forehead and neck, whispering to her. *Good girl.* Her heart is thundering. I can feel the rope about my own neck.

"The ice," says the man, because there are a thousand fine lines now.

When she's ready I slide my leg over her back and give her a squeeze with my knees, a few clicks of the tongue and an *up, up.* She surges and I slide onto her properly, getting my other leg into place and tightening my knees. The rope is still about her neck but I don't need it, I take hold of her mane and maneuver her toward the steep embankment as the cracks shudder beneath us. *This will hurt,* I tell her but she leaps up the edge, tilting me back. I'm ready for it, and I move with her, legs firm enough to keep my seat. She strains upward as her hooves scrabble for purchase and the ground gives way beneath her and then we are up and over, and the thrill that runs through her burns straight through me. Behind us the icy river has cracked open.

I press myself flat to her neck once more. *Good girl. Brave girl.* She's calm now, but I don't know for how long. She's not standing on her bad leg. Getting free might have harmed it beyond repair. I dismount and pass the rope to the man. It's rough in his bare palm, in mine. "Be gentle."

"Much appreciated," he says with a nod. "You're a horsewoman?"

A quirk of my lips. "No."

"Would you ride her home? She's from the Burns farm, not far north."

"Why'd you come get her if she's not yours?"

"I just saw her, same as you."

I consider him. "Her leg's injured. She shouldn't be ridden."

"I'll radio in a float then. You're not from around here?"

"I just moved here."

"Whereabouts?" he asks, and I wonder if he's one of those people who make it their business to know everyone in a hundred-mile radius. He has a heavy brow and a dark look about his eyes; I can't tell if he's handsome but there is something unsettling about him. "What brings you here then?"

I turn away. "Don't you have someone to radio about that horse?"

"You with the wolves?" he asks, and I stop. "We got told to expect an Australian lassie. Now how does that come about? Aren't there enough koalas for you to be cuddling?"

"Not really," I say. "Most have died in bushfires."

"Oh."

That shut him up.

After a moment he asks, "They free yet?"

"Not yet. But they will be."

"I'll alert the villagers to lock up their wives and daughters. The big bad wolves are coming."

I meet his eyes. "If I were you I'd be more worried about the wives and daughters going out to run with the wolves."

He gazes at me, taken aback.

I turn in the direction of my car. "Next time you've got an animal to track, call someone who's up to the task instead of bulldozing your monster truck through protected undergrowth." *Prick.*

I hear him laugh. "Yes, ma'am."

When I glance back it's at the horse. *Bye,* I bid her. And, *I'm sorry.* Because that damaged leg might mean freedom of a different kind.

ABOUT THE TYPE

Migrations is set in Fournier type. Fournier has a clean look on the page and provides good economy in text. Monotype, in 1924, based this face on types cut by Pierre Simon Fournier, circa 1742, which were called St Augustin Ordinaire in Fournier's *Manuel Typographique*. These types were a stepping-stone to the more severe modern style made popular by Bodoni in the late 1700s.

ABOUT THE AUTHOR

CHARLOTTE McCONAGHY is an author based in Sydney, Australia. *Migrations* is her U.S. debut and is being translated into twenty languages.